CURVY GIRLS CAN'T DATE BULLIES

KELSIE STELTING

Copyright © 2020 by Kelsie Stelting

All rights reserved.

No part of this book may be reproduced in any form or by any electronic or mechanical means, including information storage and retrieval systems, without written permission from the author, except for the use of brief quotations in a book review.

This is a work of fiction. Names, characters, businesses, places, events, locales, and incidents are either the products of the author's imagination or used in a fictitious manner. Any resemblance to actual persons, living or dead, or actual events is purely coincidental.

For questions, address kelsie@kelsiestelting.com.

Copy Edited by Tricia Harden

Cover concept by Angsty G, design by Najla Qamber Designs.

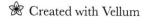 Created with Vellum

*For Little Ty, who is precious **exactly** the way he is.*

ONE

THE HOUSE WAS SO QUIET my footsteps echoed on the tile. My phone was just as silent in my hand. I kept waiting for a call. A text. *Something*. But I was running out of time. I pulled open the front door and walked onto the porch.

How could both my parents forget my last first day of school? Last year, Mom rolled out a breakfast buffet for my older sister, Ginger, and had her stand on the porch for a picture while tears rolled down my mom's cheeks.

But today? My last first day?

Crickets.

I had a contraband pop tart in my backpack for breakfast to prove it.

To be fair, my mom was in LA with my little

sisters while they filmed their first movie, and my dad was working, but I hadn't even gotten a text message. No requests for so much as a selfie.

Just for myself, I extended my phone and turned the camera on me. After tucking a loose red curl behind my ear, I smiled for the picture. I didn't want to remember this day as the one when my parents forgot about me. As the confirmation that I would always be less important than my sisters. But so far, we weren't off to a great start.

Not only was it weird to drive without my sister at my side, but I also took Mom's minivan. She got a brand-new car to shuttle the twins around, and I inherited the "mom car," which wouldn't have been bad at all if the rest of my classmates weren't driving sports cars. The second I reached the school and looked around the Emerson Academy parking lot, I could tell it would be a horrible first day—if not, year.

I pulled into my designated spot farther from the building—my parents hadn't paid extra for a closer spot—and looked around for my friend Nadira. Unfortunately, her car was one I didn't see. I sent her a text telling her I'd meet her inside and got out of the van.

The sun shone brightly in my face outside of

CHAPTER 1   3

the tinted windows. At least the weather was nice, but then again, it usually was in our part of California. I saw a girl from the basketball team leaning against a car's bumper with her boyfriend and waved. She grinned back and wiggled her fingers at me before getting lost in him again.

I wished I had a guy to walk inside with me. Maybe this would be my year for romance. My sister Ginger had met her boyfriend after second semester started, and they were still completely in love.

Feeling a little more hopeful, I readjusted my backpack and continued toward the doors. The loud guffaws of stupid guys sounded a few feet behind me, but I ignored them. No doubt freshman boys discovering their armpits could make fart sounds.

"Stop, *please*," a girl's voice said, and my stomach went cold. I turned on the spot to see Ryker Dugan and a group of football players surrounding Faith Kelley.

My blood boiled as I watched his friends pretend to corral her like a cow while Ryker sat back and laughed.

"Get out of the chute, heifer," his friend Grant said.

She fell to her knees amidst their prodding. Of course no one in the parking lot did or said anything. Ryker was the king of this school. Senior wide receiver, rich as the dessert aisle at my parents' store, and hotter than sin.

I'd spent the last year watching him bully my sister and wishing I could do something to stop him. But Ginger always stood up for herself. When he said something mean, she fought back harder. Faith was too nice, and they were crushing her.

I dropped my backpack to the ground, my fists clenching, and stormed up to them. "Stop it!" I yelled forcefully. "*Now.*"

Ryker turned his gray eyes lazily on me, his lips forming a perfectly pouty smirk. "Who's going to make us?"

This close to him, I realized how much taller he was than me. At least six inches, which was rare considering I stood at five-nine. Still, I put my hands on my hips and stared him in the eyes. "Me."

He laughed, a deep, derisive belly laugh that his friends echoed.

My cheeks got hot, and I wished more than anything my light skin didn't show my blush so quickly.

Ryker took another step forward, then another,

so his face was only inches from mine, but I didn't step back. I wasn't going to be just another girl to back down from his power trip. This was ending, and it was ending now.

His head lowered, and his eyes flicked from mine to my mouth. My stomach swooped in response, then my lips curled in disgust at him and myself. Ryker might have been attractive, but he was *ugly* inside.

Those full lips parted, and my breath caught in my chest. What was he doing?

He bypassed my mouth and leaned in, his breath teasing my ear. "You think you're going to save her? Who's going to save you?"

I sneered, stepping back from him. "I am."

His eyes danced, lighting for the first time since I'd seen him that morning. I looked away from him, breaking the spell, and met Faith's scared eyes instead.

"Let's get out of here," I told her, reaching for her hand.

Ryker put his hand on my arm. "You sure you want to start this battle?"

I narrowed my eyes at him. "No, I'm starting a *war*."

TWO

I YANKED my arm from Ryker's grip and made sure I had a good hold on Faith's hand before marching away. His friends might have been laughing, and I might have felt his eyes on my back, but I was so mad I could have boiled water for a thousand of my mom's organic food recipes.

"Um, Cori?" Faith whispered.

"What?" I snapped, still fuming.

"You're hurting my hand."

"Oh!" I instantly dropped her fingers and cringed as she shook out her hand. "Sorry, Faith."

She shrugged, hooking her fingers through her backpack straps. "I should be thanking you." She held her chin high, but I could see the tremble in her lips. It brought my anger back full force.

We reached the spot where I'd dropped my backpack, and I bent, swinging it over my shoulder. "Those guys are jerks, Faith. Karma will get them, and if not, I will."

Shaking her head quickly, she said, "No. You shouldn't have done anything. Now we both have targets on our backs."

I rolled my eyes. "I'm fat with red hair. I don't know how much more of a target I could be." I stepped from the asphalt onto the cement curb leading up to our school. The imposing façade and the Latin words inscribed over the doorway stared back at me. *Ad Meliora.* Toward better things.

Everyone at Emerson Academy was expected to do incredible things with their lives. My eight-year-old twin sisters were already on their way toward becoming famous actresses. Ginger was now at the most prestigious film school in the country. How could I ever measure up?

"Still," Faith argued, going up the steps to the school right beside me, "your life's going to get harder. Did you really want to sign up for a year of his torture?"

"I watched that guy pick on my sister every day last year. He's a coward. She just mouthed off back, and that was it. It's all a game to him, and he's not used to losing."

Faith shook her head. "He's just as bad as the *IT* girls."

My eyebrows came together. "*IT* girls?"

Her cheeks flushed, and she muttered something I couldn't make out.

"What?" I asked, entering the crowded entrance hall.

"It's just what I call Isabella and Tatiana in my head." She fluttered her lashes, barely meeting my eyes, then looked down.

She was so self-conscious. Her size and acne didn't help anything. I couldn't imagine what those guys calling her a cow earlier had done for her self-esteem. I knew from personal experience it was hard to be a big girl at Emerson Academy, even after my sister and her friends had started the Curvy Girl Club, owning their fatness instead of all the people who had picked on them.

But you couldn't let people control what you did or didn't do because of your size. There was always a way to make your assets work for you. What was a liability in the social realm quickly became my biggest advantage on the basketball court. Because of my size, I could push my way around opponents and be one of the best rebounders and highest scorers on the team.

Besides, *IT* girls was a pretty funny name for the two girls who thought they ran the school. "I like it," I told Faith. "I'm going to use it."

Her smile spread as she came to a stop in front of a locker. "It's not trademarked or anything."

I chuckled. "Maybe you should trademark it." I nodded toward the navy lockers. "This you?"

She nodded, and she looked like she wanted to say something more.

"What's up?" I asked.

She lifted a corner of her lips. "I was just thinking... it would be cool if someone finally put Ryker in his place. Then this year might not be so awful."

I wasn't planning on backing down on my promise to him. Not one bit. "Let me know if he bothers you again," I said and waved goodbye.

"See you around," she said, turning to her locker and spinning the dial.

I needed to find my own locker. It was down a different hallway, but I hadn't taken the time to find it or try my combination at the Academy's open house. I started down the east wing toward the athletes' lockers. They kept us closer to the gym so we could get to practice on time.

"Cori!" Nadira called from behind me.

A sense of relief washed over me as I turned to see my best friend. She wrapped her arms around me, her bushy hair scratching my cheek.

"You have the *worst* timing," I told her. As we walked to my locker, I filled her in on everything that happened this morning.

She leaned against the locker next to mine and said, "How have you already had a full-on face-off the first day of school? All I've done so far is forget my retainer and eat a bagel."

I laughed. "I'll trade you." I tried my combination for the third time and let out a frustrated groan. "Seriously?"

Nadira stuck out her hand. "Give me your code."

I handed her the crumpled paper with the numbers and stepped back as she worked her magic. For whatever reason, she'd always been better than me at the get-your-life-together kind of thing, despite forgetting her retainer.

Once she had the door open, she said, "Who's your first hour?"

"Aris," I said, rolling my eyes toward the ceiling. "I hate calculus." I reached into my bag and began unpacking notebooks into the empty locker. Once I found the paper that had my schedule, I passed it to her. "What classes do we have together?"

"Second hour health...Sullivan for current events...Ryker..."

My eyebrows came together as I zipped up my bag. "Ryker? Why are you bringing him up again?"

A low voice hummed behind me. "Maybe because I'm the fantasy of every girl in this school."

I closed my eyes, already picturing his stupid beautiful face. Of course Nadira had gone silent, leaving me to fend for myself.

"You're in my way," he said.

I rounded on him, ready to put him in his place for the second time today. "This is my locker."

He inclined his head toward Nadira. "I was talking to the firehouse dog."

My mouth fell open. Was he seriously calling Nadira out for her skin condition? She had been diagnosed with vitiligo our freshman year and had struggled constantly with her self-esteem since then. It was one thing to pick on someone's weight, but making fun of their skin color? How *dare* he. "You low-life piece of—"

"Cori," Nadira said. "Come on, let's go."

She began tugging me away, but I pulled back and looked Ryker square in the face. "It is *on*."

His eyes lit with glee. "I'd ask if you're ready to lose, but I watched you play basketball last year. I'd say you're used to it."

I narrowed my eyes at him. "I might be used to losing, but it should be fun watching your first time."

Ryker came forward, his lips curling into a daunting smile. "I never lose." He reached out and tucked a curl behind my ear. "But I'll have fun watching you try to get on top." He winked.

"You're disgusting." I pushed his hand away and followed Nadira down the hallway, planning my revenge the entire way.

THREE

SENIOR YEAR at Emerson Academy was no joke. By lunchtime, I'd already been assigned calculus homework, a research paper for health class, reading for British literature, and a pencil drawing for art class. How I was going to manage this, I had no idea.

With my backpack feeling significantly heavier than it had at the beginning of the day, I made my way to the cafeteria. Seeing my friends and not risking another homework assignment was my favorite part of the day.

After loading my tray, I scanned the tables and found Nadira sitting with our friend Desirae. Des sang the national anthem before almost every

Academy sporting event because her voice was just *that* good and our school wanted to show her off. Where I was tall and stout, she was short and curvy thanks to her Hispanic roots. Ever since freshman year, the three of us had been inseparable.

I took my tray and sat beside Des. "*Please* tell me we have a class together after lunch."

She finished sipping Diet Coke through her straw and turned to me. "Where are you doing your service hours?"

"With the second-grade gym class."

She frowned. "You got stuck with those germ factories?"

I snorted. "I'm actually kind of excited."

Both she and Nadira gave me a skeptical look.

"Come on," I argued. "A few hours playing games once a week can't be that bad. Where are you volunteering?"

Nadira picked at her food. "I'm helping Mr. Aris with grading freshman work."

Des gave her a teasing grin. "That's your dream come true, right? More math?"

Nadira rolled her eyes. "I'm sorry some of us actually *like* math."

"Uh huh," Desirae said, seeming skeptical. "I'm playing piano at the hospital."

"That should be good for you," I said encouragingly. "Do you think they'll let you sing?"

She shrugged. "We'll see. Maybe I could even record it and add it to my YouTube channel."

"You have a channel?" I opened the app on my phone and clicked on the search bar. "What's your handle?"

"To be determined. I'm still setting it up," she explained, tipping my phone back down. "What about current events? Are you in that?"

"Seventh hour," I said.

She rubbed my shoulder. "Yes!"

I grinned and began digging into my lunch. During basketball season, I stuck to our school's "hEAlthy" menu, but in the off-season, all bets were off. Besides, with how healthily my mom cooked and the massive amount of frozen casseroles she'd left for Dad and me, I needed a little trans-fat in my life.

Nadira leaned across the table, closer to us. "Ryker is totally staring at you."

She was obviously talking to me. And me, being the idiot I was, turned to meet his slate-gray eyes. His lips instantly quirked like I'd fallen straight into his trap, and he wiggled his fingers in a wave.

I rolled my eyes, just as frustrated as the girl next

to him who he was ignoring. Just another of the airheads who rolled their uniform skirts up three times and somehow got away with it. Ryker hooked his arm around her shoulder and pulled her close, nibbling on her ear while looking at me.

Feeling the small amount of food I'd eaten threaten to come up, I turned back to the girls. "He is so repulsive."

Nadira rolled her eyes. "Well, you basically guaranteed you'd be his target the entire year."

Des's eyes ping-ponged between the two of us. "Okay, what did I miss?"

By the time we filled her in, Des was not only disgusted with Ryker, but also seemed concerned. "Cori, you know how he treated Ginger."

"She handled it," I said. I didn't like everyone bringing up my big sister like some kind of victim. Ginger was one of the strongest people I knew.

"He made her miserable," Des said. "Remember how much happier she got when Ray started walking her into school so Ryker couldn't bully her anymore?"

"That might have something to do with the fact that Ray's completely hot," I pointed out, staring at my food. Suddenly, preservatives and refined sugar weren't looking so appetizing.

CHAPTER 3   17

"Cori," Nadira said. "Girls like us don't stand a chance against guys like him."

"Girls like us?" I challenged, lifting my chin. "What are you trying to say?"

Des put her hand gently on my arm. "We're trying to say that we care about you. Just...give it a few days to simmer, and if you want to call a full-on war, then we can get the tanks together."

Nadira nodded. "Please?"

I could see the fear in her eyes. Ryker's comment earlier had totally shaken her up. And if I was being honest, Ryker, who was currently occupied with shoving his tongue down that girl's throat in the middle of the lunchroom, had set me on edge as well. Maybe it would be better to let the vendetta rest.

The lunch bell rang, and we all parted ways to our separate classes. English composition brought another homework assignment, but my spirits felt light as I made my way to current events with Mr. Sullivan. At least I'd be seeing Des in that class.

But when I walked through the door, Mr. Sullivan pulled me aside. His mustache wobbled as he said, "Mrs. Bardot would like to see you in her office."

"College counseling already?" I asked, disappointed. Aside from having no clue what I wanted out of my future, I really wanted to catch up with Des and hear more about the YouTube channel she was setting up. Maybe I could give her some ideas on songs to cover.

Mr. Sullivan shrugged. "Not sure what the meeting regards, but nonetheless..." He made a shooing motion with his hands.

"I'm going, I'm going," I said, turning around. The hallways were nearly empty now, and it felt weird not seeing Pixie Adler as hall monitor anymore since she graduated. There didn't seem to be anyone out and about now to watch the halls. I wonder if they had just accepted that they'd never find someone as good as Pixie and given up on the whole institution of hall monitor.

Mrs. Bardot's door came up on my right, but when I rounded the doorway, there were already people inside. "Sorry," I said, backing away, then my eyebrows drew together. Why were Nadira and Des in there?

I bumped into someone behind me and turned to see Adriel Pruitt, another girl in my grade. We had a couple of classes together.

"Sorry," I rushed out.

She gave me an easy smile. "No big deal. Just got called to Birdie's office."

"I did too." What was going on here?

"Shall we?" she asked.

Dumbly, I nodded, following her the last few steps into Mrs. Bardot's office. Her finch, Ralphie, tweeted wildly at all the guests, and Nadira giggled at him, putting her finger close to the cage.

"It's okay, Ralphie," she cooed.

My eyes were on Mrs. Bardot, though. She stood at the side of her desk. "That's all of us. Please sit, girls." She ushered us toward the round table in her office.

My mind spun as I looked at the girls around me. There was Nadira, Des, Faith, Adriel, and me. The only thing we had in common was our larger-than-average size. Suddenly, I felt self-conscious about my waistline and the way my stomach rolled over my thighs as I sat down.

Mrs. Bardot clasped her fingers, showing her fingernails manicured with pencil and book decorations. "You're probably wondering why I called you here."

Nadira and I glanced at each other out of the corners of our eyes, and I said, "Yes."

"I heard about an incident in the parking lot this morning and then again in the hallway, and I have to say, I'm concerned."

My mouth fell open. This was *not* going where it looked like it was. Was this some kind of fat pity party? Mrs. Bardot was a little out there, but she couldn't be this dense.

"I have plans to talk to Ryker Dugan about his behavior, but I wanted to make sure you girls were taken care of. That you had a place to feel understood."

I glanced at Adriel across the table, who just looked confused. Des, on the other hand, had her full lips pursed into a flat line. The only thing I 'understood' was that if Mrs. Bardot confronted Ryker, it would seem obvious I'd told on him, even if I hadn't. Besides—

Faith cleared her throat. "What happened to Emerson's 'zero-tolerance' policy? Does it not apply to him?"

Mrs. Bardot wouldn't meet Faith's eyes. "Since we didn't see the incident, it's hard to make judgements like that. Besides, you girls all know that if it wasn't him, it would be someone else." She tapped her fingernails on the laminate tabletop. "Which is why I'm forming a...support group of sorts for you ladies."

My lips parted. I couldn't have heard her right.

"It's a trial run, but I want you to meet every Thursday for lunch. Mr. Davis has happily offered up the AV storage room as a private place for you to meet."

A tight ball of anger formed in my chest. "I'm not doing this."

Mrs. Bardot raised her eyebrows. "Is that so? Your parents already agreed it was a great idea." She leaned forward, leveling with me. "Look, worst case scenario, you get a private, catered lunch once a week."

"Catered?" Adriel said.

I shot her a look, and she pressed her lips together.

"This is profiling, you know," I said.

"I know," Mrs. Bardot replied. "Your commonalities are exactly why I brought you together."

I looked desperately to Nadira and Desirae. Nadira always followed the rules, but maybe Des would speak up.

"How long do we have to do it for?" Desirae asked, then glanced at me, responding to my shocked look. "Let's just get it over with."

I settled back in my chair, folding my arms over my chest.

Mrs. Bardot looked from Desirae to me. "For the rest of the semester, and potentially the year."

I opened my mouth to argue, but Desirae said, "Deal."

FOUR

SINCE I DIDN'T HAVE basketball practice after school, Dad asked if I would help stock for an hour or two at the store before heading home for dinner. I wouldn't turn down a chance to hang out with his new cute stock boy, Knox.

Driving up to Ripe, my parents' health food store, felt just as much like going home. I pulled the minivan into the parking lot and stared up at the big sign with a flashing neon banana. Ever since Ginger recovered from a near deadly case of pneumonia, this store had been their life's mission. That, and keeping her safe.

I unbuckled my seatbelt and stepped into the warm evening air. The lot was nearly full around me, which meant there would be plenty of work to do. The automatic doors slid open for me, and the main cashier, Janet, looked away from her current customer and grinned. "Hi, Cori!"

I smiled and waved so she could get back to checking out her customer, then started down aisle three, lined with organic coffee blends and cannisters of teas and herbs. Another aisle passed by with bulk offerings of grains and rice, then I reached the door that said EMPLOYEES ONLY.

The big storage room was filled with boxes, and I found my dad bent over a stack, loading them onto a cart to stock on the shelves.

"Hey, Dad," I said.

He looked at me over his shoulder. "Hey, kid. Glad you made it." The look of relief on his face was hard to miss. It almost made me forgive him for forgetting my first day of school.

"Busy day?" I asked.

He nodded. "You have no idea. Knox is slammed, the butcher counter's almost completely empty, and Janet hasn't had a break since lunch."

"Oof." I reached for a box and said, "I've got it back here. Why don't you let Janet tap out?"

"You're a godsend." He kissed the top of my head.

I smiled and got to work loading the boxes. This

was a great workout, but not quite challenging enough to keep my mind off the day. Ryker had already messed up my senior year, and it was only the first day. What would come on day two? Day fifty?

Shaking my head, I stacked the final box. I'd survived a summer watching my big sister waste away in a hospital bed. I'd taken on girls even bigger than me on the court. No way would some spoiled, promiscuous rich kid make me back down.

With a little more force than necessary, I shoved the cart to get it rolling, and a box fell off. I may have let out a few cuss words as I bent to grab the box and all the cans that had spilled out of it.

A chuckle sounded and I looked up to see Knox, the beautiful, completely off-limits college guy my dad had hired to help stock the store.

"Struggling?" he asked as he bent to help me clean up.

My cheeks heated. "Only a little bit."

He grabbed the rest of the cans in his big hands and stood. I got up as well, dusting off my jeans. "Thank you," I said.

"No problem." He grinned, flashing a set of teeth that had to be his orthodontist's best work.

"What aisle are you working? Maybe I can join you."

"Seventeen," I answered. "But my dad would probably have your head—or your job—for spending too much time with me." With how attractive he was, I couldn't tell which was worse.

He snorted. "Maybe if the store weren't completely packed right now. He won't even notice."

"True." A smile spread on my lips, but I tried to play it cool. "See you in a bit."

Maneuvering the cart around customers proved even more of a challenge. I almost ran into two people and lost a few cans on the way. Maybe "struggling" was an understatement.

Finally, I made it and began loading the cans where they belonged, taking extra care to turn the labels out and line them up with the front of the shelf. Soon, a set of hands began working beside mine, and I glanced over to see Knox in his yellow Ripe shirt.

"How's school going?" I asked.

He looked at me over his extended arm. "No classes on Monday. You?"

I groaned. "A mountain of homework and an archenemy bent on destroying my life."

With a nod, he said, "Impressive. What did you do to earn that?"

"Homework's a pretty normal part of the Academy."

Laughing, he bent to grab another armful of cans. "I meant the enemy. Did you break someone's nail?"

I glared at him but couldn't keep it up with the playful smile on his face. "I'll have you know he was asking for it."

"He? What did you do to the poor guy?"

"Didn't let him pick on a girl because of her weight, and then I got coerced into this weird support group and he won't stop looking at me." The words all came out so fast, and when I reached the end of my sentence, I had to take a breath.

Knox only chuckled softly and said, "You know, when a guy picks on you, it means he likes you."

"Oh please." I rolled my eyes. "Take that sixteenth-century nonsense back to the dark ages. Some girls actually want guys to respect them."

"True." He got out his box-cutter and began breaking down a box. "What are you going to do?"

"I don't know."

A customer wanted to look at the canned vegetables, so we stepped out of the way while the guy weighed his options. Once he had selected with a few cans of hominy, the world's grossest vegetable, Knox and I set back to work.

"Maybe you should call Ginger?" Knox suggested.

"I should," I agreed. But maybe I didn't want to. Did I want to admit that I was already in over my head when she'd handled Ryker's nonsense every day of the year? But then again, desperate times called for desperate measures.

FIVE

THE HOUSE WAS empty when I got home, just like it had been when I left. No I'm-sorry-for-forgetting-your-first-day-of-school flowers from Mom in sight. Dad still had another couple hours at the store, and I desperately needed to get a jump on my homework.

But instead of going to the kitchen table and working on it like I should have, I got out my phone and called my big sister.

I had an ugly selfie she'd taken on my phone as her contact photo, and it still made me smile. Not as much as hearing her voice, though.

"Hey, girl, hey," she said, half-joking, half not. "What's up?"

"Oh, you know." I settled into the comfy

recliner in our living room. "Living the glamorous life of an indentured servant slash high school student."

She chuckled. "Rough first day?"

"That's an understatement. Please tell me yours was better."

"Mom only called me twice, and my roommate seems really nice. We're actually thinking about heading out soon to check out a club here."

I tried to ignore the deep ache in my chest at the fact that Mom had remembered Ginger's first day and not mine. "If our mother knew you were doing that, you'd be *dead*."

Laughing, Ginger said, "That's why she doesn't know. Besides, I'm underage. What am I going to do other than rub up with some sweaty people and go home with sticky shoes?"

"Good point." I cringed, thinking of the way the floors at Spike, the under-eighteen club in town, were always covered in soda and who knew what else.

The line was quiet for a moment, something that didn't usually happen in a conversation between my sister and me.

Her knowing voice came through the line. "I'm

guessing you didn't call to chastise me about pub crawling."

I closed my eyes. How had I been so dumb? I should have just gone to get Birdie when I saw Faith being bullied. Instead, I'd gotten myself in the middle of Faith's problems and bit off more than I could chew with Ryker. "I had a run-in with Dugan." Ginger always called him by his last name because she thought it was uglier than his first. Just another form of her rebellion I couldn't live up to.

"Did he hurt you? I can call Ray and see if he'd be willing to use a little muscle."

"No, no, no." I sighed, my chest tight. "The last thing I need is to have my future-brother-in-law fighting my battles for me."

She was quiet for a moment. "Cori, you need to steer clear of him, okay? Walk into the building with Nadira and Des. Even if it means taking a little longer. Ask your teachers to sit you away from him in class. Do you understand? That guy is bad news, and I don't want you getting caught up in his games."

I could hear people talking in the background, and Ginger said something away from the mouthpiece about being there in a second.

I realized I was already dragging down her first

days at college. She should be having the time of her life, not worrying about her little sister or things going on at her old high school. "Don't worry about me," I said. "I just miss you is all. Go out with your friends, you dirty scoundrel."

She seemed uncertain, but finally said, "Okay. I'll take you out when you guys come to LA?"

"That sounds good," I said. I could wait a couple of weeks to pick her brain. After all, how much trouble could I get into anyway? "Love you, Ging."

"Love you too."

Flipping down the footrest, I got up and went to the kitchen, digging for the bag of chocolate chips my mom always hid in different places. I finally found it stuffed behind the seasonings and brought it to the table.

I video-chatted Nadira and propped my phone against my stack of books so I could get her help on algebra when I needed it. We mostly worked in silence, aside from the questions I asked every now and then.

Her mom came into the video screen behind Nadira, and she waved at me. "Hi, Cori! How was the first day?"

I gave her a look. "You heard about the fat

camp, right? It's even worse that they're trying to bribe us into it with food."

Dr. Harris smiled slightly. "Fellowship is second only to scholarship." As the dean of Brentwood U's engineering department, she was always speaking cryptically like that. I wasn't sure how Nadira understood anything her mom said.

Nadira looked up at her mom. "Almost finished here."

I waved at the screen. "That's okay. I think I managed at least a B. See you tomorrow, Dir."

I hung up the phone and stood from the table. I should have gotten a jump start on my last paper due, but I was tired. Tomorrow would be a new day. A better day.

Following Ginger's advice, I waited in the parking lot until Nadira's very sensible sedan pulled in, along with Des's cherry-red convertible. The three of us walked side by side toward the school, and thankfully, Faith was nowhere to be seen. I hoped she'd taken the same precautions to avoid Ryker.

Not that it would have been necessary. When we passed his tricked-out truck sitting in the front row of the parking lot, he had Isabella pressed up against the fender and his hand dangerously high on her thigh.

"Ugh," I said, taking my eyes off that train wreck. "Why do so many girls fall for that?"

Nadira rolled her eyes. "Tall, dark, and dangerous. It's a thing."

Des shook her head. "You have to admit he's hot, even if he is a piece of human garbage."

I started up the stairs with them. "Thank God I don't have any classes with him this semester. Hopefully we can keep it that way for the rest of the year."

"How did you not wind up with any classes with him?" Nadira asked. "There are only sixty kids in our class."

I shrugged. "Guess I'm lucky?" We stopped at the hallway that led off to the athletes' lockers. "Just like I got lucky not having to see him at the locker today."

Des giggled. "I think he's the one getting lucky."

I shoved her shoulder, laughing along. If Nadira's skin was lighter, her cheeks probably would have been bright red. As it was, she shook her head at us and walked away.

Des put her arm around my shoulders. "It's fun corrupting her, yeah?"

I put my forehead against hers. "Always."

Her eyes lit up. "Imagine what we can do with Faith and Adriel with one day a week."

I couldn't help the laugh that passed my lips. "Only you would see this forced lunch as a good thing."

"Hey." She shrugged, stepping back and running her hands over her hips. "You don't get to be this way by turning down catered meals."

I rolled my eyes. "If that's all it took, I'd have bangin' curves too."

"Oh, you do," she said.

"I tend to agree." Ryker's voice came from behind me.

My lips parted in shock as he came to stand beside me, slinging his muscled arm over my shoulders like he owned me.

I shoved it off and stepped closer to Des, my skin prickling. "Not if we were the last two people on earth, Dugan."

"We'll see about that, sweetheart." He winked and sauntered toward his locker.

Desirae gave me a look. "You're turning purple."

"And steam's about to come out of my ears." I groaned. "I can't stand him!"

"Looks like he's a little fond of you." She winked at me like he had moments earlier.

"Get out of here," I said, starting toward my locker.

She called after me, "See you later, *sweetheart*."

SIX

THE SPECKLED TILE floor stretched out before me as Nadira and I walked to our first mandatory lunch. In the email Mrs. Bardot sent us, she called it The Curvy Girl Club 2.0. I *had* to remember to tell Ginger about the cringey name later.

Nadira nudged my arm. "You okay?"

I looked back into her deep brown eyes. "I don't know. This all seems so ridiculous."

"It is." She looped her arm through mine. "But that doesn't mean it can't be fun."

"Did anyone ever tell you you're the best?" I asked, my hand on the handle to the AV room.

"Yeah, just not enough." She put her hand on top of mine and turned the handle.

The inside of the AV storage room was lined

with floor-to-ceiling shelves of VHS tapes and DVDs, almost like a time capsule. The round table in the middle of the room was absolutely loaded with a catered meal from the fanciest Italian restaurant in town, La Belle. Maybe Birdie really was trying to get on our good side.

She grinned at us from where she stood behind Faith and Adriel, her hands on their shoulders. Of course, the perpetually late Desirae wasn't here yet.

"What are we having?" she asked, coming into the room behind us.

"A bribe," I muttered to her.

"What was that?" Mrs. Bardot said.

"La Belle," I said louder, a fake smile on my face.

Nadira half led, half dragged me to the table, and I took an empty seat by Faith.

Mrs. Bardot clasped her hands over her chest, grinning proudly. "I hope you girls will find you have more in common than you think. This will be a place for you to share common challenges you might face and delight in your triumphs. And, of course, enjoy delicious food once a week. Any requests for next week?"

Des lifted her chin. "How about some lobster

tail? Seafood is supposed to be good for girls *like us*. You know, omega-3s and all."

"Sure thing," Birdie said without batting an eye.

With a smirk, Des said, "Glad to know our tuition's being put to good use."

"Look, I know you don't want to be here, but we have a donor who wants to support girls like you. Now, each of your parents agreed it would be good for you to be here, so I hope you'll give it a chance." Without providing us an opportunity to argue, she breezed out of the room and left us with our tableful of food.

The awkward silence to end all awkward silences ensued as we all stared at each other and the food.

Des reached for a serving spoon and dished pasta onto her plate. "Let's not let the food get cold."

Adriel smiled nervously. "Don't need to ask me twice." She grabbed salad tongs and dished herself a healthy helping.

Hints of parmesan and garlic hit my nose, and I couldn't say no to carbohydrates any longer. I took the serving spoon from Des and dished myself a plate. With a mouthful of food, I said, "This is still BS."

Faith shrugged. "I don't know. That did shake me up the other day." Her words didn't come close to conveying the hurt I saw in her eyes. "It wouldn't be bad to have some friends."

"You don't have friends?" Des asked bluntly.

Quietly, Faith shook her head. "Unless you count the middle-aged women my mom makes me volunteer with at our church."

Her admission made me that much angrier at what happened. "You know what? *Ryker* should be the one having a support group with the rest of the football players on how not to be a jerk."

Nadira snorted. "That would mean someone at this school actually holding him accountable for his behavior."

"Exactly," Adriel said. "Guys like him—society itself, is *never* going to change how it views girls like us, so it's on us to get stronger."

"That's crap," Des said. "That just takes even more responsibility off of them."

Faith rubbed her temples. "Can't we just forget about this?"

"No." I gestured at all of us sitting around the table, hidden away in the AV room like lepers. Here we were, five beautiful, curvaceous, lively, talented, incredible girls who were made to feel like less because of a few extra pounds. It was pure and utter crap. "This whole support group nonsense is exactly the type of thing that gives guys like Ryker power. If Birdie's not going to hold him responsible, *I* am."

Nadira shook her head. "It's not that easy. Half the school's wrapped around his finger, the other half wants to get into his pants, and the other half's too afraid of him to do anything."

Des gave Nadira a sardonic smile. "There can't be three halves—and you call yourself a mathlete."

I smiled softly, then looked each of them in the eye. "Come on, how do you want your senior year to go down? Do you want to say you laid low and hoped for better days? Or do you want to sit at the nursing home, all old and decrepit, and tell your weaselly grandkids who don't visit often enough that you stood up to the bullies and made this year —and Ryker Dugan—your bitch?"

Adriel chuckled at the curse word. "You know what? I'm in. I'm sick of being made fun of because of my size. Maybe if we can get him to stop...I don't know. Maybe everyone else wouldn't feel like they have so much power to bully us too."

Faith shook her head. "I'll do anything not to be afraid of walking to class."

Des reached out and slapped my hand. "You know I'm down."

All eyes were on Nadira now.

She looked toward the heavens and muttered something to herself. Then she looked at me. "Are you sure you want to do this? It's going to be hard. He's powerful, and he can make your life a living hell."

I grinned at her. "That's funny, because we're about to do the same to him."

Shaking her head, she said, "I know I'm going to regret it, but I'm in."

SEVEN

WITH NO FOOTBALL game on Friday, I felt a little lost. I usually spent all my time playing sports or watching them. Plus, with Dad working at the store, Ginger in college, and Mom in LA with the twins, I had the whole house to myself. Again. A girl could only watch so much TV before she lost her mind.

My phone began ringing, and I looked at the name on the screen. Mom.

I scowled, not wanting to answer, but knowing if I didn't she would just call and call until she got what she wanted.

Once I pushed the green button, I said, "Hello?"

"How was your first week of school?" she asked brightly.

My eyebrows drew even closer together. "Seriously?"

"What?" she asked innocently, as if she hadn't just ignored me for an entire week while calling my sister at least twice.

But I couldn't admit how much it hurt without sounding pathetic. She'd have her sister here to supervise me in a second, even though that was the last thing I needed...

I needed my mom.

"Nothing," I said. "It was fine."

"How was the lunch thing?"

I rolled my eyes toward the ceiling. "Great."

"Would it hurt you to say more than one word, Cori?" she asked, frustration edging into her voice.

"I was about to ask you the same thing," I retorted, moving from the couch to the kitchen in search of my chocolate chips. Chocolate could fix anything, right? Even this ball of anger blazing in my chest?

"What is that supposed to mean?"

"Nothing," I said finally, tearing open the bag. "How are the twins?"

Changing the subject was always a solid tactic

with Mom. She loved talking about her daughters. Her other daughters.

"They're great!" Mom said. "The director adores them, and they've even made friends with several of the extras around their age. And the moms on set..."

I silently ate chocolate chips while she went on and on about how fabulous the twins were and how great LA was treating them. I wasn't bitter. Nope. Not at all.

"We're so excited for you and Dad to come visit next weekend," she said. "Can't wait to show you all the sights!"

"Me too." I glanced around, desperate for a way to end this conversation that just left me feeling worse and worse with every minute that passed. "Um, Mom, I'm about to burn your casserole. I better let you go."

"Hurry!" she said, and I hung up the phone.

I leaned against the kitchen counter, resting my head on my folded hands, wishing yet again there was a football game I could watch to distract myself from the things that hurt the most.

The problem was, I couldn't think of much. After watching another movie, I fell asleep on the couch and woke up the next morning just as bored as I'd been the night before. Around ten, I gave in and texted Des.

Cori: SOS

Cori: I'm

Cori: So

Cori: BORED

Des: Are you sure you're not staying entertained blowing up my phone?

Cori: Haha. But seriously... want to do something?

Des: Mama's trying a new maza recipe. Want to come over and hang out at the beach then eat?

Cori: You had me at food.

Des: I know you. :) You wanna text Nadira?

Cori: Yeah...What if we made it a Curvy Girl Club day?

Des: I thought you hated the CGC?

Cori: The institution, yes. The girls? No.

Des: You know Mama cooks for an army. She'd be thrilled.

I started a new group chat in my *Sermo* app that let me message with anyone in our school without knowing their number. It required a group name, and I smiled sardonically as I typed in CGC 2.0.

Each of the girls agreed to come to Des's house around three, and Des sent them the address. Her family lived right on the beach, and it was honestly the best place to waste a day—or a summer—even if I couldn't get a tan no matter how hard I tried.

I sent Dad a text letting him know I'd be at Des's and threw on my swimsuit and cover. (By the way, thank god for high-waisted swim bottoms. They weren't nearly as uncomfortable to wear as the one-pieces I used to wear. Those had always ridden up and dug into my shoulders under the weight of my breasts.)

I got in the car and drove to Des's house, feeling better and better the closer I got to the beach. Her family's home came into view before me, the modern building silhouetted by the rolling blue ocean.

A couple of cars I recognized from school were there already, along with Nadira's. I parked behind her sedan and went inside without knocking.

The home opened into a view of the entire kitchen and living area, with floor-to-ceiling windows showing an even better view of their private beach.

Each of the girls sat around the bar counter, while Mama De worked in front of a massive bowl.

"Cori!" she cried, grinning at me. "*Mi amor, como estas?*"

"*Bien.*" I grinned. "New recipe?"

"Yes!" She blew at her bangs and stirred harder. "I hope you girls all have your appetites."

I patted my stomach. "You know I do."

Des came to greet me and looped her arm through mine. "We're heading out to the beach, Mama."

"Have fun," Mama De said.

As the girls and I walked through their sliding back door onto an expansive deck, I asked, "Where are your siblings, Des?"

She held up the fingers of her free hand. "Diego is kayaking with Dad, Mateo's out with his girlfriend, Adelita's hanging out with the boy next door, Marisol has violin practice, and Marco's at mi abuela's getting spoiled rotten."

Adriel caught up with us as we began walking down the stairs. "You have *five* siblings?"

Des nodded.

"And about a million cousins," Nadira added.

I laughed. That was so true. Last time I'd come to a wedding one of their family members had behind the house, I'd felt completely outnumbered by the De Leons' huge extended family.

Faith chuckled. "The more the merrier, right?"

"Exactly," Des said, letting go of my arm and

picking one of the beach chairs lined up along the shore. There were seven setting out, one for each of her family members, but it was perfect for us.

I threw my bag down on the sand, shucked my coverup and began putting on sunscreen. The sun already felt magnificent—yet deadly—on my pale, freckled skin.

Faith peered at me curiously. "How are you so confident?"

I lifted my sunglasses so I could see her. "Do I have something to be ashamed of?"

She blanched as she thought of the obvious—my extra weight—but honestly, why should I be ashamed of extra skin and fat? It didn't make me less of a person. Didn't determine my worth. I had just as much right to enjoy the beach as any girl with a size-zero waistline.

I smiled at her, hoping to lighten the mood. "It's just us here. No need to worry."

Seeming more relaxed, she took off her own dress to reveal an adorable polka dot one-piece.

"See?" I said. "You're adorable! Why wouldn't you be confident?"

"That is so cute, Faith!" Des complimented, pulling her sheer dress over her head. Her curves spilled out of the coverup, making her look like a plus-size Betty Boop.

Adriel gracefully took off her shorts and top, and soon we were all baking in the sun, the way God intended. It felt so blissful to sit out here and listen to the ocean waves.

I must have fallen asleep, because I woke up to the sound of Mama De's voice saying, "You have to try these tamales!"

I rolled over in my chair and saw her scurrying toward us in her shift dress, carrying a platter full of food. I must have been in heaven.

Des took one of the tamales first, eating with her fingers, and then Mama De worked her way through all of us, passing out the food. Mingling with the smell of saltwater, the scent of the food hit my nose, making my mouth water. I already knew it would be a hit.

The second I took a bit, a blend of sweet and spicy flavors exploded in my mouth, and I moaned loudly. "This is *so* good."

Mama De positively beamed. "You don't tell your mama that it's not organic."

I laughed. "No way, I want more of it!" I took a second helping while the other girls shared their own positive reactions.

Once we'd eaten the platter clean and Mama De Leon was satisfied with our answers to her questions about the flavor, she went inside.

Des sat up on her chair and looked us over with an evil smile. "Can't plot our revenge on an empty stomach, now can we?"

EIGHT

WE SPENT the next hour or so thinking about how we could make Ryker's life miserable, but with him, it was hard.

"He's so untouchable," Adriel said. "He has girls all over him, he's the star player on the football team, and the whole school loves him."

"So that's it then," Nadira said.

We each swung our heads to look at her, and she gawked at us like it should be obvious.

"What do you mean?" I asked.

"Well," she explained "if we want to hit him where it hurts, we have to make him vulnerable first."

Faith chewed on her lip. "But how far is too far? I don't want to be just another bully."

My mouth fell open that she would even suggest that. "Seriously? He and his friends had you trapped in the school parking lot pretending like you were a cow, and you're worried about hurting his feelings?"

"Exactly." Des shook her head. "Nothing we do to him will ever be as bad as what he's done to you."

"How do you know?" Faith asked cautiously.

"Because," Adriel said quietly. "He's never had to wonder whether he's good enough."

"Exactly," I agreed. Even though I was confident in my body, other people treated me like I shouldn't be. Not to mention, I constantly had to wonder about whether I deserved anything I had. My parents were always worried about Ginger getting sick or the twins succeeding in acting. I had nothing special enough to keep their attention. But we'd get *Ryker's* attention once this was all said and done.

"So where do we start?" Des asked. "Football? Girls?"

"What if..." Faith started, looking shy. "What if we started with his truck?"

I blanched. "I thought you were worried about

going too far, and now you want to mess with his vehicle?!"

"No, no, no," she cried. "My parents own a dealership, and they never let a car go on a test drive without making sure it smells good."

My lips turned up as I caught on to her idea. "How can we make it stink?"

Adriel gazed over the water. "Looks like we have plenty of material right here. A fish would make it stink for a week!"

We spent a good hour scanning the shore for a dead fish until Des pointed out we could probably just get one from my parents' store. I agreed to grab one from Ripe, and we parted ways. Adriel said she had dance practice, and I needed to get home to Dad for our weekly video call with Mom, the twins, and Ginger.

I made it home just in time to find Dad sitting at the table, opening his laptop.

"You're cutting it close," he said.

"I know, I know," I replied, already running to my room to change. I hurriedly threw on an Emerson Academy T-shirt and sweatpants, then jogged to the table.

The twins' faces were already on the screen, along with Mom's.

"They had to put in a fake tooth since I lost one!" Tarra cried.

Cara nodded excitedly. "It looks so real though. They say they use them on kids all the time."

Dad chuckled as I slid into the seat beside him. "Sounds like an adventure."

"It is," Mom agreed. "But I'm so proud of them. The director said they're the most respectful kids she's ever had on set."

Dad positively beamed. I'd never seen his cheeks get so high under his red beard. "That's great, girls, keep it up!"

Ginger's face popped onto the screen. "Sorry, class ran long!"

Mom narrowed her eyes but said, "You better be on time next weekend!"

"Wouldn't dream of being late," Ginger said. "Cori and I have a lunch date on campus."

Mom's smile matched Dad's from earlier. "I'm so glad you two are still staying so close." She sniffed. "Melts your mother's heart."

"*Mom*," Ginger and I said at the same time.

"Hey," Cara said. "*We're* supposed to be the ones talking in unison."

We all chuckled, and even though we were all apart, for a moment, it felt like we were together again. Sure, the twins got on my nerves sometimes with their constant singing and saying things in unison, but they were still my sisters. And Ginger was my rock, even if she couldn't see that in herself. And Mom... she was still my mom.

"Cori," Mom said, "how's the Curvy Girl Club going?"

Ginger smirked. "The new and improved version, right?"

I rolled my eyes. "We're getting a lobster dinner out of the deal, so I can't complain too much, right? Fat girls are supposed to be bought with food after all."

"Cori," Mom admonished.

Dad jumped in. "She actually hung out with them today at the De Leons', right, Cori?"

I could tell he was trying to make things easier for Mom, even on a video call, and it melted me. Just a little.

Mom raised her eyebrows. "Did they feed you GMO corn again? I told them—"

"We had a good time," I said. Which reminded me, I needed to get a fish from the store before Monday...

For the rest of the hour, we talked about college for Ginger, the store, and the twins' role in the movie, and then we said goodnight. Before I went to bed, I sent a text to Knox.

Cori: Any chance you can grab a raw fish from the store for me without Dad knowing? The stinkier the better.

Within a few minutes, he replied.

Knox: Should I be worried?

Cori: Probably.

Knox: In that case...

Knox: Meet me Monday in front of Waldo's. 7 am.

NINE

WHOSE IDEA WAS it to get up at this ungodly hour? Oh yeah, mine. The things I'd do for revenge.

After making sure Dad had already left for the store to unload the truck, I trudged out of bed and went to the bathroom to get ready. No way would I look my second best in a close encounter with Knox or with Ryker.

I tamed my curly mane with a straightener, put on my school uniform, and hurried out the door. The path to Waldo's Diner was a familiar one. I couldn't count how many hours I'd spent there with Nadira and Des just hanging out or celebrating a win with the basketball team. That place was like a second home at this point.

When I pulled into the parking lot in front of the silver building, I saw Knox's car almost immediately. His windows were rolled down, and I took a second to sneak a peek while he wasn't looking.

Knox was good-looking, but not in the football player-y way Ryker was. With a slim body and shaggy hair, he could have easily fit in on a soccer field or playing frisbee with friends. Grinning, of course.

I parked the minivan a few spots away from his and got out to see his trademark smile. "Hi there, accomplice."

He got out of his car and looked around, pretending to be nervous. "Are you sure you want to do the handoff here?"

I noticed the storage bag with a disgusting looking fish—head, eyes, and all—in his hand. "Do you have a better place?" I teased.

He shrugged, making the fish flop. "I don't know, but I'm starving. You have time for breakfast?"

I checked my watch, even though I knew I did. I just had to do something to keep from squealing. "Sure," I said casually. "I can get yours, you know, for risking your clean record and all."

He bit his lip. "I knew you'd make it worth my while."

My cheeks heated instantly, and I turned toward the restaurant. "Well, let's go. I want to see Chester."

Nothing could kill a blush like Chester, the sweet old man who hung out in the restaurant like he owned the place. He was always there, getting endless coffee refills and chatting with anyone who walked by.

I pushed inside the door, making the bell ring, and my favorite waitress, Betty, waved and said a cheery, "Good morning!"

"Morning," I said back, echoed by Knox behind me.

Just as I expected, Chester sat in his regular booth, the morning paper spread before him.

"Morning, Chester," I said to him.

"Hi there." He smiled back at me and lifted his cup. "How's your sister liking college?"

"She's living the dream," I answered honestly. "How's Karen and your kitten?"

He chuckled. "It's hardly a kitten anymore. But they are both great."

I smiled and waved goodbye so Knox and I could

take a booth. I didn't have tons of time before school started, and I wanted to sit across from him as long as I could. After Betty took our orders, Knox eyed me.

"Do I want to know why you requested a fish on a Monday morning?"

I drank deeply from my sugary coffee. "You're the one who wanted to get up this early."

He laughed. "Don't avoid the question."

I rolled my eyes. "There's this guy."

He snorted and had to set his coffee cup down so he wouldn't spill. "That was so not where I was expecting that to go."

I was blushing again, this time at the idiocy of the idea. Seriously? I was putting a fish in his truck? It all seemed a little junior high. But then I remembered how hopeless and hurt Faith had looked surrounded by Ryker and his goons. What a brave face Ginger had put on each morning just to walk into the building.

"It's hard to explain," I said finally.

"Yeah?"

I nodded.

"Well, answer me this...what are you doing with it?"

"Putting it in his truck."

Knox outright laughed, and now my cheeks really were red.

"Do you have any better ideas?" I demanded. "I have to get back at him somehow."

"What? You can't just pull a classic move and hide his clothes after gym class? You have to hurt Harry?"

"Harry?" I asked, confused.

"Oh, it's what I named the fish."

I rolled my eyes, laughing. "I think Harry will be fine. Ryker, on the other hand, will not be. I'll make sure of that."

His lips parted. "Ryker? As in Ryker *Dugan*?"

"Yeah," I said. "Who else?"

Suddenly serious, he said, "Cori, you can't do this."

My eyebrows came together. "Why not?"

Shaking his head, he swirled his spoon in his coffee. "You know my dad used to work with his dad?"

"No." I hadn't even heard of Knox before Ginger told me a cute college guy had started at the store. And somehow, despite all my social media stalking, I hadn't checked out his dad's LinkedIn. "Why is that important?"

"Because," he said. "My dad was one of the top

dock workers at the marina before Trent Dugan felt threatened by him. And do you know where my dad is now?"

"Living a bright and happy life?" I asked, cringing all the while.

"Working airport security because no one in the boating industry would even *think* of hiring him after Trent Dugan got through with him." There was a shadow on Knox's face, showing just how much the betrayal had hurt his family.

I reached across the table and rested my hand on his. "I'm so sorry."

With half a smile, he drew his brown eyes to mine. "I hope you'll be careful when it comes to this guy. The apple never falls far from the tree."

My throat felt tight, and I swallowed. "Maybe that's true, but then what? Ryker keeps being a bully for the rest of his life, destroying entire families? Or maybe he has a chance at learning his lesson?"

"Is that what this is, a friendly helping hand?" Knox asked, a knowing look in his eyes. "Or is it revenge?"

Unable to hold his gaze, I flicked my eyes down to my half-eaten eggs, the yolk spilling into my hash browns. "Why don't you let me worry about that."

"I hope you will." He stood, reaching into his pocket.

"You don't have to pay," I said. "I can get it."

He shook his head, a somber smile on his lips. "That's fine. Just...take care of Harry for me, will you?"

"Of course."

He dropped a couple of bills on the table and walked out of the restaurant, waving to Chester on the way.

Through the broad diner windows, I watched him pull away. Despite his warnings, I knew what I had to do. Ryker Dugan had messed with the wrong girl.

TEN

WE AGREED to hide the fish in his truck during football practice. That would at least keep him occupied, and if we did it in the middle of practice, no one should have been walking through the parking lot.

Still, we had Adriel stationed near the front doors of the school and Nadira on the other end of the parking lot to make sure no one found us.

"Hurry up, hurry up!" Des whispered.

I followed her and ducked down behind a Jeep.

Behind me, Faith said, "Do you really want to do this?"

"Yes," I whispered. "If nothing else, to get Harry out of the car."

Des glanced back at me. "Any word from Adriel

or Nadira?"

I shook my head. My phone was blissfully vibration-free.

"Let's get this over with," Des muttered. She crawled forward, well hidden between a Hummer and Ryker's truck. It was perfectly shiny, as if he took it through a car wash each morning before getting to school. It honestly wouldn't surprise me.

I sneered at the shining paint. "Pass me the tape."

Nervously, Faith handed me a roll of black tape. "Dad says this will stick for life."

"Good." I rolled to my stomach and crawled over the pavement to get underneath the truck. It was lifted high enough that I had plenty of room. When I got under the spot where the driver's seat should have been, I unzipped the plastic bag that was Harry's temporary home.

Trying to keep my face away from the disgusting, dripping juices, I pulled off a strip of tape and secured Harry to the underside of the truck. If our plan went well, it would stink up Ryker's vehicle without causing permanent damage. If we got really lucky, he'd never find out it was us.

My phone vibrated in my back pocket, and I froze.

"Cori!" Des hissed. "Was that you?"

I finished slapping the tape on and rolled out of the way as fast as I could, ditching the plastic bag under the pickup. And yeah, littering wasn't cool, but neither was being caught and getting expelled for taking care of a problem the principal should have covered.

I sprang to a crouch and followed the girls away from Ryker's pickup. A few rows over, Des stood up, talking casually. If singing didn't work out, she had a definite career in acting.

Faith was so nervous she just smiled way too big.

"I got a text," I said casually and got my phone out.

Nadira: SOS. PRACTICE LET OUT EARLY. HURRY UP.

Loud mooing sounds came from a few feet over, and I saw none other than Ryker Dugan with a pretty, skinny girl clinging to his side, followed by a group of his friends.

"Looks like the herd's in town!" Grant called to a bunch of guffawing laughter.

I rolled my eyes. "Let's get out of here."

"Going to feed?" another player called.

Des lifted her hand in the air, making a gesture

that could have gotten her detention. It just made the laughter louder.

"Come on, Red," Ryker called after us. "Scared so easily?"

I closed my eyes and clenched my fists, keeping pace beside my two friends.

"There's the herd dog!" Grant called, and I looked around to see what he was talking about. Nadira was standing beside us now, and my blood was *boiling*.

"Everything okay?" Adriel asked, coming up on our left.

I let out a sigh. We'd fallen right into the trap.

"Sooey!" Ryker yelled. "Come get your slop!"

Another guy laughed. "They can drink my slop. Come and get it!"

The girl giggled loudly.

Des pretended to gag herself, but kept walking, dragging me along beside her. Faith's eyes were watering, and Adriel's chin was just as high as it was when she did ballet.

"They're not going to feed," Ryker said. "They're going to slaughter. They've fattened up plenty to make some good steak."

I spun on my heel, ripping my arm from Nadira's protective grip. "The only meathead around here is you," I hissed, closing the several yard gap between us. Walking up to him when he was surrounded by his band of idiots felt like swimming in the shark tank, but I didn't care. I'd bite back. "And you'll have to let me know what being slaughtered feels like after the game on Friday. Have fun losing."

His lip curled, and his gray eyes were hard as stone. "You think you're cute, don't you, Red?" Everyone around him fell deathly silent, and I didn't hear any noise coming from my friends either.

I rolled my eyes.

"Why don't you stop acting tough and give up." He nodded his chin toward my friends. "Unless you want your friends to pay too."

Suddenly, I felt a lot less confident than I had before. Still, I bluffed, raising my chin and meeting his eyes. "Don't worry, I can handle the bill on my own."

At that, I turned and marched toward my friends. Their expressions were equal mixtures of shock and horror as I reached them, but I just said, "Let's get out of here."

"Week two," Nadira muttered. "Already off to a great start."

ELEVEN

FOR THE NEXT FEW DAYS, I felt like my heart was on edge. Maybe I felt guilty about sticking a fish to the underside of Ryker's car. I kept waiting for whispers about his vehicle's odor, but nothing.

At least, not yet.

On Thursday, we had steak and greens, at Adriel's request. She said she was training for nationals.

"Placing could mean the difference between performing with a well-known dance company or going down as someone who *used to* dance."

Faith opened her mouth, then shut it.

"What?" I asked her.

"Nothing." She began cutting through her steak, although it hardly required the provided knives. In fact, my piece hardly required chewing it melted so well in my mouth.

The set of Adriel's shoulders became defensive. "What, Faith?"

"I just..." She set down her fork and knife. "Are you worried they won't take you because of your size?"

Adriel's lips set. "If I dance well enough, my size won't matter." She seemed like she was trying to convince herself. But I wasn't about to try and talk her out of it.

"What about you, Faith?" I asked. "What's after high school?"

She shrugged. "My parents want me to go to college and study business. Marry well. Live an entirely boring life."

I frowned. "Is that true?" I couldn't imagine someone's parents just expecting them to get married and start popping out babies. "There has to be more."

She pushed a piece of lettuce around her plate. "Not for someone like me."

I wanted to ask her what she meant, but Des said, "Oh my gosh!" She was looking down at her phone.

"What?" I asked, my heart sinking. We'd been

caught. How did people ever rob banks and stay quiet about it? Would this guilty feeling ever go away?

She turned her phone to me to show her YouTube app. "My last cover got thirty thousand views!"

"No way!" I cried.

Nadira grinned. "Of course it did! You have an amazing voice!"

Adriel lifted her cup of bubbling Diet Coke. "A toast, to Desirae."

Des held up her glass. "My friends call me Des."

Adriel's lips turned up. "To Des."

We clinked our cups together.

"To Des," I said.

She grinned. "And to showing this world that curvy girls deserve to be heard."

I smirked. "We're going to be heard alright." One way or another, we'd get our message across.

After lunch, my classes flew by, and I went to my locker to get my books before picking up a shift at the store. I grabbed what I needed and my nearly empty bag of chocolate chips, then shut the door to see Ryker standing only inches from me, holding up a bag with a mottled piece of... *something*.

I jerked back, my heart racing. Once I realized what it was, I sent him a glare, then turned and walked away, going faster than normal.

Busted.

He followed me, easily keeping my pace with his long legs. The hall had cleared out just enough that he could walk beside me unimpeded. "No, 'hello, Ryker,' 'how are you, Ryker'?"

"I usually only speak to my *friends* like that," I said icily.

"I am a friend," he said, no friendliness in his voice at all.

I gave him a look and pushed out the school's front door. Knowing I was going to have to deal with him one way or another, I stepped to the side and waited. Also, going down a long set of stairs with my enemy beside me didn't seem like the smartest idea.

"What do you want?" I asked.

He held up the bag, his dark eyebrows raised.

"Afternoon snack?"

A growl sounded low in his throat, and I couldn't help but laugh. "Caveman doesn't look good on you, *Dugan*."

"Is that so?" He stepped menacingly forward,

and I backed up until my back hit the hard brick wall. He had me cornered, and he knew it. Liked it —I could tell from the glint in his eyes.

I lifted my chin, even though it put my lips inches from his. I would not look away from those chilling gray eyes. Would stand my ground even on legs that felt as firm as unset jelly.

"My car was starting to smell like fish, and I thought some chick had left her underwear behind or something."

My lip curled in disgust. "You're nasty."

He put his hand on the wall by my head, making me aware of every bit of his body near mine, of the charge of hatred that existed between us. "*Then*, my guy comes out from detailing the truck and brings me this." He rattled the bag, making poor Harry flop lifelessly. "Of course, I got a new pickup out of the deal, but I was fond of my old one. Now, you wouldn't have anything to do with this, would you, Red?"

"My name. Is Cori." I pushed away from him and went to the stairs, despite the fear and adrenaline racing through my blood. "And I want nothing to do with you." I held on to the railing and started down.

Behind me, he said, "You're going to have to do better than that if you want to win this war, Red."

Under my breath, I promised, "Don't worry, I will."

TWELVE

THE NEXT MORNING OVER BREAKFAST, I reminded Dad that I'd be at the football game. It was about the only time we really got to talk, since he got home late and left for work early. Without Mom around to help pick up the slack at the store and the house, I knew it had been hard for him.

"How late do you think you'll be out?" he asked, finishing up his bowl of cereal.

I raised my eyebrows. Dad asking me about my curfew? This was a new one.

Noting my surprise, he said, "You're a senior, Cori, and there are plenty of things I'd do over with Ginger if I could. I want to give you the chance to prove you're responsible before I take away any of that trust."

My heart swelled at the idea, at the fact that my parents were coming around to seeing me as a person and not as a walking danger to herself. "Is eleven alright?"

He nodded. "I'll wait up."

I smiled and stood up, going to kiss his cheek. "Have a good day at work."

"You have fun at the game." He reached out and brushed my cheek with his thumb. "And be *safe*."

"I will," I promised, thinking to myself that Ryker was the only one in danger of being humiliated. I wasn't sure how, but I would start phase two tonight. Hopefully the girls had a plan.

As Dad left, I sent a text to the group chat.

Cori: Want to watch the football game with me tonight?

Faith immediately replied.

Faith: YES. Anything is better than sitting with my parents.

Des: It's a date. :)

Adriel: I can come after dance practice. Is it okay if I'm a little late?

Cori: Of course!

Nadira: You know I'm game. Get it?

Des: Eyeroll emoji. ANOTHER pun?

Nadira: That's the goal. Hey-oooo

I laughed out loud and tucked my phone in my pocket. Tonight was going to be fun.

After lunch, Mrs. Bardot's voice came over the school's PA system reminding seniors to go to their volunteer assignments. "If you've forgotten your assignment or have questions, please come find me in my office," she finished, and a loud crackle signaled the end of her speech.

I waved goodbye to Des and Nadira, then started outside.

So far, I'd managed to avoid Ryker, but I hadn't been able to miss his obnoxiously fancy—and new—truck sitting in his parking spot. As I walked down the stairs, trying to keep the strong wind from affecting my modesty, I glared at the shiny monstrosity.

It had to be the newest model, one with all the upgrades, and its grill gleamed back at me like even the truck knew it was supposed to be evil. Thank goodness I'd be able to spend the afternoon with the second graders, helping the elementary school gym teacher with PE and getting my mind off Ryker.

The elementary school was in a building on the opposite end of the Emerson Academy campus, so I put in my headphones to listen to music on the walk. I turned the volume up loud so I could hear it over the strong wind and kept my hand bunched on my skirt. I was *definitely* wearing pants tomorrow.

Finally, I reached the elementary school building, and the second I put my hand on the front handle, my skirt blew up all the way. I dropped the handle and pushed the fabric down, absolutely mortified, even though I hadn't seen anyone outside.

A large hand reached around me, pushing the door open, and Ryker's voice said, "Ladies first."

My mouth fell open as I turned to take in his smirking face. "You didn't—"

"See your Tuesday underwear?" His eyes smoldered. "Absolutely." He nodded toward the open door. "Go inside."

I didn't like taking orders from anyone, much less Ryker, but standing out in this wind wasn't doing me or my hair any favors.

I backed in through the door and pressed the

buzzer so we'd be let inside. "What are you doing here, Dugan?"

"My name is Ryker."

I smiled sweetly at him. "I know. What I don't know is why you're following me."

"You mean other than the view?"

My cheeks flushed, and I turned away, pressing the buzzer again. Come *on*.

The door clacked as the lock lifted, and I dragged the heavy door open as fast as I could, hitting myself in the forehead. Pain spread across my face not nearly as bad as the embarrassment blooming everywhere else.

"Smooth, Red," Ryker said, taking the door. "Why don't you leave the heavy lifting to the guys."

I glared at him, knowing full well there had to be a red line on my forehead. "You better get away from me."

The elementary school receptionist, Mrs. O'Haire, came out to greet us. "Our volunteers are here!"

My mouth fell open, and all I could think was... *Oh hell to the no.*

Maybe I didn't think it, because she looked at me, her penciled-in eyebrows drawn together, and said, "Excuse me, Miss Nash?"

I shook my head, feeling the heat of Ryker's smile prick at my back. "Nothing."

"We know where to go," he said.

"Great," she replied. "Let me know if you have any problems."

Oh, I had a problem, and he was walking right beside me, a smug grin on his face.

"Just stay away from me," I said as we reached the gym.

He lifted his hands. "Whatever blows your skirt up, darlin'."

Ugh. I opened the double doors to the gym, careful not to dome myself this time, and walked inside. Ms. Anaheim had the kids lined up on the bench, and when she saw us, she said, "Class, welcome our volunteers, Cori and Ryker!" She started clapping, and the kids cheered along.

When the noise died down and she had them settled again, she said, "You know Ryker from the football team. He's the wide receiver, the one who catches the long passes from the quarterback and scores some Drafter Touchdowns!"

The kids stared at him like he was some kind of god, and I felt sick to my stomach. He was *so* not this cool.

"Cori plays on the basketball team, scoring baskets for our Lady Drafters!"

I had to keep my eyes down as the kids turned their admiration on me. I so wasn't used to getting attention. How had Ryker stood so proudly? Probably because he was always the center of the universe, at least in his opinion.

For the first part of the class, Ms. Anaheim wanted the students to get used to us and vice versa. She sent Ryker and me to opposite ends of the court to play an ice breaker game with the kids.

I learned that a girl named Anna had lost seven teeth in the last year and a boy named Frederick was saving dog poop in his backpack for his mom's flower bed. (I might need to tell Ms. Anaheim about that one).

They were all so cute, and I swore Ms. Anaheim had the dream job. Playing sports with kids all day? Sign me up.

Across the gym, I could see Ryker's smile and hear giggles from time to time, but I had my doubts about his abilities to be a good, kind role model for children. Maybe if Ms. Anaheim saw him as unfit, he would have to find a different volunteer service —maybe I wouldn't even need to see him every Friday.

When our shift was over, Ryker walked with the kids to their class, but I hung back with Ms. Anaheim.

"How was he?" I asked. "With the kids?"

She smiled. "He was great."

I couldn't help the surprised look that crossed my face. "Really?"

"I know he has a bit of a reputation, but he was great with the kids..." She looked at me. "You both were."

My lips turned up. "I had a lot of fun," I answered honestly. For the first time since I'd learned Ryker would be volunteering with me, I had a little bit of hope. Maybe this wouldn't be so bad after all. Besides, how much damage could he do with a teacher watching?

THIRTEEN

WALKING to the football field for the first game of the season felt like being home.

The air was beginning to feel more like fall with the undercurrents of a chill that was yet to come. Even though it wasn't quite cold enough to warrant it, I had on a beanie that felt warm and cozy and made my hair curl away from my face in a way that I loved.

I held my phone in my free hand and scanned the home stands for my friends. It seemed like the entire town had to come to watch the first game of the season, and I couldn't blame them.

I was about to text Des to see where she was before I remembered that she'd be singing the national anthem. Anytime we had a home game, she was our music teacher's go-to. Instead, I looked for Nadira's telltale curly hair and found her several rows up from the front. Faith sat next to her, and they looked deep in conversation. Their growing friendship brought a smile to my lips. Faith needed someone on her team, especially after what I'd witnessed the first day of school.

I climbed up the steps to the front, saying hi to a few of my classmates on the way, and walked up to Faith and Nadira. They both greeted me, and Faith offered me a thermos and a Styrofoam cup. "My mom made hot chocolate if you want some."

"It's heavenly," Nadira said over her cup that was slowly fogging up her glasses.

"In that case…" I took the cup and held it steady in both my hands as Faith poured some steaming liquid inside. Taking a careful sip, I found it was just as good as my friend had promised. "You *have* to give me this recipe," I said.

Faith grinned. "That would be amazing. You're welcome to come over and drink some any time, but my brothers are a little obnoxious."

I shrugged because she wasn't wrong. Faith had two older brothers in college and one younger brother who was a junior. He actually played as the football team's tight end, and if Faith weren't his sister, he probably would've been right there with Ryker, picking on her.

After another sip, I turned my gaze toward the football field where our home team was warming up. Ryker and the school quarterback were along the sidelines, passing the ball back and forth. Ryker had his helmet off and tossed to the side, revealing his strong jaw and the black marks painted under his eyes.

I didn't know how it was possible, but he looked even more intimidating on the football field than he ever had walking the halls of Emerson Academy. Especially with his muscles bulging on his arms with each throw and catch of the ball.

As if he felt me staring, his eyes panned over the stands, and even though there were hundreds of people around me, it felt like he was seeing right through me. He smirked once before turning his eyes back on the quarterback and tossing the ball back his direction.

"He was so looking at you," Nadira said.

Faith giggled. "Probably worried you might prank his pickup again. Did you see he got a new one?"

"Actually..." I told them about my run-in with

Ryker the day before and how he divulged getting a new truck because his last one had smelled bad.

Nadira's jaw dropped open. "Why didn't you tell us yesterday?"

"Or today at lunch?" Faith added.

"It's been a long day." I sighed and shook my head. "You won't believe who I'm volunteering with either."

Nadira's mottled hands covered her mouth. "You're kidding."

"Nope," I said, popping the P. "I swear it's like the universe is conspiring to make my senior year the worst one possible."

Faith frowned as Mr. Davis came over the PA system, announcing Des singing the national anthem. She stepped up to centerfield, holding a microphone and looking stunning in her tight jeans and formfitting Emerson Academy jacket. Everyone around us rose and listened as she sang the most beautiful performance I'd heard her do yet.

Nadira filmed the entire thing on her phone, and when it was over, she said, "This better go on her YouTube channel."

"Definitely," Faith agreed.

"Excuse me," I heard and looked up to see Adriel shuffling down the benches toward us. She looked adorable with her hair above her head in a tightly wound bun. I needed to ask her how she did that because anytime I attempted a twist, I just looked like I had a wimpy man bun.

"How was dance practice?" I asked her instead as Faith poured her a cup of cocoa.

"Intense," she said. "I feel like the studio director's being harder on me than everyone else."

"Why?" I asked.

Her gaze darkened, but she simply shook her head. "I'd rather not think about it." She gestured toward the field where Des had just been. "That sounded amazing."

I agreed with her and turned my eyes to the field as well. Whatever was happening with her at dance practice was obviously too raw to touch right now. My eyes fell on Ryker and Grant standing in the middle of the field doing the coin toss with the captains of the other team.

After the toss, it was customary for the captains to shake hands. I could only imagine the crushing grips that Ryker and Grant were offering their opponents right now. I watched with morbid fascination as he and Grant walked back to the team and begin preparing for the first play of the season. I recognized the intensity on their faces because I felt it on my own during basketball season. I loved the feeling of standing at the tip-off line, knowing all my practice and hard work could come down to a single moment and I would either fail and learn or win and push harder, but there was no giving up.

Des joined us about halfway in to the first quarter, and I had to go through round two of filling everyone in on Ryker's truck situation.

"So, basically, he's untouchable," Des said. "Ruin the truck and he'll just get a new one."

"Yep," I said flatly.

"Then it's on to the girl situation, right?" Des asked.

"I'm in," I answered. "Should we start planning tonight?"

"I'm down," Adriel said. "A strawberry milkshake from Waldo's sounds amazing."

Faith grinned. "Make that a chocolate shake, and I'm in."

Nadira frowned. "Are you sure Waldo's is the best place to go tonight? It'll be packed with football players and cheerleaders, and there's no way they're going to see the five of us together and not make a scene."

My heart ached for all of us. How was it okay that these people on the football field could make others feel this way, make us afraid to go out to a restaurant to eat, and just got to go on with their happy, carefree lives?

"That's exactly why we have to go," I said. "We need to show them that they don't own us. Their actions can't control us anymore."

Faith chewed on her full bottom lip. "But what if they do make a scene?"

I pressed my lips together and smiled. "We drink our milkshakes like the cows they think we are."

Des rolled her eyes, laughing. "Only you."

"And you." I pointed at her. "And you and you." I pointed out the other two. "We're in this together. Curvy Girl Club 2.0, right?"

With a grin, Adriel said, "Ryker is going down."

FOURTEEN

EMERSON ACADEMY WON the football game 33-14, and Ryker scored 28 of those points. After the final buzzer sounded, his teammates lifted him on their shoulders, parading him around the field.

The cheerleaders formed a human tower, and the girl at the top kissed Ryker on the cheek.

"Barf," Des said.

"Right?" I agreed, turning away. "Let's get out of here."

We took separate cars to the diner so we could leave after on our own, and on the drive, I kept thinking about Ryker and the life he lived. How silly I'd been to think a mere fish could even dent his perfect reality. We'd have to do something that rattled him as much as his taunting rattled us.

I pulled into the diner, which was already slammed with customers. On nights like this, my favorite waitress, Betty, told me they just premade milkshakes in every flavor because they knew they'd get ordered before they melted.

As I parked, my phone chimed with a message in our group chat.

Faith: Was it a bad idea to come here?

Nadira answered before I could.

Nadira: It's never a bad idea to spend time with friends. <3

My lips softened into a smile. Nadira was right. Sure, we wanted to get revenge against Ryker, but that didn't mean we shouldn't enjoy each other's company as well. I tried to focus on that as I got out of my car and began walking toward the door.

Inside, the big booth at the back was completely empty. Everyone saved that one for the football players and cheerleaders who'd come in on their high horses when they were done primping after the game. Part of me wanted to go sit in it, but then I saw Nadira wave from a booth midway down the diner. She and Adriel were already there, and I joined them, sitting next to Adriel.

"How did you snag a booth?" I asked, shrugging off my jacket. "It's packed in here."

Adriel giggled. "You know Nadira tackled someone for it."

I laughed out loud. That was so not Nadira. "That girl couldn't hurt a fly."

Nadira eyed us over the menu. "If you must know, I helped Betty clear the dishes, and she said we could have it."

"You're such a saint," I said, grabbing a menu of my own, even though I already knew what I'd be getting. Chocolate shake and French fries. Plus ranch. I'd alternate dipping between the ice cream and dressing, and it would be heaven. I was already drooling just thinking about it.

Faith hurriedly got into the booth next to Nadira and said, "Made it!"

Adriel chuckled. "Was that ever in question?"

She shook her head, shucking her jacket. "Just didn't want to get caught around the football guys on their way in."

My smile quickly fell, but I tried to put it back in place. "Well, you're here now. Unlike Des, who's always—"

"Fashionably on time?" Des said, getting into the booth beside me.

"Exactly what I was going to say," I said with an eyeroll to Adriel behind my menu.

She chuckled, and Des sent us both a look that said we were being children. Maybe we were, but it was fun.

Faith straightened uncomfortably, and a hush fell over the diner as the door clanged open. I followed her eyes to see Ryker walk in, wearing jeans that framed his muscular legs, a tight T-shirt, and his letterman jacket that hung off his broad shoulders.

Grant and Fletcher flanked him, walking in alongside him like the gods they thought they were. For a moment, his eyes flicked over me, but then he was distracted by person after person congratulating him on the game and his ridiculous number of touchdowns. Part of me was afraid Ryker would stop and confront me, but when he passed by our table without stopping, I felt a little disappointed.

What was wrong with me? Why did I like arguing with him so much?

I couldn't ponder on it too long because Betty came to our table and took our orders. Within minutes, she had our milkshakes on the table and promised the fries would be ready in a few minutes, hot from the fryer.

"You're incredible," I said, grinning at her.

She winked. "Just doing my job."

After she walked away, Des said, "Tell us, evil mastermind. What's next on our revenge plot?"

All of my friends' eyes turned on me. In avoiding their gazes, I glanced over to the booth where Ryker sat, a girl curled on his lap.

"We could try to break up his booty call?" I suggested.

"How?" Adriel asked. "She seems pretty invested to me."

I turned to Des. "You've had boyfriends before. What was a deal-breaker?"

She rolled her eyes. "I'm single. What wasn't a deal-breaker?"

Nadira gave her a look. "You're so picky. I'd just be happy to have someone even remotely interested in me."

"Same," Faith said, sipping from her drink.

Adriel shook her head. "Come on, guys. You have to see that you deserve better."

"Exactly," I agreed. "So be real, Des."

She rubbed her arm, deep in thought. "Oh! You remember that one guy I dated? The one who was a clown at birthday parties?"

Adriel snorted while Faith just looked horrified.

"Unfortunately," Nadira said as I nodded.

"I think the final straw—besides the whole

clown thing—was that he started taking calls from other girls *while* I was on dates with him."

"Ugh," Faith said in disgust.

"Mhmm," Nadira agreed. "But it's not like we can call him. He'd just know it was us."

Adriel perked up. "Actually..." She got out her phone and began tapping on the screen. After a moment, she showed an image of a scantily dressed woman with text that read ONE DOLLAR PER MINUTE! CALL ME NOW.

I nearly snorted out my milkshake and started coughing. "Oh, this is good." There was a spot to put in your phone number and card info, which meant we could have someone on the phone with Ryker in seconds.

The other girls burst out laughing, and Des happily drummed her hands on the table. "I think I have his number!" She began scrolling through her phone and within seconds was giving Adriel the number along with her father's credit card information.

"He won't notice the charge?" Adriel asked.

Des shook her head. "Not unless it's over 2k."

Adriel and Faith's mouths fell open, but Nadira and I were used to the lenient way Des's family handled money. To the De Leons, money wasn't a precious resource, just something that came and went as you were living life.

Adriel looked from her phone to the rest of us. "Ready?"

We nodded, and she pressed the button. Then we turned to his booth and waited.

Our table was just close enough that we could hear his phone play the lyrics of a rock song in his pocket, and I watched with glee as he shifted the girl in his lap to pull out his phone. After eyeing the number, he seemed to shrug, swiped the screen, and held the phone to his ear.

I watched as his expression transformed from confused to amused. With a wide smile on his face and his shoulders shaking with silent laughter, he said something into the mouthpiece and tapped a button on his phone.

The guys—and girls—around him leaned in to listen, suppressing laughter of their own.

"I can't look anymore," I muttered, turning back toward my food.

"Me neither," Nadira agreed. "Anyone else have any bright ideas?"

Adriel shook her head. "I'm out."

Faith turned back to us, her eyes wide. "Oh dear lord no."

"What?" I looked over at Ryker to see his friends lifting him into the air.

"Ryker! Ryker! Ryker!"

Laughing, he slipped down from their shoulders, took the girl who had been on his lap, and dipped her into a low kiss. The entire restaurant burst into applause.

Everyone except for us.

FIFTEEN

I ROLLED into the driveway at exactly 10:59. The front porch light was on, which meant Dad was still up, so I pulled my keys and hurried to the door. No need to get my trust card revoked over a minute. No, if I was going to blow it, it would be a Fourth-of-July-level explosion.

I slipped my keys in the lock and twisted the dead bolt before pushing inside to find Dad sitting in front of the TV. At the sight of me, he lifted the remote and turned down the volume.

"Watcha watching?" I asked.

He nodded toward the screen. "Just some old western Ray told me to watch. Ever heard of *Lonesome Dove*?"

I shook my head, but that was nothing new. I'd

never heard of half the movies Ginger's boyfriend wanted me to watch. "Is it any good?"

He shrugged and scrubbed his face, showing just how tired he was. "Ready for tomorrow?"

I nodded. "What time are we leaving?"

"Eight. And don't be up too late tonight. Your mom would never forgive us if we didn't leave on time."

I chuckled. "She might even make Aunt Rosie come stay with us."

Laughing, he said, "I don't know who that would be worse for. Rosie, who'd miss her dog, or us, who'd be constantly under surveillance."

"Rosie's dog," I said immediately.

"Good point." With a sigh, he got out of his chair. "I'm heading to bed. Make sure you're packed and ready on time."

I nodded and watched as he padded back to the bedroom in his plaid pajamas and the leather old-man slippers I always made fun of. Tonight though, I didn't feel like teasing. Mom being in LA with the twins was obviously taking a toll on him.

I made a mental note to pick up a couple more shifts at the store and maybe order something for him so he didn't have to keep eating frozen dinners at the store or old casseroles.

On the way to my room, I passed the den. It was probably the least used room in our house, with books lining the wall, a sofa bed in case guests came to visit, and a big rocking chair where Ginger used to take her breathing treatments.

The machine was gone now, but I could still picture her, sitting on her phone with the breathing apparatus hooked around her face. I shuddered and continued to the room we used to share.

I couldn't wait to see her again and just check that she was alright. It was like our parents' paranoia about her safety had rubbed off on me, and I worried that she was doing her breathing treatments, that she kept her inhaler filled and with her.

As I put on my pajamas, I considered ways I might ask her about her asthma without annoying her. She wanted to be independent, but at the same time, I wanted to know my sister was safe.

With my pajamas on, I went to the bathroom, washed my face, pulled my wavy hair up in a bun and went back to my room. As I lay in my bed, I could hear Dad's chainsaw snores coming from the master bedroom. The muffled rhythm of it sent me fast to sleep.

As we neared LA, skyscrapers silhouetted by soft blue mountains stood out in the windshield. I stared at the sight in awe, wondering where I might be living this time next year. With the basketball season only a couple of months away and college application deadlines looming, I might be finding out soon where a scholarship could lead me.

"What's the plan?" I asked.

He ticked his fingers off on the wheel. "Breakfast at the twins' apartment, then you and Ginger hang out while Mom and I pick up some school supplies for the girls, and then we'll meet back together at the set so you and Ginger can have a tour."

"Simple enough," I said as he merged into another lane. This freeway had six lanes on each side, and I got stressed just thinking about driving on it.

Dad didn't seem nervous, but he did stay quiet as we drew closer and closer to our destination. Mom and Dad had rented an apartment for the twins near the set so they wouldn't have to spend so long in the car after work days, which I heard could be brutal for them.

The apartment complex seemed nice enough,

although there was more asphalt than grass and more palm trees than any other form of life.

Dad said they were in U52, so we followed the signs to the U building, then parked between a Beamer and a topless Jeep. I imagined the glamorous lives people lived here, driving around in convertibles and taking off to the beach at a moment's notice.

The idea that I could be doing the same someday put a smile on my face as we got out of the car.

We reached unit U52, and the second Dad knocked on the door, Mom had it flung open and pounced on Dad, locking her arms around his shoulders. "I missed you!" she cried between kisses.

The twins and I gave each other a look, but it was hard not to gawk at my sisters. They looked at least fourteen or so with the false eyelashes on their eyes and mature clothes they were wearing.

"You look so grown up!" I cried.

Tarra grinned, while Cara grinned to show off her missing tooth. I took both of them in a hug, holding them tight. "I missed you!" I said.

From behind me, my mom said, "I missed you too, you know!"

Forcing a smile, I stood to give her a hug. She

put her arms around me and squeezed me. "You've been eating the meals I prepped for you, right?"

"Yes, Mom," I said.

"And you haven't found the chocolate chips."

I smiled. "Nooo."

Laughing, she released me and said, "Let's show you inside."

We walked into a one-bedroom apartment I'd only seen on video calls. It had plenty of windows and a view of the pool below.

"Girls," Mom said, "why don't you show your dad around the complex?"

I didn't need to ask to know she was only referring to the twins and that I was about to be grilled.

As the twins and Dad left, Mom said, "Do you want some tea?"

I sighed and sat at their four-person dining table. "Can we just skip to the interrogation?"

Mom's hand stalled on the kettle, but she quickly recovered and flipped up the handle on the sink to fill it. "I'm curious to hear about school. According to your counselor, you made quite a stir the first day."

I reached into my purse, grabbing my phone to check the time. Shouldn't Ginger be here to whisk me away?

"How are you liking the Curvy Girl Club 2.0?" she asked.

I put my head in my hands. When Mom said Curvy Girl Club, it sounded so lame. Like she was talking about my "little friends" or hanging up a first-grade finger painting. Didn't she know I was nearly eighteen? That I'd done just fine on my own while she was busy worrying about Ginger's asthma and the twins' acting career?

The kettle clanged as she set it on the stovetop, and I lifted my head.

Mom's brows creased in the middle. "Are you having a headache?" She came closer and put her hand on my forehead, and I scooted away from the table, feeling completely smothered.

"Stop!" I said, backing away. "Mom, I'm fine. I can handle myself." My chest heaved with the force I needed just to take a breath.

Her green eyes assessed me, seeing too much before she turned back to her tea kettle. Steam was beginning to come from the spout. Even though it probably wasn't ready, she poured herself a steaming cup and got out a bag of her favorite ginger lemon tea.

I watched her, ready for the other shoe to drop. Ever since Ginger graduated high school, it was like we didn't know how to be around each other. But maybe that was because I was always an afterthought when it came to my mom and my sisters.

Instead, she sat at the table with her tea and said, "The people on the set are nice enough. They have a snack table the girls would absolutely devour if I let them, and they even agreed to start ordering some healthier options from our store."

I took her in, noticing the lines around her eyes and the tired way she dipped her tea bag into her mug. My heart ached for her. It was probably lonely here, going from being a stay-at-home mom to being a set mom, surrounded by people from a completely different world. But that didn't change the fact that I'd been flying under the radar in the one place I should have been noticed.

Mom opened her mouth to say something more, but a loud knock sounded on the door.

"I'm here!" Ginger yelled through the door. "I'm only fifteen minutes late!"

As Mom walked to let her in, I thought Ginger was right on time.

SIXTEEN

WITH GINGER HERE, the focus quickly shifted off of me and on to her. There were questions about her breathing treatments, the college's pharmacy, and whether or not Ginger thought she needed a backup nebulizer.

Dad and the twins came back just in time to hear Ginger telling Mom the health department had left bowls of condoms on the coffee tables in the dorms' common area.

Mom was blushing as red as the beets in the omelets she had delivered, but when Dad and the twins asked, she said she was flushed and gulped down a glass of ice water.

Ginger winked at me, and it was that moment I noticed an extra piece of silver in her ear. "You got your tragus pierced?" I reached out and moved her curly hair out of the way to take in the piercing. "It looks epic."

Dad snorted. "Nothing says 'epic' like shoving a needle through your skin."

Ginger rolled her eyes. "It's supposed to help with migraines, Dad. It's medical."

Mom was on the scene in two seconds flat. "You're having migraines? Do I need to send you some more turmeric supplements?"

Ginger laughed, shaking her head. "Not yet, but I hear finals get pretty rough."

Mom shook her head. "Just make sure to sanitize it. I've heard of people getting nasty infections from new piercings in college."

"I will," Ginger promised and then asked Dad about the store, easily changing the subject.

That was a skill I needed to learn for myself. Instead, I got so worked up, I just wanted to fight and argue. On the other hand, Ginger had the rest of the conversation flowing smoothly and finally said she was ready to take me to campus.

Without argument, Mom agreed, saying she and Dad and the twins would be spending some "much needed" time together. That didn't sting. Not at all.

Ginger and I walked out to her car, and when we were safely inside, she said, "Freedom!"

I hugged the dash of her car and said, "I've missed you so much! The minivan just isn't the same."

"Should I give you some privacy?" Ginger asked, buckling in.

Laughing, I sat back and slipped my own belt over my lap. "That's okay. I missed you too. Kind of."

She shook her head, smiling the whole time. As we drove across town, she asked me about school and my friends, and of course, Ryker. When I told her about my revenge plot, her jaw fell open. "No stinking way."

I nodded nervously, not sure whether she'd be proud of me or admonish me like Knox had.

"You're crazy."

"Is that a good thing?" I asked. I honestly couldn't tell, especially with her eyes focused on traffic.

"I don't know," she said. "I just hope you're being careful."

"What's he going to do?" I asked. "Call me some names? So what?"

I immediately felt bad for saying it, because that

was exactly what he'd done to Ginger, and it had been a big deal. She'd constantly been on guard against him, and she shouldn't have had to be the tough one in that situation.

"You remember Shiloh Jones, right?" she asked, turning onto the UCLA campus.

I thought back to the guy who had been neck and neck with Ryker our freshman year. He and Ryker had to compete for playing time in the football games, and I remembered the evil looks they had always sent each other until Shiloh transferred halfway through the season.

"What about him?" I asked.

"You remember when he moved?"

I nodded. "His dad got transferred or something."

"No," Ginger said, her voice low as she pulled into a parking spot in a sparse lot. She put her car in park and met my eyes. "Shiloh's dad got handed a choice—move out of Emerson or have his career destroyed."

I covered my mouth with my hand. "*What?*" It was the second time I'd heard of the Dugans' path of devastation, but I couldn't believe Ryker's dad would stoop so low over something so trivial as playing time as a freshman.

Ginger nodded, her lips pressed together. "Shiloh's older sister told me before they moved away, but of course they had to keep it hush-hush because they were worried the Dugans would do something worse."

I lowered my hand to my lap as a fearful feeling built up in my chest. What had I gotten myself into? What had I gotten the girls into?

"Losing isn't an option for you now," Ginger said. "You either win or lives will be ruined. Do you understand?"

Slowly, I nodded. What had started out as a ploy for revenge was quickly becoming so much more. "You'll help me, right?"

"Of course." She put her hand on my lap. "I'll do whatever I can from here."

I swallowed and nodded, trying to still my nerves. "Thank you."

"Now"—she opened her car door—"it's time I show you the future." We got out of the car, and she spread her hands in the air. "Picture it, a life without the constant oversight of our parents. Friends in all directions. And a buffet. With non-organic food."

"Sold," I said with a laugh and followed her to campus.

We got into her dorm room, which she shared with a girl named Rachel. Ginger said she was gone most of the time, though, hanging out with her boyfriend or working late hours at a local coffee shop.

I stared around at the space lined with twinkle lights and brightly colored posters and throw pillows. Although a fourth of the size of our room at home, it was beautiful. It looked like freedom.

"I can't wait to get out of the house," I muttered. "I swear, half the time Mom doesn't even remember she has a fourth daughter."

Ginger frowned, sitting at her desk chair and offering me Rachel's chair. "What do you mean?"

"She hasn't even asked me how school went. And when she does ask me a question, she doesn't even wait to hear my answer. It's like I'm invisible."

Ginger shook her head, sighing. "I can't believe I'm sticking up for Mom."

"But?" I said.

"*But*, some space has really helped me see that she cares. She's just...misguided sometimes."

I shook my head. It was fine for Ginger to say that. For how much our mom smothered her, at least she paid attention.

"Here." Ginger slid her desk drawer open. "I

have something I think will help." She lifted a quart-sized ziplock filled with chocolate chip cookies. "Ray's mom gave them to me, but I think you may need them more." She grinned and passed me the bag. "To get you through until you find the next bag of chocolate chips."

I held the bag of cookies like the gold that it was. "If it was ever in question, you've won the best sister award. Don't tell the twins."

Ginger laughed and crossed her heart with her pointer finger. "It's our secret."

SEVENTEEN

I HELD the studio guest pass around my neck and looked at my name written in black permanent marker. Mom and the twins walked ahead of us, showing the set that looked like deconstructed portions of a dollhouse. Everywhere else I looked, there were cameras and cords and people. The floor was unlevel under my feet for all the taped down wires.

For some reason, I had imagined stars strutting around in fancy clothes and living the dream life. Instead, it seemed more like the grocery store. Everyone simply went about their business and then checked out.

As I watched a couple filming in front of a green screen, I had a whole new respect for the twins and what they were doing. Acting wasn't just some holiday where they got to do online school and spend half a year away from home. No, it was work, but the way their eyes lit up as they spoke about it, you'd never guess.

How had my eight-year-old sisters already found their calling? I was almost eighteen and still had no idea what I wanted to do when I "grew up" aside from play college basketball, and there was a whole lot of life to live after those four years.

I tried not to think about it as we left the studio and went out to eat at a nearby vegan restaurant Mom had discovered. We sat around the table in highbacked chairs made of woven bamboo, and I lifted the menu to see what might have a chance of filling me up.

Mom hadn't even glanced at her own menu. "You know, I've already seen several big names here." She put her hand on Ginger's wrist. "Maybe I can put in a good word for you for an internship?"

Ginger looked at Mom over her menu. "Unless you want my career to die before it starts, don't. Nothing's lamer than my mommy stirring up business for me."

Mom shrugged, picking up her own menu.

"Have it your way. Paul, see anything that interests you?"

Dad shrugged. "Is there something here that doesn't have wheatgrass in it?"

Ginger and I giggled. Dad usually went along with Mom's health food kicks, but this vegan restaurant was taking it a little far. I didn't even see vegan ice cream on the menu.

Tarra patted Dad's arm. "Just go with the chickpea burger. It's the most edible."

Mom pretended to be upset while I stifled laughter.

The waitress came to our table and said, "What can I get for you?"

Dad immediately ordered the chickpea burger, making us all laugh again. For the next hour, the six of us spent time together around the table like the family we used to be in our home. I kept thinking about what Ginger had said about giving Mom a chance, but being around her this weekend was just showing me how much I'd been hurt over the last eighteen years. Moving on from that wasn't as simple as a change in perspective.

Dad paid the check and we all went to the parking lot, where we'd part ways again. It was time for him and me to go home, to say goodbye to more than half of our family.

Ginger hugged me tightly and said, "Hang in there. It gets better."

"I hope so," I said before turning to the twins and saying goodbye.

As if comforting me, Cara said, "We'll be home before you know it."

I smiled and put my forehead against hers. "You will be. And then we'll have to fight over the bathroom again."

She laughed. "Maybe we can get Mom and Dad to build another one with all the money we'll be making."

"Yeah, yeah, yeah!" Tarra whispered excitedly. "We'll butter Mom up about it first, and then Dad will have to go along."

"You know what they'll say," I reminded them. "'Cori's going to be out of the house in a year, and then you'll have the bathroom all to yourselves.'" I'd heard the same line myself with mine and Ginger's names swapped out.

The twins gave each other a look that told me they were doing that creepy twin telepathy thing. Smiling exasperatedly, I shook my head and said,

"Tear it up on set, yeah? It's kind of cool having movie star little sisters."

They grinned back at me and said, "We will," in unison.

Chuckling, I walked to Dad's car and got in. He gave a final goodbye to Ginger and the twins and got in alongside me.

With a contented look, he began backing out of the lot. "Back to reality, huh?"

Which really meant back to being alone. Back to fighting a losing war. Back to not knowing what I wanted to do with my life but moving forward anyway.

I let out a sigh and leaned against the window, watching the city fade away and give way to my hometown, to "reality."

EIGHTEEN

I LEFT for school late on Monday, so I completely missed my chance to walk inside with the girls. Almost all the spots in the parking lot were full, including Ryker's with his brand-new truck with slick black paint and evilly gleaming rims.

I passed the monstrosity, swerving into my parking spot and jamming the van into park. If my mom found out I'd gotten a tardy, it would mean weeks of extra chores and increased supervision. As much as I'd like to have Mom's attention, I'd rather earn it than be punished with it.

I hurriedly grabbed my backpack from the passenger seat, climbed out, and smoothed my uniform skirt. As I rushed toward the front door, I heard the sound of soft sobs. My eyebrows furrowed together, and I looked around, trying to tell where they were coming from.

A few cars over, I found Isabella sitting on the ground against her Bugatti. She had her knees pulled tightly to her chest and mascara streaming down her cheeks.

My first response was to turn and run away. When it came to the bullying department, Isabella and Tatiana, who Faith referred to as the IT girls, were nearly as bad as Ryker. But she saw me, and I couldn't walk away. Not even when she turned her teary face away from me and said, "Keep walking, ginger. Don't you have a soul to find or a stepmom to bother?"

I rolled my eyes. "Even you know that was weak."

She half-laughed, half-snorted, giving me the courage I needed to walk a couple steps closer.

"What's going on?" I asked.

She looked at me, taking me in. She rolled her dark chocolate eyes as if thinking *to hell with it* and said, "I'm so tired of Ryker."

My eyebrows furrowed together, confused by what she meant. "I didn't know you two were dating."

"We're not," she said, letting out an annoyed

sob and then wiping at her cheeks. "I just thought eventually he'd break Coach's no-dating rule and be with me. Just me. But he wouldn't even have sex with me!"

My lips parted, shocked at what she'd said. First that she'd even told me, and then at the words and what they meant. I was about to ask her about Coach's no-dating rule when she started talking again.

"God, I can't even believe I'm telling you this. I'm pathetic." She pushed up from her spot on the ground and walked to the driver's side of the car. "Don't tell anyone about this, or I'll *ruin* you. Do you understand?"

Slowly, I nodded.

As the engine roared to life, I realized I needed to get out of there or I really would be late.

The tires squealed on the pavement as she backed out. Watching her taillights whip around the corner and onto the main road, I realized Isabella had given us just what we needed. If we could get Ryker to date someone, to fall in love, we could get him kicked off the football team. And no football? That meant no status, no girls, no superiority.

I needed to keep my friends close and my enemies closer.

At lunchtime, I finally got to tell my friends my new idea. The five of us all sat together, huddled around a table, as I told them my plan, not to be Ryker's enemy, but his friend. Maybe more.

"You're crazy!" Nadira cried. "Weren't you the one declaring war on him?"

I glanced over to the jock table where Ryker sat laughing at one of the dumb football players who had French fries sticking out of each nostril. "You play chess, right? This isn't the final move."

Nadira pressed her lips together, but Faith shook her head. "Won't he know it's just a ploy?"

"No way," Des said, answering for me. "He's so obsessed with himself, he wouldn't see any reason why Cori wouldn't want to be his friend—or more."

Adriel's mouth fell open. "What if he tries something? Are you going to go through with it?"

The thought of Ryker touching me sent a strange, confusing warmth to my cheeks, but I said, "That is *not* going to happen."

Nadira took a bite out of her chicken salad sandwich, shaking her head. "You know, maybe you should major in psychology next year. Figure out what kind of disordered thinking is making you want to go into the literal lion's den with this guy."

It was then that I had to tell them the truth of what Ginger and Knox had told me, every sordid detail. When I finished unveiling it all, I said, "If you want out, I understand, but losing isn't a choice for me. I don't even want to think of what people like the Dugans could do to my parents' store or to the twins' acting career. Losing isn't an option for me anymore."

For a moment, the entire table was silent, but each nerve in my chest was knotted into tight, painful balls.

Finally, Nadira put her hand in and said, "I'm here with you. You need someone smart to help keep you in check."

I half-smiled. "Thanks, Dir. Although, you know how stubborn I am."

She snorted. "Stubborn? That's the understatement of the year."

I rolled my eyes and waited for the others.

One by one they agreed to help, and my eyes felt hot. In the last few weeks, I'd learned who my true friends were, and they were sitting around me.

"We're in this," Adriel said. "Who knows?

Maybe we'll make Emerson Academy a better place to be for girls like us."

Des nodded. "And make his life hell along the way."

My lips tugged into a smile. "Did you have anything in mind?"

"Actually..." Faith began, surprising us. "Adriel, do you have any extra leotards?"

NINETEEN

AFTER SCHOOL, I got to my locker early and stared at the bag of delicious chocolate chip cookies Ginger had given me. Ray's mom made the best cookies, and I'd been saving these, telling myself I would only eat one of the twelve per day. That would be nearly two weeks of deliciousness.

But if basketball had taught me anything, it was that big wins took big sacrifices.

"You should probably quit staring at those cookies like you want to make out with them," Ryker said from behind me, nearly making me jump out of my skin. He chuckled. "Little jumpy, are we?"

I shook my head, forcing a deep breath. It was

hard to focus with him standing so close to me, his broad shoulders only inches from mine.

To help bolster my mental clarity, I took the bag and stepped back. "Actually, I wanted to give these to you."

His gray eyes flitted over the treats in my hand, back to my face. He didn't seem amused. "What's this, Nash?"

The strength in his voice took me aback. "A peace offering?"

His gaze narrowed, the dark fringe of his lashes becoming even more pronounced. "I don't buy it. What's in it for you?"

My eyebrows drew together. Now I was getting frustrated. "I'm just trying to be nice! What do you want from me, Dugan?"

"The cookies. Hand them over." He extended his hand flat, ready for me to drop the bag in his palm.

But now I wasn't so sure. I narrowed at my eyes at him suspiciously, but undeterred, he wiggled his fingers.

With a sigh, I dropped the bag with my precious cookies into his palm.

Slowly he took a cookie out and then dropped the bag on the floor, stepping on it with his dress shoes. He leaned in closer, so his minty breath tickled my cheek. "Next time you try to buy me, do better." With a smirk, he took a bite of the cookie he hadn't destroyed and walked away.

I narrowed my eyes at his back. He might have won the battle, but like hell if I wasn't going to win this war.

At the store, the meat guy was out, so Knox and I got stuck with the lovely job of cleaning out the fish tanks.

Except they weren't really fish tanks. They were ice boxes where giant fish corpses lay for all to see like a walking processional.

I had steaming hot water filling a bucket while Knox lined a rolling trash can with a bag to catch all of the ice and garnishes.

When the water had nearly reached the top, I dumped some bleach in and capped the bottle.

"Whoa," Knox said with a laugh. "Are you trying to clean or fill a swimming pool?"

"What?" I asked. "We don't clean with this stuff at home. Is that too much?"

"You needed maybe a capful," he said. "Two if you're being crazy."

I rolled my eyes and laughed. "I do like to live on the edge." I gripped the bucket and carried it from the food preparation area to the front cases. I watched people walking by as I set it on the floor.

Knox gloved up and lifted a giant salmon from the ice, then waggled it at me. "Cori, tell me, how's my pal Harry doing? He always was a great guy."

Stifling a smile, I looked at Knox's cute green eyes, then back to the sad-looking fish. "Harry served boldly, but unfortunately, he didn't make it back."

"Noooooo," Knox wailed, making the fish shake like it was sobbing.

Over the meat counter, I could see customers watching us with amused looks, and my cheeks heated. "We better get to work before someone tells on us for having too much fun."

He shook his head as he put the fish on the meat counter, preparing to cut it into smaller slices for sale. "Your dad's not that bad."

"Not compared to some people." I got a big cup and began scooping ice into the trash can Knox had wheeled over.

"Speaking of not-so-great people, how's your feud going with you-know-who?"

I tried to focus on the task at hand, but still felt frustrated. "Not so great."

He chuckled. "Evil plan not going...to plan?"

I finished scooping the ice and stared at him. "If by 'not to plan' you mean I got all my chocolate chip cookies crunched and have only succeeded in making him cooler, then you are spot on."

"Ooh, I know what will make you feel better," Knox said, holding up a big butcher knife.

I snorted way too loud, which just made both of us laugh. "I'm a lover, not a fighter," I said once my laughter subsided.

"No way," he said, chopping poor Harry's friend in half so we could package and sell it. "You don't start battles with a Dugan without being ready for a fight."

"True," I agreed.

"So what's phase two?" he asked.

An evil smile crossed my lips. "Well, it involves a leotard, if that tells you anything."

Knox set the knife down and pretended to bow to me. "My hero."

I laughed and continued cleaning up the stinky fish pit. "A hero would have a better job."

"I don't know," he said with a smile that warmed me from the inside out. "I think mine's pretty great."

TWENTY

DURING OUR CURVY Girl lunch on Thursday, Adriel passed me one of her "pinkest, frilliest" leotards, and I stored it in my bag for safe keeping.

"But how are we going to get it into his locker without someone knowing it was me?" I asked. "It would be a little suspicious of me to sneak into the boys' locker room in the middle of the day.

Adriel frowned. "They always make that part look way easier in the movies."

Nadira swallowed her bite of sushi, then clicked her chopsticks together. "Do we really need to keep it a secret if he already knows Cori's against him?"

I lifted an eyebrow. "That's a good point, but I feel like there's a difference in outright doing it and suspicions. One could have me expelled."

Des mimicked Mrs. Bardot's voice. "Not if no one *witnessed* it happening."

Adriel rolled her eyes. "There are cameras all over this place. If they wanted to see something happen, they would."

"Exactly," I agreed. "Which means it has to be a boy, right?"

Nadira looked around the table. "I don't see any of those in here, do you?"

I groaned. "But maybe we could talk your brothers into—"

"No, no, no," she said. "No way would they put basketball at risk by getting expelled."

Adriel frowned. "None of the guys at the ballet studio would go near that locker room. Not that I blame them."

"Same," I said, frowning too. We were running out of options to make this work. "Des, isn't Diego on the football team?"

She looked town at the table, fiddling with her chopsticks. "I don't know, Cor... I don't want to get him involved in something that could go so wrong, you know? He's on the same team as Ryker."

Des was just protecting her brother, and I knew they'd all gone out on a limb to support me in this crazy scheme, but I couldn't help feeling disappointed.

"I guess that's it then," I said, trying to battle the heavy spot in my chest. "Maybe it's time to just give up."

"Wait..." Nadira said. "Wasn't your sister best friends with Aiden Hutton's sister?"

"Yeah, she was at my house like three weeks ago. And?" I was having a hard time keeping my mood up knowing the consequences of my actions against Ryker would surely come soon.

Nadira leaned forward, something shining in her dark brown eyes that I couldn't quite understand. "His mom's a teacher...with access to keys and maybe a little pull in the Academy's disciplinary actions. And he's on the cross-country team." She shrugged. "Seems to me if you wanted to get something done, he'd be the person to talk to."

My eyes lit up as a small spark of hope burned brighter in my chest. "I'll catch him today after school. Thanks, Dir."

She tilted her head to the side. "You know I'm going to regret this."

"Not at all," I grinned, standing as the lunch bell rang. "I'll see you all with your camera phones after lunch tomorrow."

I knew my only chance of catching Aiden and talking to him in private was after school. So I stood outside the guys' locker room exit after school like a creep.

The first guy who walked out of the locker room caught sight of me and smirked. "Looking for some eye candy?"

I glared at the sophomore with a senior sense of entitlement. "I'd tell you to beat it, but I'm sure you do that enough already."

His smirk quickly faded, and he curled his lip, letting an ugly word fall out of his mouth before jogging toward the practice field.

I'd be lying if I said his words didn't sting a little, but I reminded myself that behavior was on him, not me. If he had an issue with my size or my actions, he could take it up with his diary or someone who actually cared.

Another couple of guys dressed in football pads jogged out of the locker room without noticing me, but I saw Aiden step out in running shorts and a T-shirt.

"Aiden!" I said, pushing off from the brick wall. "Hold on."

He looked at me and seemed confused. "Cori?" He looked around like there should be someone else with me. "Everything okay?" Dark hair fell over his forehead, and he pushed it back as he waited for my answer.

"Yeah, kind of," I said, stalling. Where was the handbook on asking someone to swap the devil's usual pitchfork for a tutu?

"Um, I have to start walking that way or I'm going to be late." He jerked his thumb over his shoulder toward the street leading to the winding golf course where the cross-country runners practiced.

"I'll walk with you," I said, falling into step beside him and feeling awkward as hell. Aiden was one of those guys who was nice to a fault. I almost didn't know what to do with myself around him. Did people like that understand sarcasm?

And then I almost kicked myself because why was I asking Mr. Nice Guy to help me out? This plan was destined to fail before it even started.

"I'm guessing you didn't just want to join me on a stroll," he said with a teasing smile.

His banter broke the ice enough that I said, "No, actually, I need some help." It all sounded so dumb in my head that I rushed it out as quickly as possible.

"I need someone to trade Ryker's gym clothes for a leotard and then somehow take away his uniform so he can't just wear that to the volunteer period."

Aiden stumbled and barely righted himself. His gaze swiveled around—there was another runner several hundred yards ahead of us and another person barely leaving the school. When he swung his blue eyes back to mine, he seemed confused. "Why?"

I looked toward the cloudless blue sky, not even remotely knowing how to explain. "You know Faith Kelley?"

He nodded. "I'm with her in like three different classes."

"Then you know how nice she is?"

He nodded again. "One of the nicest girls I know."

"Do you also know Ryker and half the guys on the football team pretended to corral her like she was a cow our first day of school?"

Aiden cringed. "No. Come on." He raked his hand through his hair. "Really?"

I pressed my lips together and nodded. For once, I didn't need more words to get my point across.

"So by putting a leo in his locker, she'll feel better?" he asked.

The meaning behind his words hit me. Getting payback on Ryker wouldn't take away the hurt of what he'd done to Faith, to my sister. We both knew that. This was about something more. "It won't make her feel better. The damage has already been done, but maybe he'll think twice before putting someone else through the same stuff." I met his eyes, begging him to understand. "Look, you know how much your sister struggled because of her size. We both know how amazing and kind and talented she is, but she still suffered at the hands of people like Ryker. Wouldn't it be good to give him a taste of what it feels like? Just once? Let him know that public humiliation isn't something to inflict on someone else?"

For a long moment, Aiden took me in, considering all I was asking him. The person behind us caught up and passed where we stood before Aiden finally said, "I'll do it."

I could have done a happy dance right there, but instead I said, "Thank you, Aiden. You have no idea how much this means."

His smile was easy as he backed away. "Yeah,

yeah, now go back to your board with red yarn and thumbtacks, ya evil genius."

Laughing, I began backing up as well. "I'll text you about the...thing."

"Sure," he said and turned, jogging toward the golf course before he even had to begin practice.

I had a grin on my face the entire way back to the school, thinking of how Ryker would react the next day and how *adorable* he'd look in a pink leotard.

TWENTY-ONE

AFTER STOCKING shelves for a couple of hours, I went home to an empty house, again. Mom called to check in with me, but I cut it short, saying I had a lot of homework to do. Actually, for the first time since school started, I didn't have any homework. Although, that could have had something to do with the football game tomorrow night.

Even though our teachers acted like academics were the most important thing at the Academy, they took sports just as seriously. Athletes practically ruled the halls, which might have been one reason why Ryker used to pick on my sister but always left me alone. As a starting player on the basketball team, I had an advantage.

Rather than think about that confusing double

standard, I got out my laptop and started looking at colleges. Although I probably wouldn't officially sign with a university until basketball season, I needed to at least apply and decide on a major. Besides, Coach Clark recommended I reach out to some coaches to make sure I was on their radar when the season began.

The only problem was, how did I decide where to go? I thought of applying where my friends were planning to attend, but Des's top pick of Julliard definitely didn't have a basketball team. (Not to mention my absolute lack of musical talent.) Nadira planned to attend MIT with Brentwood U as a backup plan since she would get free tuition with her mom working there.

But Brentwood U was too close for comfort. Being so near home would just remind me of how little I meant to my parents. I wanted to get out, see the world, finally make a name for myself where I wouldn't be overshadowed by Ginger's health problems or the twins' acting skills. Then I would find out—if Mom and Dad made it a point to visit me, to see my space, even if it wasn't convenient—maybe they cared. If not...

I shook the thought and focused on my computer. I clicked through to a map and thought about places I might want to live. My whole life had been spent in Emerson, and we hardly traveled because of the store or Mom's fear of Ginger's asthma getting triggered by an allergen she wasn't used to.

I zoomed in on Florida, thinking of how amazing the beach would be and how fun it would be to live in a spring break destination. But then I thought about hurricanes and what the humidity would do to my curly hair and kept scrolling up the coast. Duke had an incredible program, but at five-nine, I probably wasn't tall enough to get much playing time on the women's team. That would leave me doing all the grueling practices only to sit on the bench at games. No thank you.

Any farther north, where multiple feet of snow could fall in a day, was out of the question. I'd only seen snow once, and that was on vacation with Aunt Rosie. It could stay there. So that left out pretty much the top half of the United States.

I chose a few Division II colleges in the lower Midwest and then wrote down a college in Hawaii on a whim. As I sat back from my computer, it hit me. I'd be leaving soon, moving away, and I would get to live my own life on my terms. But no matter how exciting that was, I realized how few people would remember me here.

My parents would be occupied with their other children and the store. My friends would be chasing their dreams on the East Coast. And soon enough, Emerson Academy and even my basketball coach would forget me too.

I hoped, by teaching Ryker a lesson, I could at least leave my mark on Emerson Academy's culture, even if it wouldn't remember my name.

TWENTY-TWO

THE GIRLS WISHED me luck before I went to the locker room to change for volunteer class. I dressed in my Emerson Academy cotton shorts and slipped on my regulation white tennis shoes, thinking of what was happening in the boys' locker room. Ms. Anaheim had asked us to change for gym class, and I could only imagine her face when she saw Ryker in his "outfit." Or Ryker's expression when he realized he had no other options.

With a smile on my lips, I walked out of the girls' locker room and started down the empty halls. Half the students had gone off-campus for their volunteer work, and the others were surely already at their stations.

As I walked past the music room, I could hear

the bold vocals of Des's voice, and I smiled at the sound. She said she wanted to make it big someday, and I knew she would. I couldn't wait to go to one of her concerts—with a backstage pass of course.

I stepped out of the school building and started down the stairs, enjoying the feeling of sunshine on my skin. My cheeks heated as I remembered last week and the unfortunate wind. Thank goodness for shorts and today's lack of a breeze.

On my way to the elementary school, I looked over my shoulder every so often to see if I could catch a glimpse of Ryker. I wasn't sure what I was expecting—maybe a shout of frustration echoing across campus when he realized his gym clothes had been taken from his locker? Then, when he went to Coach Ripley's office inside the locker room —likely dressed in his underwear—Aiden would snatch his uniform and run. (He was good at that.) Ryker would be left to find Coach Ripley's office locked and no other options to wear.

Maybe I was a little nervous about Aiden getting caught, but he'd reassured me this morning that he'd be careful.

The elementary building loomed before me, and I pushed through the front door and hit the buzzer. Mrs. O'Haire waved at me through the glass office window and hit the unlock button for the doors.

I made my way down the tiled hallway, remembering what it felt like to be a little girl walking these halls. Des had been my best friend since kindergarten when she shared her candy cigarettes with me at lunchtime, but Nadira had come into our lives later, in fifth grade.

Her dad had landed the head coach position at Brentwood U, and her mom was hired as a professor in the engineering department. Nadira had been the best help as I learned long division that year and hasn't stopped saving my butt since.

As I approached the gym, I realized some of the kids in that very room would be making their best friends for life right now. I hoped they knew how precious those friendships would become.

I opened one of the double doors and walked inside to see the gym set up like a giant obstacle course. The kids were already at one end, stretching.

When she noticed me, Ms. Anaheim traded the lead spot with Anna and walked toward me with a smile on her face. "What do you think?" she asked once she got close enough.

I scanned the course, noting the small inflatable,

the padded mats, colorful cones, and rolling squares. "It looks so *fun*."

Grinning, she said, "I think the kiddos will love it. Are you excited for the relay?"

"Relay?"

With a nod, she answered, "We're going to have a girls versus boys relay through the obstacle course. I thought it could be fun to have you and Ryker bring up the rear."

The thought of Ryker in a leotard racing through the obstacle course struck my funny bone, and it took all I had not to bust out in laughter. "Totally fun," I agreed.

She glanced at the watch on her wrist. "Any idea where Ryker is? He should be here by now."

I pressed my lips together and shook my head, trying to look as innocent as possible. "No idea what could be holding him up."

Okay, I was definitely failing at this lying thing. My lips were twitching like even they didn't like the lies coming out of my mouth.

Just then, the door opened and Ryker barged inside, wearing the same bright pink leotard that had been in my bag this morning.

I covered my mouth with my hands to hide the fact that my jaw was basically on the floor. The pink leo clung to his body, showing off the ripples of his abdominal muscles. He'd worn a pair of spandex shorts underneath, which hugged his defined thighs. For shoes, he didn't have ballet flats but black tennis shoes with black socks that stretched halfway up his calves. But meeting his eyes was the best part.

They were so dark the slate gray looked almost black, but they weren't dark enough to hide the mutiny within them. I tried not to laugh at how frustrated he was because this was *exactly* the reaction I'd been hoping for. But the second his eyes left mine, his lips stretched into a broad smile, completely at odds with his earlier expression.

My eyebrows drew together at his sudden change in expression. Was Ryker Dugan going crazy, or had I missed something?

Beside me, Ms. Anaheim asked, "Ryker, why aren't you in your gym uniform?"

Not, *why are you in a pink leo?* Or *why are you grinning like a fool?*

He stretched his smile even wider, despite the giggling from the second graders across the gym. "I thought this could be a really fun way to teach a lesson today. You know, gender positivity and all."

I didn't even bother hiding my eye-roll. That wasn't even a term, and Ryker was as far from feminist as it got. If anything, he'd probably be asking his future wives—because there were sure to be many—to make him sandwiches while he sat on the couch with a beer in hand.

Ms. Anaheim just shook her head with a sigh. "I'll let it fly this week, Ryker, but next week, wear your gym uniform like I asked."

Ryker sent her an apologetic smile and said, "Of course, Ms. Anaheim."

Turning away from him and his nonsense, she approached the students, and we followed behind her. Ryker leaned toward me and muttered, "I'm assuming this is your handiwork."

"Don't flatter yourself," I said, even though I would have loved nothing better than to claim all my glory like an evil villain. "Besides, I was here on time, unlike someone else I know."

Unfazed, Ryker said, "So now I know you have people on the inside. Who's the mole?" There was a deadly lilt to his voice.

I ignored him, along with the fear fizzing in my stomach, and continued to the students. Anna rushed up to me and gave me a big hug, followed by a couple of her friends, Abigail and Bailey.

"Hi, girls," I said. "Are you ready to kick some boy butt today?"

Bailey giggled. "You said butt."

I laughed, remembering the age when words like butt were funny. "I sure did," I whispered.

Abigail extended her pinky finger. "Pinky promise we're going to win?"

I slipped my pinky through hers. "I'll do my best if you do."

She shook it and then followed the rest of the class lining up behind the inflatable where Ryker stood near the back of the line. All the girls kept looking at him while the boys gave him sideways glances like they weren't sure what to make of the getup.

One brave girl finally said, "You look like a ballerina!"

That lead to a cascade of comments, including one from a little boy who called, "Do a leap!"

Ryker jumped through the air and twirled in a display of athleticism and grace I didn't know he possessed. As he came to the back of the line beside me, I gave him a confused look.

He shrugged and said loud enough for everyone to hear, "Football players practice ballet too so that they can have good footwork on the field. I take private lessons at least once a week. Sometimes more."

The boys in the class jostled each other, making promises that they would start practicing ballet too so that they could crush it on the field when they got old enough to play on the Drafters football team.

I rolled my eyes. Of course Ryker would take something that should have been completely humiliating and turn himself into a hero.

When he looked my way again, he had a smug smile on his face like he knew he was winning. I stared straight ahead and muttered, "You're going down."

"We'll see about that, Nash," he said.

Ms. Anaheim yelled, "Ready!" raising her black and white checkered flag. The kids fell into an excited hush.

"Set!" She waved the flag toward the ground and yelled, "GO!"

The boy and girl in the front of each line took off at a sprint, climbing up the inflatable and then sliding down it. Then they danced and dove and sprinted around the course while all of us cheered for one or the other to win.

There were sixteen kids in the class, so we had some time before Ryker and I would face off. I only hoped that we would begin on an even playing field, because I could not wait to smother him into the ground.

I cheered and shouted for the girls so much I thought I might lose my voice before the football game tonight. That was fine, though, because cheering for Ryker's team wasn't nearly as appealing as cheering for my own.

Finally, our turn arrived. The girls and boys had been neck and neck the entire time. As Anna sprinted to me, her arm extended, I said, "You're going down, Ryker."

He laughed harshly, poised to take off. "In your dreams."

Anna slapped my hand, and I sprinted alongside Ryker, flying up the inflatable. It wobbled dangerously, but we both pressed on, undeterred. We slid down to the bottom, barely keeping the whole thing from toppling over.

We sprinted to the cones, and I worked my feet as fast as I could, already out of breath. Once we passed the cones, there were tunnels to crawl through. I dove into mine, cringing, because there was about a fifty percent chance I'd get stuck inside, but Ryker's shoulders were just as broad as mine, so I'd take my chances.

The tunnel rolled, and I shimmied out of it on

my back before flipping over and running to the line of tape we had to walk on like a tight rope. I kept my eyes on the blue tape, hearing Ryker's easy breathing beside me. I definitely needed to start getting in shape for basketball.

Finally, we reached the last part of the course: the small square carts. Since I definitely couldn't fit on one, I grabbed two from the rack, put a knee on each, and pushed off as hard as I could. Seconds after taking off, I realized I had severely misjudged my direction. My carts were careening toward Ryker and even bailing from them wouldn't help.

I completely crashed into him in a collision of muscles and plastic and wheels and flesh. And, oh my god I could feel his abs. We skidded to a stop, him over me with his hands flat on either side of my head. His chest was heaving, and his full lips were parted so I could smell his minty breath.

Then I had the most horrible thought: if I ignored his personality, I could see why girls were attracted to him. There was a spark in his gray eyes that I hadn't quite noticed before, a faint scar above his right cheek. And his lips. They were the subtlest shade of pink.

Those lips turned into a smirk, and he said, "Are you ready to lose now?"

My voice was breathy as I said, "What do you mean?"

With his eyes on mine the entire time, Ryker extended his right arm and placed it across the finish line.

TWENTY-THREE

DES and I walked together toward the bleachers for the football game, each holding our own bag of popcorn from the concession stand. The band was going to play the national anthem tonight, which meant we had her to ourselves the entire game.

I picked a piece of buttery perfection from my bag and ate it. "Popcorn has to be the best part of Friday nights."

Des considered her bag, then the football field, then looked at me like I was crazy. "Not the muscled jocks in tight pants?"

"I mean, that's not bad, but..." I held out a few kernels. "This is better. I can never get my popcorn at home to turn out this good."

"So now I know what I'm getting for Christmas. A popcorn machine."

"Won't fit in my dorm," I said, scooting out of the way for another fan to pass by. As I fell back into step beside Des, I said, "I know what I'm getting you."

"What?"

"A guy in tight pants."

She snorted, nearly choking on her own bite. "That will *definitely* fit in my dorm." Laughing, she said, "Speaking of guys in tight pants, you haven't told me how it went with Ryker."

I'd wanted to tell the girls how it went down when we were all together, mostly because I didn't want to reveal the godlike status he'd gained for himself—or the way my stomach had fluttered with him on top of me. But I couldn't hold it in anymore.

I reached into my pocket, flipped the picture I'd covertly taken of him walking into the gym, and held it out for her to see.

Thank goodness the sidewalk was even because her jaw fell open, and I was pretty sure she would have tripped if we'd been on bumpy ground. She skidded to a stop and took the phone in both of her hands, clutching her popcorn bag in the crook of her elbow. "Holy Greek god in tights."

I rolled my eyes, taking my phone back. "You're going to get drool on the screen."

She caught up with me as I continued walking and said, "Seriously, Cor, if you don't want to date him, I will."

"We're supposed to be in a war, remember?" I asked her. Although there was a weird surge of...something in my stomach at the thought of Des dating him. Revulsion? It had to be. He was the epitome of a bully, using his power to make others feel small.

Raising her eyebrows, Des replied, "All's fair in love and war, remember?"

Shaking my head, I said, "It's so annoying. Every time I think I've one-upped him, he finds a way to come back, better and stronger. So far, he's gotten a new truck, a literal parade out of Waldo's, and now the adoration of a bunch of second graders. And what have I gotten out of the deal?"

"A picture of Ryker Dugan in a leo?" she said suggestively.

I rolled my eyes. Hard.

With a shrug, she said, "Maybe you're not hitting

close enough to home yet." She began climbing the bleachers, and I had to fall into step behind her so we could fit up the stairs with people walking by. "When he falls in love with you, it'll be easier to crush him."

I shook my head. "When," I muttered. "As if."

"Do you see them?" she asked over her shoulder.

I glanced in roughly the same spot we'd sat last time and found Nadira, Faith, and Adriel just a few rows closer to the field. "Over there," I said, pointing.

Des led the way to them, and we both settled into the bleacher seats, the coolness of the metal seeping through my jeans. Under the darkening sky, it was almost cold outside. I pulled my beanie farther over my ears, just taking it all in.

Something about sunset and stadium lights just felt right to me. I would definitely miss this when I went to college, but then again, I could attend college games and watch college players. The thought made me smile. Even if I couldn't find someone to date at the Academy, there had to be someone in a bigger school that would be the perfect fit. Maybe someone from the basketball team...

"Earth to Cori!" Nadira said, followed by Desirae's elbow jabbing my side.

"Ow!" I said, rubbing the spot where she'd nudged me. "What?"

Faith leaned over so she could see me. "Tell us about Operation Tutu!"

I shook my head, smiling, and reached for my phone to show them the photo I'd gotten of Ryker.

A burst of giggles quickly erupted through my friends, and I glanced around to make sure no one was watching us.

They weren't. We were our own island at Emerson Academy—different in our sameness. And the fact was, no one cared about us unless they could use us to make themselves feel better.

"Send it to me?" Faith said, passing me the phone back.

I shrugged. "Sure." As I typed in her number, I told them about what a complete bust the day had been.

"Maybe not yet," Faith said with a small smile. She tapped at her phone with Adriel and Nadira looking over her shoulder.

Soon, my phone pinged with a message. The photo inside showed Ryker in a pink tutu with a pink background behind him and a caption that said, King Tutu.

I snorted and immediately hit save. "This is golden."

Des leaned her head on my shoulder. "Ready for it to go viral?"

"What do you mean?" I asked.

She bent over her phone and shared the photo to social media, tagging some of the biggest accounts at Emerson Academy. Since so many children of the rich and famous went to school with us, there had to be millions of followers all combined.

"Oh my gosh!" Adriel held out her phone, showing us line after line of posts with Ryker in his leotard with the hashtag #rykerina.

Des's eyes widened at her own phone. "It's trending!"

"Already?" I asked. Now that I looked around, I could see why people weren't interested in us or the game. They were all looking at their phones, sharing their screens with their friends. Even the parents in the crowd seemed to be obsessed with their phones.

The girls and I looked at each other in shock. Was this our first big win?

A squeal sounded in front of the bleachers, and

I turned my head to see the cheerleaders' peels of giggles as they gathered around a phone.

Oh yeah, it was a win.

Des said, "Pretty sure Aiden deserves a Nobel Prize."

"Or at least a thank you," Adriel said.

I totally agreed and glanced around the stands to see if I could find him. He sat with his girlfriend, who was completely adorable in her white knit cap and Emerson Academy sweater, which was so big on her it obviously belonged to Aiden. As if he felt me watching him, he turned to me and winked.

I kept my smile to myself and turned back to the girls. At least we had one ally.

The captains of the football teams did the traditional coin toss, and I watched Ryker move across the field, the perfect picture of intimidation. I wondered how he could get into that persona so easily.

A small part of me wondered if there was more to the reason why he always had to be on guard, why he always had to be the alpha. Was it just the way his dad had raised him, or was it something more?

More importantly, why was I thinking about this? I should have been having fun with the girls, but instead I was focusing on a guy who I didn't even like. Despised, was more like it.

I turned back to my friends. Des had traded places with Adriel to ask Nadira something, so I asked Adriel how dance was going. She'd mentioned training for a major competition last week.

Her smile faltered, and she kind of shrugged. "It's going fine. It's just..." She let out a heavy sigh. "We're having trouble finding a dance costume for the group dance that will fit me, and the studio owner wants me to lose weight."

My face fell—I had been there before. Not being able to wear the same clothes as everyone around me and struggling to squeeze into the limited options in a store. There was nothing worse than realizing no matter what you did, there just wasn't anything for you, nothing to make you as pretty as the other girls who got to wear the cute clothes in smaller sizes. "I'm so sorry," I said. It was all I could manage.

She shook her head, blinking quickly. "It's not my job to find a costume that will match everyone's. That's a studio director's job. And my mom's already offered to help with alterations and decorations. There's no reason why I should change my size for the sake of an outfit." The fierceness in her voice took me aback, but I nodded. That was good. She needed to be a fighter, especially as a dancer in a sport where most people were petite and delicate.

"Good for you," I said.

She smiled a little bashfully and shrugged. "What about you? Are you getting excited for basketball season?"

I nodded, instantly feeling the heat in my eyes. Honestly, I wanted nothing more than to have a basketball in my hands and feel the smooth lines against the dimpled orange leather. I felt more at home on the court than I ever did in my actual house.

I had a sense of purpose in basketball like I felt nowhere else. All I had to do was get the ball through the hoop or try to stop someone else from doing the same. Life was a little more complicated than that.

The whistle blew on the field, and I looked just in time to watch the opposing team kick the football far, far, far to the other end of the field. Ryker was there, catching it in his hands. He darted down the field, expertly dodging his opponents, and even jumping over one person's arms as they dove for his ankles.

For a moment, I thought he looked like he was at home too. Maybe we had more in common than I ever thought.

The team ended the first quarter ten points ahead, and when the buzzer counted down with Emerson in a fourteen-point lead, the crowd chanted, "Rykerina! Rykerina! Rykerina!"

My eyes went wide as I looked to the girls. They might have been cheering his name, but it felt like it could be mine.

On the field, Ryker shucked his helmet, holding it at his side, and stared at all of the people who typically worshiped him, a look of confusion on his face. He probably thought they were getting his name wrong.

I'd watched as his expression changed from confused to furious. He met my gaze in the stands, and I wiggled my fingers in a smug wave.

He stormed off the field without a backward glance, but if he'd looked back, he would have seen me smile and join in the chant.

TWENTY-FOUR

THERE WAS no way we were going to end the night without going to Waldo's to bask in our victory. And not the Drafters' win, but ours. The Curvy Girl Club 2.0 had earned some definite points tonight in our war, and we needed to sit back and celebrate before aiming another punch.

When I arrived at Waldo's, there was no text from Faith asking if it was okay to walk into the restaurant. There was no fear in my gut about whether or not we were doing the right thing. Not even when I walked into the diner and saw Ryker in the booth with his friends, a murderous expression on his face.

As I settled into the booth across from Adriel, I

was half surprised to see him at Waldo's at all. Without a girl in his lap, no less.

Des scooted in the seat beside me, followed by Faith, while Nadira sat by Adriel. The five of us had always felt a little awkward together before, but we were starting to feel more like a group. I was beginning to wonder how it had always been Nadira, Des, and me before without Faith and Adriel to complete us.

Betty brought a round of waters for us, looking flustered with a pencil tucked into her curly hair and a bead of sweat dripping down the back of her neck.

"How are you holding up, Betty?" I asked.

She blew up her bangs and said, "I'll be doing a lot better when that lot gets out of here." She subtly tipped her head toward the rambunctious crowd of cheerleaders and football players who acted like they owned the place every Friday night.

"Same," Nadira said.

But Betty's comment got me thinking. "Why are you always working on Friday nights anyway? Can't you trade shifts with someone?" It struck me just how often I saw her here. Almost as much as that sweet old man Chester, who was as much a part of the restaurant as the boomerang tabletops. I understood why he might want to drink his coffee around the hustle and bustle and chat up customers, but didn't Betty have a family to get to or a boyfriend to spend time with?

Taking out her pad, she shook her head. "Not much else to do. Mama's pretty good on her own as long as I make sure she gets her meds after I get off work."

So Betty was taking care of her mom. I lifted my lips in a half-smile. "She's lucky to have you."

"Thank you," she said sweetly, then leaned in. "Milkshakes are on the house tonight. Same as last time?"

We all nodded emphatically and thanked her half a dozen times before she breezed away to check on the rest of her customers.

"I had no idea she was taking care of her mom," I said, looking down at the blank surface of my phone.

"Me neither," Nadira said.

We were all quiet for a moment, thinking to ourselves, and then Des nudged my arm. "Don't look now, but Ryker is staring right at you."

My lips parted, and despite her clear instructions, I instantly turned my gaze onto slate-gray eyes that were looking right at mine.

"I said *don't look*!" Des cried, and I realized that every head in our booth had turned toward the one Ryker sat in.

Instantly, my cheeks heated, and I turned my focus back toward the laminate tabletop, tracing the boomerang pattern with my eyes.

There was a mass shuffling as my friends turned back toward me, and Des said, "Oh crap."

The worried tone in her voice had me looking up, and, oh crap was right. "Is he coming this way?" I asked, even though I knew the answer.

Ryker Dugan was walking toward our table.

Toward us.

Toward me.

A metal cup plunked on the table in front of me, and Betty said, "Chocolate for you, sweetie."

Oblivious to the hand grenade coming our way, she passed out the rest of our milkshakes and said, "Enjoy, sweethearts!"

The other girls managed various thanks, but I couldn't speak because Ryker was standing at our table now, staring me down.

"Cori," he said.

I squared my shoulders, cleared my throat. "Rykerina."

His jaw ticked at my use of the nickname. He

closed his eyes and opened them on me again. "Can I talk to you?"

He wanted to...talk? "Sure." I waited, but he seemed even more annoyed. Even more controlled, in the oddest of ways.

"Outside?" He tilted his head toward the door for emphasis.

I looked to the girls, and they didn't even bother hiding their shocked expressions. I made a mental note to *thank* them for how absolutely *helpful* they were being and folded my arms on the table. "Why should I?"

"I had an idea for volunteer hour I wanted to run by you," he said flatly, like anything would do to get me out of the booth.

Nope, I was enjoying watching him flounder a little too much. "I'd love to, but..." I took a long sip of my shake. "Betty just brought me this, and I'm fat, you know, so I'm not going to pass up a chance for a milkshake."

Ryker's fists clenched at his sides, but before he could speak, I said, "We were kind of talking, so... see ya next Friday, Rykerina."

With a vein throbbing on his forehead and his jaw so tight his teeth should have shattered, he turned and walked away.

Instantaneously, the girls burst into a quiet chorus of squeals and applauses.

"Oh my gosh, Cor!" Faith cried. "That has to be the first time any girl has ever turned down Ryker Dugan."

Des fanned herself. "I'm practically on fire from the tension."

Nadira pursed her lips. "Wait for the other cleat to fall."

"Cleat?" Adriel asked.

Nadira looked around at us to explain, then gave up. "Cleats? Like the shoes they wear on the field?"

"Come on, Dir." Des gave her an admonishing look. "Let her have her victory."

"I will." Nadira sipped on her milkshake, then added, "For now."

TWENTY-FIVE

THE NEXT MORNING, I woke to a text from my sister around eight.

Ginger: #Rykerina? I'm assuming this has something to do with you?

My lips easily spread into a smile, even though mornings were usually *not* my thing. Still, if news about last night had already reached UCLA, that was a huge deal. I pushed my messy hair off my forehead and then gave my phone my full attention.

Cori: I have no idea what you're talking about.

After sending the text, I went to social media and typed in the #Rykerina hashtag, smiling as I read through all the posts talking about how cute he looked in a leo and whether or not it was an update to the EA uniform.

A notification slid down my screen, showing Ginger's next messages.

Ginger: Sure.

Ginger: But whoever did it deserves a massive high five and a bag full of chocolate chips. The package will be at your door AFTER Dad leaves and before you go in for your shift.

Okay, that was enough to get me out of bed. I'd already blown through Mom's hidden stash and hadn't grabbed any more yet.

I pushed back the covers and stood, stretching so far I accidentally hit the ceiling fan chain, making it clang against the glass. Speaking of hashtags... #tallgirlproblems.

Ginger: Be sure to give it to the person who deserves them. ;)

I looked down at my phone as I left the room and typed back my response.

Cori: You know I will.

After going to the bathroom, I walked into the living room just in time to see Dad grabbing his keys off the hook.

"You're up early," he commented with a surprised look.

I held up my phone. "Ginger woke me up."

His expression softened, and I could see how

much he missed her in just a look. It made my heart hurt—he'd never miss me that much when I left for college.

"I'm going to get food," I said before he could say anything more to make me wallow in a pool of envy.

The doorbell rang, and I immediately cringed. If Dad saw I'd gotten a package, he'd wait for me to open it, and then he'd know about the contraband chocolate chips, and then Mom would find out what Ginger was doing with her credit card, and it'd be a whole bag of worms.

"I'll get it!" I said quickly.

To which he said, "I'm already on my way out. I got it."

Which left us both arriving at the front door, him in a banana-yellow Ripe shirt and me in my slouchy basketball pajamas with a barely tamed bedhead. The things I'd do for chocolate.

But when Dad opened the door, I didn't see a delivery guy in a brown outfit. No, there on my front porch, in light washed jeans and a tight navy-blue tee was Ryker Dugan.

Dad's eyes immediately pinballed, drawing conclusions so far from the truth, even a lie couldn't adequately categorize it. I instantly blurted, "What're you doing here?"

"I'm here to see your dad, actually," Ryker said with a smile that brightened each of his features. "Cori and I go to school together," he explained to my dad.

Who was this? The good twin? The only expressions I'd known Ryker to have were fury, derision, and mild amusement.

Dad must have looked just as surprised as I did because Ryker added, "May I have a minute, sir?"

Sir? Oh, he was laying it on thick.

"Of course," Dad said, stepping aside. "Come to the kitchen, son." As he guided Ryker toward the kitchen, Dad turned to me, looking for an explanation. Of which I had none.

"I'll come with," I said.

Dad shook his head. "Maybe you should get dressed."

It was then both Ryker and I fully realized what I was wearing. Short shorts with little basketballs printed all over them, a scoop-neck tank top, and a bright pink sports bra. My cheeks immediately felt hot as I noticed the amusement in Ryker's eyes.

I would have turned to walk—no, run—to my

bedroom and change, but then he would have seen the back of my too-short shorts, including my dimpled butt. Instead, I nodded meekly and backed away.

My hip jabbed into something sharp, and a vase on Mom's hall table nearly toppled over. I bent to grab it, realizing just how exposed I was as my shirt rode up my back. What the heck was I thinking, wearing this to bed?

Oh yeah, that *Ryker freaking Dugan wouldn't show up at my house at the butt crack of dawn*!

I hurried to my room, firing off two identical SOS texts—one to my sister and one to the Curvy Girl Club 2.0.

Cori: SOS. RYKER DUGAN IS IN MY HOUSE TALKING TO MY DAD.

I nearly added that he'd seen me half-exposed in old pajamas, but decided for time's sake to keep it short.

I dug through a pile of clean clothes I'd neglected to fold and flung them behind me until I found a pair of stomach-smoothing leggings that also shaped my curves and a flowy blouse. Then I snatched a hair tie from Ginger's desk that she made me promise not to fill with all my stuff.

Oops.

I threw my hair up into a messy bun, then

skidded into the bathroom to wash my face and throw on a layer of foundation and mascara. All the while, thoughts and fears of what Dad and Dugan could possibly be talking about flooded my mind.

What could Ryker possibly have to say to my dad anyway? He wasn't going to tell on me, was he? Did bullying a bully fall into the whole "loss of trust" category? Or would it be something even more conniving, as only Ryker could do?

I ran down the hallway and slowed just in time to walk oh-so casually into the dining room, where my arch enemy was shaking hands with my father.

I looked between the two of them, my eyebrows furrowed together, waiting for an explanation and getting none. Instead, Dad said, "We'll see you tomorrow evening. Be here at five."

"I'll see you then, sir," Ryker said. He turned his thousand-watt smile on me, and I'd be lying if I said my breath didn't catch, just a little bit. "I'll see you then, Cori."

Ryker let himself out of the house, and I stared at my father. "What just happened?"

Dad watched through the front window as Ryker got into his ridiculous truck. "That young man asked my permission to date you." With a chuckle, he shook his head and scratched at his beard. "You know, if someone would have told me having my daughters date would be this pleasant, I never would have believed them. It's almost too good to be true."

There were a thousand things I could have said, but my mind was still stuck on one word. "Date?" I asked, just to make sure I'd heard it right. There had to be a mistake here.

"Wait until your mother hears we're making another visit," Dad said, walking toward the door. "She'll be thrilled."

"Why are we visiting?" I asked.

"So she can meet him, of course!"

"Wait!" I said, following him out the open door. "I don't want to date Ryker."

Dad's face immediately fell. "Oh, hon, I'm sorry. I already told him yes... You wouldn't mind sticking it out one night? I'd hate to disappoint the kid."

Dad was worried about *Ryker's* feelings? That guy didn't have a heart, much less feelings. "Dad, I—"

"I'm sorry, Cor." He looked at his watch. "I'm already running late. Can we talk when you come in for your shift?" He'd already unlocked the car.

I let out a sigh. "Sure."

"Thanks, kid!" He got into his car and began driving away.

Just as he'd turned the corner, a big brown delivery truck arrived, and I muttered, "Just in time."

TWENTY-SIX

WHEN I GOT BACK to my phone, there were missed calls and a thousand and one messages, each in the same confused, panicked tone.

I shoved a handful of chocolate chips in my mouth and immediately dialed Ginger.

She picked up instantly and said, "What in the world is going on, Cori?"

"I don't know!" I cried, pacing from the living room to the kitchen and back. If there were a Grand-Canyon-sized path worn by the time Dad got home, it wouldn't be a surprise. "He showed up at the house this morning acting like someone I've never even met before and asked Dad if he could go on a date with me!"

"WHAT?!"

I held my phone away from my ear, but her reaction was exactly the right level of panicked and confused. "Of course Dad stuck to his rule that anyone who wants to date us has to have dinner with the family first. I don't know what Ryker's playing at, but it's *crazy*! And now apparently we're all going to LA so he can meet Mom!"

I heard Ginger muttering something in the background of the phone, and then she said, "Jordan's here too. You're on speaker."

Thank God because I needed all the backup I could get! "Help!" I cried.

Jordan said, "Did you tell your dad you don't want to go out with Ryker? Seems like that would be a good way to get it shut down."

"Of course I did." I rolled my eyes toward the ceiling, digging for more chocolate.

"And he said?" Ginger asked.

I mimicked Dad's voice. "Oh, I already told him yes, and your feelings don't matter, so just tough it out for a two-hour ride in the car round trip and a dinner *with your mother*."

Ginger let out a groan. "They're the worst."

"Maybe it's not such a bad thing," Jordan added hopefully.

I stared at my phone, and Ginger must have

been staring at Jordan the same way because Jordan said, "What? Didn't Ray's pre-date dinner with your family go horribly wrong? Your parents acted like they didn't want any of their daughters dating before they saw how amazing Ray is. They'll make the dinner so awful, Ryker will have no choice but to turn the other way and run."

For the first time since Ryker arrived at my house this morning, I felt relieved. She was right. My parents had been so rude to Ray he'd practically run out of the house and Ginger had cried herself to sleep. Thankfully, Ray hadn't given up on her. He'd even walked her to class every day, protecting her from Ryker's taunting...

He'd protected her from Ryker.

"Ginger!" I cried. "Please tell me you can get Ray to come to this dinner and put the fear of God in Ryker. *Please*."

"Brilliant!" Jordan cried.

"I'll ask," Ginger said hesitantly. "But we'll have to see. He's pretty busy training a new ranch hand... In the meantime, talk to your friends. Why do I have a feeling Des would have some ideas?"

"Because she's an evil genius," I answered, smiling despite myself. "Thanks, Ging."

"Of course. See you tomorrow."

I closed my eyes. "See you tomorrow."

When I hung up, I looked through my other notifications, and seeing missed calls from all four of my friends, I did one group video call. After hitting dial, I licked the melted chocolate from my fingertips. Quickly, each of their faces filled a portion of the screen, and they all peppered me with questions at the same time.

"One at a time!" I yelled, then as they quieted, I decided it would be better to start from the beginning. I filled them in, thankful I could see their shocked looks, just so I could confirm that I wasn't the crazy one here.

"He's insane!" Adriel said, making me feel that much better. "He's just getting you back for standing him up at the restaurant."

"I know. But now I have this dinner with him. What am I going to do?"

Des quirked a brow. "You're going to look hot and make him miserable."

Nadira nodded emphatically. "Plus, if Ginger and Ray are going to be there, Ryker's going to be squirming."

I raised my eyebrows. "Since when did you get on-board?"

"Since he came to your house!" she said,

followed by the closing of a door. She lowered her voice and said, "It's one thing for us to chase him down; it's another for him to come looking for trouble."

"Exactly," Faith agreed. "I think this is fun for him."

I put my hand on my forehead. The thought of this being some sort of weird foreplay for Ryker made me want to vomit.

Des said, "Maybe he's turning the tables."

"What do you mean?" I asked.

"Maybe he's playing games back. He probably thinks you're just like every other girl who's going to fall at his feet and hand over your heart."

I laughed. Out loud. Because that was the most nonsensical thing I'd ever heard. I knew who the real Ryker was, and I hated his stupid bully guts.

"Do you want us to come help you get ready tomorrow?" Nadira asked.

I gawked at her. Nadira was the farthest person from a girly girl I'd ever met. Pretty sure the last time she wore makeup was for prom because Des practically strapped her to a chair with her dress shawl.

Nadira quickly shook her head. "Des will be

doing the primping. I'm just here for moral support."

Laughing, I said, "You can all come over. Des, *please* bring some snacks."

In the background of Des's phone, I heard her mother shout, "OF COURSE!"

Giggling, I said, "See you guys tomorrow."

As their faces turned to black, I closed my eyes and held my phone against my chest. Everyone had told me I was out of my league. I just hadn't believed them until now.

TWENTY-SEVEN

WHEN I MADE it to the store, Dad waved me back to his office, and we had lunch together—a couple of frozen dinners that were about to expire. Dad focused on his computer while I scrolled through my phone.

In between bites, I glanced at Dad, realizing he was completely absorbed in his work. Tilting my screen toward me, I typed in Ryker's name on Facebook. His profile picture was one of him in his football uniform. His slate-gray eyes stared back at the camera, his face partially obscured by the gridded mask on his helmet. Dark black lines shined beneath his eyes, and his lips curled dangerously.

He was a formidable opponent on the field, and he was starting to look like one in real life too.

Half the posts on his feed were from our schoolmates congratulating him on the game, girls being a little too obvious in their innuendos. I rolled my eyes. None of them even had replies, as if Ryker thought he was too good to bother.

"Well," Dad said, "better get back to it."

I snapped my eyes up from my phone and nodded jerkily. "Sure." I opened my mouth to talk to him about Ryker, but decided to give up. What was the point when my voice didn't matter? I had no choice but to take this into my own hands.

Sliding out of the extra chair he kept in the office, I got up and left to get back to work. The store always got a big shipment Monday morning, which meant we had to clear out space for new product and make sure nothing expired stayed on the shelves. (Even though Dad said expiration dates were a scam meant for people to throw out perfectly good food and spend money on new stuff.)

As I stepped out of the office, I passed by EA's health teacher, Mrs. Hutton, and Aiden, who had a cartload of groceries.

"Hey," I said, giving a wave. "Stocking up?"

Mrs. Hutton nodded while Aiden gave her a sideways look.

"This is just a regular haul," he teased. "She

could open her own store with the size of our pantry."

Mrs. Hutton laughed. "Let's just say your parents should be happy they have teenage girls instead of boys for the way this one eats."

I wasn't sure about that—Ginger and I could give anyone a run for their money—but I said, "Hey, running takes a lot of energy, right?"

Aiden nodded. "Thank you!"

Mrs. H shook her head at her son. "Thank goodness for unlimited meal plans in college. Have you settled on a place yet, Cori?"

I almost wished I hadn't stopped to talk because I'd submitted applications to a few colleges and hadn't heard anything. Not that that was unusual. Ginger had waited months to get her acceptance letter from UCLA. Still, the nerves of it all was something I'd rather avoid. "Still deciding," I said simply and changed the topic to Aiden. "What about you? I bet you have colleges knocking down your door."

His cheeks pinked at the recognition. "A few."

"Should be deciding any day now," Mrs. H answered with a pleased smile.

"Good luck," I said honestly. "I better get to work."

We said goodbye, and I headed toward the back of the store. I'd start with anything still in boxes, breaking them down, and then work my way forward with a cart.

When I reached the back room, I saw Knox was already at work. His muscles stood out against his Ripe shirt as he bent over a box, ripping back the flaps and breaking it down.

"Hey," I said loud enough for him to hear me over the ripping of tape and cardboard.

He turned over his shoulder, hazel eyes meeting mine. "Hey, Cor."

His words hit me right along with a crazy idea. What if *Knox* dated me? He was cute, and nice, and funny—even if half of his jokes included floppy dead fish. Plus he cared enough to help me and warn me about Ryker. And we'd eaten breakfast together...

Was this more than a harebrained idea? Was there something there?

Suddenly, the room felt a lot smaller, and the back of my neck felt hot.

"Need a box cutter?" Knox asked, standing and reaching for the shelf where we kept them.

Silently, I nodded, and when he handed it to me, my hand shook so much I almost dropped it.

"Thanks," I said finally. Why hadn't I seen what was right in front of me all this time? Was it that I didn't believe a guy like Knox could be interested in a girl like me? Or was there more to it?

I didn't have time to psychoanalyze, not with him working and me standing awkwardly behind him. So I got to work on the boxes, trying to come up with a non-pathetic way to ask him to ask me out.

Turned out there wasn't one. Not that I could think of with him working right beside me. I thought and thought and *thought* for hours while we broke down the boxes and loaded up the trailer we used to hold cardboard recycling.

"You've been quiet today," Knox said as we walked back into the store after our final load.

"Just distracted, I guess," I said, not bothering to add that it was him I'd been distracted by.

"Yeah," he agreed. "It felt like there were more boxes than usual."

I nodded. "I think Dad's been moving a lot more product these last few months."

"That's good, right?" He dropped his box cutter on the shelf and extended his hand for mine.

"I guess," I replied as I handed him mine. "A lot of work."

After he put it on the shelf, he turned toward me and smiled. "Some of the best things in life take a lot of work."

Was there more to what he was saying? I tried to decipher it in his hazel eyes, but he grabbed one of the carts and started toward the door. "I'll take produce?"

I nodded. "I'll start at the other end."

With a smile, he said, "Meet you in the middle."

We went to opposite ends of the store, and I got lost in the monotony of pulling products, checking the dates, and moving on. My cart was nearly full by the time I met Knox in the cereal aisle.

"Race you?" he asked.

My lips spread into a smile. "You're going down."

"We start back to back," he said, positioning his cart to face one end of the aisle. I backed mine up to his, and even though our backs weren't touching, I could feel his proximity.

"Ready?" he said.

"Set," I continued.

He waited until both sides of the aisle were clear. "Go!"

I took off, twisting packages and putting them back as quickly as I could. My eyes darted over the items, now familiar with the expiration dates and where to find them. The effort made my breathing speed and my muscles hum with excitement. I was so winning this race.

We couldn't be too loud because it wasn't quite time for the store to close, but the farther from him I got, the more nervous I became. Without glancing back, I couldn't tell how much progress he'd made or how much ground I needed to make up, but I wasn't taking my eyes off the prize.

Finally, I reached the end of the aisle, checked the very last product, and yelled, "Done!"

He yelled, "Finished!" at almost exactly the same time, and I was about to argue that I'd said it first, but then someone started clapping beside me. More than one someone.

Dad and Janet appeared around the aisle, amused grins stretching across their faces.

Dad chuckled and said, "That's what I call employee motivation."

My cheeks flushed, and I heard Knox's voice come closer. "Do I get a bonus for winning?"

I spun on him. "You didn't win! I clearly said 'done' first!"

Janet laughed gleefully. "I saw a tie."

"You know what a tie means," I said, turning back to her. "Two losers."

Knox chuckled. "I'll settle on a tie then."

Dad's smile stretched his mustache and beard. "I say I have two winners who get to head home a little early."

"You sure?" I asked.

He nodded. "I'm proud of you two."

Knox grinned. "Thanks, Mr. Nash."

There he went, being all polite. He *had* to be father approved.

We went to grab our things from the employee lockers, and Knox elbowed me. "Look at you, making daddy proud."

I rolled my eyes as I got my purse. "Please, he'd have to notice me first."

Knox's smile faltered, but he said brightly, "Looks like he noticed you alright. What are you going to do with your extra hour?"

I shrugged. "Sleep? Homework? The world is my oyster."

He chuckled, following me toward the front door. We waved goodbye to Janet on the way outside, and as I saw our vehicles parked toward the back of the lot, I realized I had about fifty yards left to suck up my courage and ask my question. But how?

I decided with an innocuous question. "What are you up to tomorrow?"

"Homework. Sleep. The world is my oyster," he teased.

I chuckled, shaking my head. This had to be it. "Knox, I—"

His eyes looked from me to a cute red car pulling into the parking lot. It drove right up to us, and as the vehicle approached, I saw a cute, petite blond inside. She slowed right beside us and said, "Hey, baby!"

Baby? My eyes widened, and my heart fell, and my stomach tried melting into the pavement like I wished I could have.

"Hey, Court!" Knox said, the smile just as clear in his voice as it was on his face. He was happy to see her. As the blond turned off her car and stepped out, Knox said, "Cori, this is my girlfriend, Courtney."

Although our names were similar, that was where our commonalities ended. This girl barely cleared five-two. She tucked herself into Knox's side like she and her sleek blond hair were designed to be there. And not only that, but she was also wearing a skirt and *heels*. The only time I'd worn heels was for prom pictures last year.

I felt something I usually only felt at home.

Invisible.

Inferior.

"Nice to meet you," I said, trying to keep my voice from shaking.

"You too," she said brightly. "Knox has told me all about what a blast you are at work!"

So he'd told her about me? And from the looks of it, she wasn't even remotely threatened. But I'd never heard about her. Why? "How long have you two been dating?" I asked, in what I hoped sounded like a friendly, curious tone.

"A week or two," Knox said easily, smiling down at her.

"We've been friends forever though," she said, smiling back just as happily. It made my heart sink, just like my hopes.

Was everyone on the planet destined to find love aside from me? I mean, it was pretty bad that the first guy who'd been forced to sit through one of my family's pre-boyfriend dinners was someone I absolutely detested.

She looked from Knox to me and brightened. "Hey, maybe you want to grab supper with us?"

"Yeah," Knox agreed. "That would be fun!"

"Thanks for the offer, but I better get going," I said, because if I stood there any longer, I might just cry. Not for Knox, I was happy for him. Nope, I had a big fat pity party waiting for me at home and a family dinner to ruin.

TWENTY-EIGHT

EVER SINCE GINGER and I got old enough to work at the store, Mom decided we should save Sundays for helping around the house and studying or working on homework. Even though Mom was in LA with the twins for filming, her rule of no working on Sundays carried over.

Of course, that rule didn't apply to Dad. The last time he'd taken so much as a weekend off from the store was to go with Mom for the twins' audition. He hadn't even taken the whole day off when my team competed at State basketball, working until the last second and showing up halfway into the second quarter.

Mom called me around nine in the morning—too late for me to pretend to be sleeping, but too early for me to be fully dressed and functional. Brushing back my hair, I swiped my phone to answer and saw my mom's perky face.

"Hi, sweet pea."

"Hi, Mom," I replied, leaning my phone up against the box of cereal on the table and continuing to eat.

"Excited for tonight?"

I lifted my eyebrows. "Dad told you I asked to cancel, right?"

"Oh honey. I thought you'd be happy to see your sisters and me." She seemed disappointed as she stepped onto their balcony and sat on a reclining chair. "And you know Ray's coming too? Ginger said he really wants to make sure Ryker is a good guy for you."

For the first time since seeing Knox's girlfriend last night, I smiled. "Really? Ray's coming?"

She nodded. "Just for you!"

My heart seemed to fray a little at the edges. Ray had set aside his busy schedule running his family's ranch just for me, and he wasn't even family. At least, not yet. He still needed to put a ring on my sister's finger and become an official Nash family member.

"Where should we take Ryker to eat?" she

asked. "There's a nice steakhouse a few blocks over we could try."

The wheels in my mind turned. If Ryker was going to ruin my night, I could make sure he didn't get a good free meal out of making me suffer. "Can we go back to that vegan place? It was *so* good last time."

"Yes!" She nodded quickly. "I'm so glad you liked it. I'll make us all a reservation."

"Great," I replied, taking another bite of cereal. It was that perfect mixture between crunchy and soft, and I was seriously wishing I had some chocolate chips to add to the bowl, but I'd stress eaten them all the day before.

"Now, onto the chores," Mom said, all business. "Have you seen the things I added to the list?"

Here we go. I shook my head and rested my cheek in my hand.

She went through a list of items she wanted me to clean and then some things she wanted me to check on, like how much we had left of our cleaning supplies and whether or not she needed to send some casseroles home with us. "And make sure you get the cleaning done. I'll have Dad check tonight and tell me."

I turned my eyes toward the ceiling and immediately regretted it because Mom said, "Cori Marie Nash, what is with the attitude?"

It might have been a rhetorical question, but I didn't care. "I don't know, Mom, maybe it's the fact that I have my first pre-boyfriend dinner tonight and you didn't bother asking me anything about the guy. Most moms would at least be a tiny bit curious. You know, what's he like? Is he cute? Do I even like him or is *Dad forcing this dinner to save face?*"

Mom rubbed her forehead. "Tell me about him, Cori."

I pulled my head away from the phone, just as disgusted with her as I was with the tears stinging my eyes. "I want you to ask because you're interested, not because you're guilty."

She sighed, looking genuinely remorseful. "I'm sorry. Can we start over?"

I blinked quickly, but when that wasn't enough, I wiped at my eyes. "It's okay. I'll just see you tonight."

"Bye, honey, love you," she said quickly.

I said goodbye and hung up the phone feeling wide awake but completely drained at the same time. How could Mom and I have the same DNA and exist on such opposite wavelengths? I didn't understand, and what was worse, she had no drive to understand me.

I got to work on the cleaning, because I knew it needed to happen before my friends arrived, and when it came time to text her about the questions she had for me, I kept my answers short and sweet.

When Nadira arrived fifteen minutes early to help me get ready (as was her standard), she immediately noticed something was off.

"What's going on?" she asked, following me to my room.

I thought about shrugging it off, just focusing on having a good time with my friends, but decided to tell her the truth instead. Nadira knew me too well for me to pull off a lie anyway.

"My mom just gets to me," I said, dropping onto my bed while she sat in my desk chair. "I swear she does anything she can to show me she has as little interest as possible in my life."

Nadira frowned. "Is Ginger sick again?"

My eyebrows drew together. "No, why?"

Her shoulders lifted slightly. "It just seems to be worse when she gets all wrapped up in Ginger's problems."

The words hit me hard. I didn't want to be jealous of the attention Ginger got. It was definitely warranted, even if Mom took it too far at times. "I don't know. Maybe a part of me thought it would be better when Ginger went to college and Mom wouldn't have her around to fuss over all the time, you know?"

My friend nodded, her tight curls bouncing. "I feel the same way at school. Like I do all the right things and yet it's like I'm invisible. No one sees me. Or at least they don't care to."

I leaned forward and squeezed her hand. "I see you."

She smiled at me. "And after Des gets done with you, Ryker is going to see you for the threat that you are."

Leaning back, I said, "You think so?"

"Oh yeah," she reassured. "He's scrambling now."

A devious smile formed on my lips as I realized Nadira was right. Ryker may have caught me off guard with his move, but I was still in charge here. I'd had years of experience dealing with my family, and he had no clue.

The doorbell rang throughout the house, and Nadira grinned at me. "It's go time."

TWENTY-NINE

MY ROOM quickly became a flurry of girls, makeup, hair supplies, and snacks sent by Faith's mom.

I took a bite of my scotcheroo and moaned. "These are so good, Faith."

Rolling her eyes, she said, "I'd tell my mom, but she doesn't need her ego to get any bigger."

"What do you mean?" Adriel asked, unclamping the curling iron and grabbing another tress of my hair.

All eyes were on Faith, except for Des, who was still digging through my closet for an outfit she liked for tonight.

Faith turned her gaze down, looking at her own half-eaten scotcheroo. "I don't know... She's just on all these volunteer boards where everyone tells her and Dad how incredible they are for adopting me. And my brothers are practically gods amongst men in my parents' eyes. Now they're thinking about getting a foreign exchange student so they can 'help' someone else."

I hardly knew how to take in all that information, but one piece stood out. "Wait. You're adopted?"

The color in her cheeks became more pronounced. "When I was little. It's not a big deal. But when it comes up, people always tell my parents what saints they are for adopting me."

She tried to say it lightheartedly with a roll of her eyes, but I could see the pain that lived behind her words. And I got it. When someone said her parents were saints for adopting her, that made her a burden.

"We'll keep the scotcheroo secret to ourselves," I promised, and she smiled gratefully.

"Agreed," Des said, stepping out of my closet. "Now the secret we need to *stop* keeping is your curves." She held out two of my dresses and said, "Are these dresses or pillowcases, Cor?"

I raised my eyebrows. "What does that mean?"

She shook them at me. "They have no shape!

Where's the ruching? The tuck at the waist? The neck line to show off your cleavage?"

I would have shrugged, but the way Adriel was flying around me with the curling iron—it was better to stay still. "I basically live in my uniform and basketball shorts," I said.

"I can tell," she said drily.

"*But,*" I continued, "I think I have a few blouses toward the back that could work."

With a determined look, she went back into the closet, disappearing behind the racks of clothes.

Nadira looked dreamily at me. "Adriel is killing it on your hair, Cor."

Adriel grinned as she set the curling iron on Ginger's commandeered desk. "What do you think?"

I turned in the chair to look at the mirror hanging above the desk and gasped. "How did you do this?" I asked, gingerly touching the loose waves Adriel had put into my hair. "I've never seen it look this good, not even on prom night."

Adriel stood behind me with a bottle of hair spray. "Hold still for a sec."

I froze as she misted my curls, and a soft floral scent fell over me.

"Perfect," she said.

"Almost," Des added, holding up a white blouse with a stone-washed denim jacket and black skinny jeans. "Pair these with some killer heels, and he won't know what hit him."

With a grin, I took the outfit to the bathroom and wiggled into it. I hardly ever wore jeans—for good reason—but Des was right. These brought out my curves and showed off my hips and thighs. The white shirt contrasted them perfectly, and the denim jacket was the perfect casual piece to keep me from looking like I was trying too hard.

After changing, I took a fresh look in the mirror, delighting in the natural makeup Des had applied earlier that gave my skin a fresh, dewy look, and the gentle curls framing my face. I looked incredible, and as I narrowed my eyes, deadly. Ryker wouldn't know what hit him.

Adjusting my denim jacket, I stepped out of the bathroom and strutted to the bedroom. The girls burst out in gleeful compliments, clapping their hands together and demanding I do a turn.

I spun in a circle, feeling confident in myself and the way I looked. I savored the feeling, both of being at home in my own body and of having friends who were one hundred percent on my side.

Des waggled her eyebrows. "You should send a pic to that hot bagger at your store."

"He's a stocker," I reminded her, going to the closet to grab my chunky heeled boots. "And he has a girlfriend."

"What?" Nadira pouted. "He's so cute."

"Stocker?" Adriel asked. "Like the dangerous kind?"

I giggled. "No, he just makes sure the shelves are stocked."

"Much better," Adriel said with a giggle. "Can we see him?"

"Des, you do the honors," I said. I sat beside Faith on the bed and began lacing up my boots. With my being a basketball player, I had thick, muscular calves, and most boots didn't fit. These were the exception. Plus, with three-inch heels, they'd put me almost eye to eye with Ryker. On a level playing field.

As Des held her phone out, Adriel fanned herself and Faith said disappointedly, "He has a girlfriend?"

"Yup." I finished lacing up my boots. "And she's adorable. Just like a life-size Barbie doll."

"Naturally," Nadira said. "I swear, people like that are magnets for each other."

I frowned. "I don't know. I kind of thought Knox and I had...something. But apparently it was all in my head."

Des put her hands on my shoulders, making me look into her amber eyes. "Cori, tonight is not the night to worry about some guy who's off the market. It's the night to worry about us." She gestured to herself and the other girls.

"You guys?" I asked, confused.

She nodded. "This whole time, you've been saying you want to teach him a lesson, let him know what it feels like to be on the other end of the bullying. Of the tormenting. Keep your eyes on the prize. If he tries to date you, really date you, we'll get him off the team."

I nodded. She was right. As usual. "I've got this."

Faith smiled at me. "I don't know if I ever told you, but thanks, for that day. Standing up for me. Most people wouldn't have."

I leaned across the gap separating us on the bed and gave her a tight hug. "Any time, girl. You deserve it."

Nadira looked pointedly at her watch. "We need to go. Unless you want him knowing all of us put you together for the dinner?"

My eyes widened, realizing how desperate that would make me look. "Absolutely not. You guys have to go." I stood, taller than all of them in my heels. "I'll walk you out."

We scurried down the hall, Faith carrying a nearly empty glass pan, and I opened the front door for them. The sun streamed into my light eyes, and I squinted against the change in brightness.

"Let us know how it goes," Des said, walking backward to her cherry-red car.

"I will," I promised.

Adriel sashayed around the Eat Ripe sign and Faith crossed the lawn to her car. Within minutes, they were all out of the driveway, and I was still standing in the doorway, enjoying the silence that always came before metaphorical storms, when my dad pulled into the driveway with Ryker in the passenger seat.

THIRTY

I WANTED to run inside and hide and pretend I hadn't been standing on the porch. Ryker probably thought I was waiting for him like a lost puppy or something. Like all the other girls who fell for his good looks. He was nothing more than one of those disgusting cherry marshmallow-flavored chocolates hiding amongst all the good caramel ones.

Instead of hiding, I stepped farther out into the light, trying to embody all the confidence I'd felt earlier.

Dad and Ryker got out of the car, and the sun glinted off of Ryker's movie-star sunglasses. His mouthwateringly good looks unveiled as he stepped around the car, revealing his biceps pulling at the sleeves of an open gray button down over a black shirt. His dark-wash jeans contoured against his muscular thighs down to his white sneakers.

Cherry marshmallow, I reminded myself, keeping my mouth firmly shut.

Dad walked toward me and said, "I just need to change my shirt and I'll be ready."

I nodded, standing on the front porch with Ryker. He lowered his glasses just so I could watch his eyes slowly scan my body.

A chill traveled down my spine, and my breathing sped as I wondered what he thought about what he saw.

He lifted his glasses over his eyes. "Cori."

"Rykerina." I folded my arms over my chest.

His lip curled, and I smirked, knowing I had already gotten to him.

"Excited for our date?" he asked.

Cori-1, Ryker-1.

"It's not a date," I reminded him. "And I'm surprised you'd give up an evening with someone you actually like to ruin mine."

"How else was I supposed to get a second alone with you?" he asked, tilting his head so I could see his eyes over his sunglass frames. The wind shifted, and I caught the scent of his cologne. It filled my nostrils, intoxicating and weakening me against the words that came next.

I opened my mouth to give him reason one of a million why we shouldn't be alone together, but Dad opened the door, stepping out in khakis and a plaid shirt with the sleeves rolled up.

"Ready to go?" he asked, rubbing his hands together.

"Yes, sir," Ryker said, but I shook my head.

"I have to get my purse."

Dad nodded. "We'll be in the car. Be sure to hurry. Mom has reservations."

"Sure," I said, stepping inside. Wouldn't want to keep Mom waiting for *my* date. Inside the house, I immediately relaxed. Like it took a whole layer of brick and drywall to block the effect Ryker had on me. He was so infuriating.

I went and got my purse from the key hook, then went to my room and got a pack of gum and some lip gloss from Ginger's desk. No way would I be caught looking less than my best tonight. Especially not with Ryker looking like *that*.

Taking one last deep breath, I walked out of the house, locked the door, and faced this night, head on.

Dad had the car running, and I could see him

and Ryker laughing about something in the front seat. *Why* did they get along so well? I didn't understand it. Was Dad that clueless, or was Ryker just that good?

I went to the back seat and sat in the middle so I could keep an eye on them both. Maybe from back here I could get a picture of texts he was sending and show my parents for proof that Ryker shouldn't be let within a hundred yards of our family, or any girl for that matter.

Once I had my belt on, Dad backed out of the driveway and started toward my own personal hell. I had an entire hour in the car with Ryker—possibly more depending on traffic—and I knew Dad wouldn't let the trip be filled with music too loud to talk.

"Now, Ryker, how do you feel about vegan food?" Dad asked. "Because my wife picked a vegan place for tonight—but between the three of us, I can probably sneak us a hamburger afterward."

My mouth fell open as Ryker chuckled. Was Dad seriously offering Ryker non-organic food behind Mom's back? He never would have done something like that for me.

"That won't be necessary," Ryker said. "My

mom's a vegetarian Monday through Thursday, so I know my way around a vegan menu."

"Monday through Thursday?" Dad asked, voicing my own question.

Ryker spread his large hands over his jeans. "Vegan options aren't always available at the social outings she goes to on the weekends."

"Ah," Dad said, but something seemed off to me.

"The outings she goes to?" I asked and immediately regretted it as Ryker shifted to look at me.

"They're usually plus one," he said shortly. "No children allowed."

The emotion behind his voice was hardly detectable, but it was there. I pressed my lips together, promising myself not to ask another question about him. Especially not one that would make me feel sorry for him.

"You're welcome to family movie nights when the girls get back from filming," Dad offered. "When Laura's around, we always put up a movie and make a big to-do about popcorn and Cori's favorite chocolate chips."

"Chocolate chips?" Ryker asked.

"She's crazy about the things," Dad said. "Drives her mother nuts since she can never find them when she wants them for a recipe. Hides them all over the place."

Ryker's lips turned up in an amused smile, and my cheeks felt hot. I looked out the window at the ocean passing in the distance and wished it could swallow me whole.

"What was Cori like as a kid?" Ryker asked innocently.

I narrowed my eyes at him, but the second Dad looked at me in the rearview mirror, a smile on his face, my expression softened.

"She was precious," Dad said. "Trouble on two feet the second she could walk. Always getting into things and causing a stir."

"Nothing's changed," Ryker said, making my neck get hot right along with my cheeks.

"No, it hasn't." Dad chuckled. "She used to always want to dance along with the radio. It was right where she could reach it, and when it was off and she thought no one was looking, she'd dance over to it, all sneaky, with the biggest grin on her face. Of course the second we saw her going that direction, she'd take off at a run to push the buttons." He laughed at the memory, and my heart melted.

It had been forever since I'd heard him share a

good memory about me, especially with all his focus on the store and my sisters.

"That sounds adorable," Ryker said, ruining the moment.

"It was," Dad agreed. "And she's still my little girl, so you better treat her right."

Ryker turned to me, a smirk on his full lips. "I promise I will."

THIRTY-ONE

I'D NEVER BEEN SO happy to see Ray's muddy truck in all my life. My eyes landed on it the second we pulled into the restaurant's parking lot, and I could have kissed him for showing up.

"This is the place," Dad said, turning off the car.

"Can't wait to try it," Ryker replied, continuing his butt-kissery. "Let me get your door, Cori."

Dad gave an impressed nod, looking at me in the mirror. "A gentleman. I like him already." He got out the car while I stared down Ryker through the tinted window.

Mom waited near the front of the restaurant with the twins, Ginger, and Ray, and Dad went to join them. When Ryker opened my door, I stood to full height, meeting his eyes. Still, he was a couple of annoying inches taller than me.

"What are you playing at?" I demanded.

"Is it a crime to like a girl?" he asked, his voice silky smooth.

"In your case? Absolutely."

He chuckled, sliding his arm around me and letting me out of the cage he'd created. I followed along just long enough to elbow his ribs and stepped forward, strutting toward my family so Ryker could see *exactly* what he'd be missing out on forever.

Ginger immediately came to hug me, whisper-yelling, "THIS IS CRAZY!"

We both turned to watch Ray extending his strong hand toward Ryker.

"Dugan," he said in his charming country way, but there was nothing sweet about the death grip he placed on Ryker's hand. "Heard you're interested in our girl."

Ryker stood even straighter, eye to eye with Ray. "I am."

Ray lifted his eyebrows and stepped away. "This family protects its own."

Ryker lifted his chin. "I don't see why they'd need to. Cori does a good job of that on her own."

Dad clapped his hand on Ray's shoulder. "And here I thought I was supposed to be the one showing up with a shotgun." Dad chuckled. "Come on in, sons." As Dad led Ray and Ryker into the restaurant, Ginger and I stared at each other. Ray was the ace up my sleeve, and Dad had made him nothing but a joker.

"What is happening?" I whispered.

She shook her head, just as clueless as me.

Before we went inside, Mom made sure to give me a hug. "You look beautiful, honey."

I gave her half a smile and nodded. "Thanks, Mom."

She left her arm around my waist and we walked inside together until I was left with the only empty chair, right next to Ryker's.

Tarra sat on the other side of me, and as the menus were passed out, I made a point to give her my full attention so Ryker knew just how little I was interested in him.

"Tell me about the studio, Tarra," I said. "How much longer do you think you have?"

She excitedly launched into an explanation of how filming actually worked, from the hour it typically took to get one minute of screen time to the stand-ins who helped the crew get lighting right before she and Cara could step in to do their parts.

Then she said, "Have you done any acting, Ryker? You look like a movie star."

Ginger, Ray, and I all rolled our eyes, but Ryker said, "You and your sisters are the ones who look like movie stars. You're all so beautiful."

Mom and the twins smiled, while Ginger and I did the twin thing, mirroring looks of disgust.

"You're laying it on a little thick, Dugan," Ginger said.

"Ginger!" Mom admonished.

"What?" Ginger asked, disappearing behind her menu.

Ryker leaned in a little closer, his breath tickling my cheek, and asked, "What are you getting, Cori?"

I gave him a look, leaning away, and said, "What about you, Monday-through-Thursday vegan?"

Ray arched an eyebrow. "What?"

Ryker shook his head. "It's a long story, and the waitress is coming, so…" He nodded his head toward the pretty girl waiting on us.

It seemed like she had a hard time deciding between the cowboy at my sister's side and the wannabe boy band singer at mine. The way her eyes bounced between the two was kind of comical, really. "I'll have a Caesar salad," Ray said, putting her out of her misery. "And my girlfriend will have a raspberry wedge salad."

Ginger smiled at him, happily nodding along.

Their relationship was so sweet. I loved how Ray did those old-fashioned touches with her, even though it wasn't my thing. I didn't want a guy speaking on my behalf—I wanted him to step aside and let me lead.

Maybe that was why I'd always had trouble finding the right guy. High school boys weren't used to a woman who knew what she wanted, much less one who would make it happen one way or another.

Which was why I'd thought Knox might be a good bet, but...

"Cori," Mom said. "Your order?"

I realized everyone was waiting on me, so I quickly asked for the chickpea burger and returned my menu to the pretty waitress, who Ryker hadn't looked at once. He was on his A game tonight. I had to hold on to the hope that it would only be a matter of time before he revealed himself and his sleazy nature.

"So, Ryker," Mom said. "What do you want to do in college?"

"Play football," he answered easily, taking a sip of his water.

"You sound like Cori," Mom said, shaking her head. "She just wants to play basketball. You both forget student comes before athlete."

I shook my head as Ryker took me in. I so wasn't in the mood for another lecture.

"You can learn plenty in sports," Ryker said. "Teamwork, leadership, dedication, determination. Even if you don't make it pro, the connections made on a team can last a lifetime."

Ray's jaw ticked. "Connections are no replacement for knowledge and hard work."

I wanted to agree with Ray. I got where he was coming from, running his family farm and all, but Ryker and I came from a different world. At the Academy, who you knew was just as important as what you knew.

My mom folded her napkin over her lap. "Both valid points."

She was *agreeing* with Ryker on not needing to know a major? Who was this woman posing as my mother?

"Ginger?" I said. "Can you come to the bathroom with me?"

She stood up before I even got the sentence out, and Mom chuckled. "Girls."

Ignoring everyone, I beelined for the restrooms, or at least where I thought they were. Turned out that was the kitchen, and I had to make the awkward walk of shame toward the actual bathroom where Ginger was already waiting for me.

She stood near the sinks, and the second I got in there, she said, "What is *happening* out there?"

"I don't know!" I cried. "But who is that woman pretending to be our mother?"

"And who is that guy pretending to be Ryker?" she asked. "I've *never* seen him on this good of behavior."

"He said he wants to talk to me on my own and this was his only way to do it." I leaned back against the wall but accidentally hit the paper towel dispenser, and it whirred, spitting out more brown paper. I sighed and stood back up. "He's got me all flustered!"

"He's putting on all the moves, that's for sure." Ginger folded her arms over her chest. "What does he want to talk to you about?"

"Probably the picture of him in a pink leo that's all over the internet."

She rolled her eyes. "He has a hundred thousand more followers on social, thanks to that. He shouldn't be too upset."

I shrugged with my hands out to the side. "I'm out of my league here, Ging."

She tapped her chin thoughtfully. "It's obvious Mom and Dad are going to give him the go ahead, right? Why not go out with him and see what he has to say?"

My eyes widened. "My sister, the one Ryker bullied for months, wants me to spend time with him? What am I missing here?"

"Maybe you'll get something to use against him? I don't know, but if you keep going at this blind, it's clear he's going to win."

I nodded slowly, my stomach churning.

She put her hands on my shoulders, making the seams of my denim jacket press into my skin. "If anyone can do this, you can."

My lips parted. "What do you mean?"

She gave me a sardonic smile. "Cori, you know you're special. Out of all of us, you've always been the one who goes for what you want, no questions asked, no assistance needed. You've got this."

With her words bolstering me, I squared my shoulders and walked back into the lion's den.

When Ginger and I reached the table, all the food had already been delivered. As I neared my seat, Ryker stood up as well, which then caused Ray to stand up, and we all stood awkwardly until Ginger and I took our seats.

This was the worst pre-date dinner ever, and that was including the one where our parents had practically kicked Ray out of the house. I needed to say a rosary or sprinkle holy water or burn some sage around the twins so they wouldn't have to go through this kind of torture.

As we sat down, Mom and Ryker resumed a conversation about the benefits of using chickpeas, soy, or turnips for meat substitutes. It was the lamest thing I'd ever heard, and if I thought for a second it wouldn't bore everyone else to tears, I'd film it to tease him more.

Instead, I sat quietly, picking at my horrible meal until everyone was done eating. Dad paid the check, although Ryker offered to, and then we made our way to the door like the awkward group we were.

Once outside in the cool evening air, Ray said,

"Why don't you say goodbye to the girls, Paul? I can walk Ryker to the car."

Dad chuckled. "Boys will be boys, right?" He passed Ray the keys, and I stood beside Ginger as we watched them walk away. Dad and Mom and the twins were too busy saying goodbye to even notice the tense set of the boys' shoulders or the measured way they took their steps.

"What do you think they're talking about?" I whispered to Ginger.

She shook her head. "Ray's probably putting the fear of God in him."

"Good," I muttered, folding my arms across my chest. What I wouldn't give to be a fly on the car window, listening to their conversation.

"Come here, girls," Mom said, interrupting my thoughts. She put her arms around Ginger's shoulders, along with mine, and said, "I'm so proud of you two."

We both looked at her in shock.

"What?" I asked.

She smiled and said, "You have become such good girls that you're attracting very respectable boys. It says something about your self-worth that these guys are willing to go through all of this to be with you."

Ginger started coughing, no doubt at Mom calling Ryker respectable, and I merely shook my head. "Don't worry, Mom. You won't be seeing too much more of Ryker anyway."

She frowned, glancing at the boys standing by the car, their arms folded over their chests. "Why is that?"

I looked at them too. Ryker was attractive—tall, lean, deep eyes you could stare into, but any girl with self-worth had to look past all that. "He's just not the guy for me." Or for any curvy girl for that matter. We deserved better.

Dad and the twins approached us. "We should probably get on the road," he said.

I sighed, turning to Ginger and giving her a hug. Even though I liked having my room to myself, I missed her. Missed having my partner in crime a few feet away.

Then I hugged Mom. The tension between us was just as palpable as her curly hair tickling my cheek.

"We should be done filming in a month," she said, cupping my cheek. "And when I get back, I promise we'll make time to talk, just you and me."

Her promise brought tears to my eyes. "I'd like that," I said honestly. Maybe her treatment of

Ryker was more about me and less about him—a peace offering I hadn't quite understood.

She kissed my cheek, and after I said goodbye to the twins, hugging them both, Dad, Ginger and I walked to the car. Ray and Ryker amicably shook hands, confusing me even more. Ginger and I exchanged a look, and I made a mental note to text her later and ask why the heck Ray was acting like Ryker wasn't the enemy anymore.

As Dad got into the car, Ryker stood by the passenger door to let me in.

"Wait," I said, stopping him from opening it. I looked up at him, into his eyes, which looked pale in the streetlights. For a moment, I searched them. Looking for the evil. Looking for the hate. But I didn't see it. "Why are you doing this?"

His head tilted down as he spoke to me. "I'll explain. When we get to your house, I'm going to ask your dad if I can take you for a burger, because you and I both know that vegan food was awful."

It took all I had not to smile.

"Will you come with me?" he asked.

Maybe it was because I was actually hungry. Or because I couldn't detect even a hint of malice in his voice. But for whatever reason, I said, "Yes."

THIRTY-TWO

I TEXTED GINGER FIRST THING, asking what had transpired between Ryker and Ray. Then I sent a group chat to the girls.

Cori: I'm not sure what's going on, but Ryker asked me to go out with him tonight. I'm going to see what he wants.

Des: You know he wants that *peach emoji*

To which I immediately replied with an eyeroll emoji.

I tapped back to my message thread with Ginger, but she still hadn't replied. I sent her a string of question marks, hoping she'd speed it up, but nothing. Not even those bubbles to reassure me she was replying.

No, all I could do was stare at the back of

Ryker's and Dad's heads as they talked about boating. Apparently, Dad's family used to sail a lot because he was saying things to Ryker I didn't even understand.

A bit of jealousy welled inside me, because Dad never talked to me like this—like I was a friend he wanted to know more about and not just a child to protect.

As we pulled into the parking lot of Ripe where Ryker's black truck gleamed in a spot away from the store, he shifted to face my dad.

"Sir," he began, "I'd like to thank you for the opportunity to meet your family tonight and the chance to get to know you a little better."

"The pleasure's been mine, son." Dad extended his hand for a shake. "If my daughter will have you, it's alright with my wife and me."

What? Dad actually acknowledging my choice in this? Miracles were possible.

"Well, I'm glad you said that, because I was wondering if I could take you up on your offer and take Cori for some burgers?"

Dad looked at me, actually checking with me, and I nodded.

"It's fine with me," he said. "Be back by ten thirty."

That gave us two hours, and I could hardly even believe he was letting me stay out that late on a school night. I couldn't help but think that would never fly with Mom. How much would things change when the twins finished filming and she was around to micromanage us again?

My door opened, and I realized Ryker was holding it for me. I picked up my purse and scooted out of the seat. "See you later, Dad."

He lifted his hand in a wave, and then Ryker hit the button on his own keys, making the taillights flash.

As Dad drove away, I realized this had been a terrible idea. What was I doing alone in a parking lot with a person I'd declared war on? Who'd smashed my chocolate chip cookies to a pulp? Who'd pretended my friend was a cow in a chute? What kind of sick person did something like that?

I gritted my teeth as he let me in the passenger door of his pickup and held on to the righteous anger as I buckled in. With the seatbelt firmly in place, I folded my arms over my chest, reminding myself to guard my feelings, and my heart.

My phone vibrated as he got in, and I checked it. A message from Ginger.

Ginger: Ray says he thinks Ryker might have changed, but something's not sitting right with me.

Cori: What? Why???

Ginger: I don't know. He said it was a gut feeling. Just be careful, okay?

Ginger didn't need to tell me twice. I locked the screen before Ryker would have a chance to look over my shoulder.

Quietly, he started his pickup, and the engine roared to life. The dash lights flashed blue, and he easily put the truck into drive. Music played softly—country from what I could tell—and my mouth fell open.

"What?" he asked.

I shook my head, quickly sealing my lips. "Nothing, it's just…you didn't strike me as a country boy."

His lips turned up in one corner. "What, you have to walk around in cowboy boots to like country music?"

I arched a brow. "No, but the truck makes a lot more sense now."

He laughed softly, and it was so different from what I'd heard from him before. I had to wonder if I'd ever heard him laugh in a non-derisive way.

As he drove down the main road in Emerson, he said, "Your family's nice."

I rolled my eyes. "More like embarrassing. I'm sure your parents don't talk on dates about what you were like as a baby."

"No," he said quietly. "But then again, they've never met one of my dates."

I snorted, thinking of the revolving door of girls Ryker kept on his arm. "It would be too hard to remember all their names, right?"

"No, because they never cared enough to."

The implication behind his words didn't escape me, and for once, I found myself speechless. And somehow in an odd kinship with Ryker. Again. Tonight was the first time the entire family had done something purely for my benefit, but he wouldn't understand that. All he saw was a family with quirky parents and too much red hair, not reality. And I didn't trust him enough to let him know how lonely that reality felt at times.

His headlights panned over Waldo's Diner, and I stared into the windows as he parked. The restaurant was a little slower since it was a Sunday evening. I recognized Aiden and his girlfriend, Casey, in one window. She was laughing, and even from here I could see the love in his eyes.

"Are you coming?" Ryker asked.

"You want to be seen with me?" My voice came out more bitter than I'd wanted it to, but the sentiment remained the same.

His eyes held mine as he said, "Why wouldn't I?"

I narrowed my gaze. "You might be a jock, but I know you're not dumb."

Instead of replying, he opened his door and got out. I'd expected him to walk into the restaurant, make an order to-go, and walk out, but instead, he crossed the front of the pickup and opened my door.

My mouth must have been open because he said, "Come on, Cori, you know you're hot."

Mouth closed. "Say that to my size sixteen jeans."

His eyes heated as he took me in. "Whatever size they are, I like them. Especially on you."

My stomach fluttered before my mind could catch up. I rolled my eyes and got out. "Lay off, Dugan."

I walked into the diner ahead of him, feeling his eyes on my jeans the entire time. Was he being serious, or was this just another one of his games? He was good on the field, but a true player made the world their playground.

Without waiting for Ryker, I sat in a booth right near the bathrooms so I'd have an escape route if necessary. I wasn't above locking myself in a stall and waiting until I could get some backup to pick me up.

Ryker slid into the booth across from me like he owned the place. Actually, everywhere he went, he had that sense of being at home in a way I'd never been—not even in my own house.

"Cori?" Betty said, almost like she didn't trust it was actually me. She looked between Ryker and me, her hand limp around her pen.

"Hi, Betty," I said brightly, happy to see her. But her eyes flicked to Ryker, saying *what gives?* I shrugged, not knowing myself.

"Chocolate shake and fries, thanks," Ryker said, not even making eye contact with Betty.

I stared at him before turning to Betty. "I'll have a chocolate shake, a cheeseburger, cheese fries, and a Coke. Oh, and if you find someone in the back who actually has some manners, I'll take him too."

She smirked. "I'll see what I can do." Without taking any notes, she walked away, leaving me with an incredulous Ryker.

"What was that about?" he demanded, his jaw tight.

I leaned forward across the table, my eyebrows together. "Do you not realize how rude you are? Or do you just not care?"

"Rude?" he demanded. "I told the waitress thanks!"

I rolled my eyes. "Only you would call treating *Betty* like a servant polite."

His head tilted to the side. "Am I missing something, or is she not wearing a Waldo's Diner T-shirt? Her literal *job* is to wait on us."

I scoffed. "So just because it's her job to be our waitress we shouldn't treat her like someone with thoughts and feelings and goals and—"

He scoffed right back. "Give me a break, Robin Hood."

"What's that supposed to mean?" I demanded.

"It means you surround yourself with all these people who are weaker than you because you want to be the best. You want to *save* them. Newsflash, sweetie, you're not Jesus, and they don't need saving."

Repulsion so strong wracked through me, it was a miracle I was still in the seat. "As opposed to what? Some guy who walks around in his letterman jacket and picks on fat girls because why? They're a little bit different?"

"I'm doing them a favor," he said, lifting his chin. "Everyone wants high school to be roses and rainbows, but that's not real life. The world's a hard place to be, and anything I do to them is *peanuts* compared to the reality coming their way."

My lip curled. "Reality? What would you know about the real world, living in your mansion on the beach with your rich parents who give you no rules and going to a school that lets you get away with anything you want? Huh? You think that's the way the rest of your life is going to be?" My breathing was coming fast now, firing up along with my anger. "Someday you're going to be fat and bald and sitting on your couch boring your wife to tears talking about the good ol' days. And those girls? They're going to have an *amazing* life. And they won't even give you a second thought."

I got up, thinking my former exit plan wasn't good enough. I started walking toward the door and met Betty, who held two milkshakes in her hands. "I'm sorry, Betty," I said, angry tears hot in my eyes. "I'm not hungry anymore."

I pushed out the door and started walking as fast as I could in the general direction of home. At least I'd be a little closer when I finally got in touch with one of my friends who could pick me up.

"Cori!" a voice yelled, but it wasn't Ryker's like I'd been expecting. I turned to see Aiden jogging my way. "Cori, are you okay?"

I wiped at my tears, feeling beyond stupid. "I'm fine." My voice cracked, giving me away.

"What's going on?" he asked, his dark eyes shining in the streetlights. "Why are you here with Ryker?"

"It's a long story," I said, feeling more exhausted than I ever had. How did I even begin to explain the craziness that was this entire weekend?

"You're not... dating him, are you?" The disgust at the idea was clear on Aiden's face.

"No, no, no, absolutely not."

Ryker's pickup pulled along the sidewalk where Aiden and I stood, and the door opened as Ryker got out.

I closed my eyes, and Aiden gently put a hand on my arm. "Do you want a ride home?" he asked.

"Cori," Ryker said, ignoring Aiden completely. "Let me give you a ride. Please?"

I opened my eyes to see Ryker glancing between Aiden and me.

"I can walk," I lied to both of them.

Ryker stepped to my other side, his hand on my opposite arm. "I'm sorry for what I said back there. Can we just...talk? In the truck?" His voice strained, and it was clear how uncomfortable he was doing this at all, especially in front of Aiden.

Then it hit me. Ryker had *apologized* for something. Had I heard him wrong?

I searched his gray eyes, and they seemed honest. Instead of looking at Ryker, I spoke to Aiden. "I'll be okay."

Aiden's eyes flicked from me to the boy with the ridiculous truck. "Are you sure?"

I nodded. "I'll see you in school?"

"Sure." He glanced back to the restaurant where his girlfriend's thin frame was silhouetted against the lights. "Text me when you get home?"

"Sure," I agreed.

Without another word, he turned and jogged back to her.

Ryker opened the truck door for me.

I looked between the plush leather interior and the gray sidewalk. Finally, I got in. As the door shut behind me, I sealed my fate.

THIRTY-THREE

AS SOON AS Ryker walked to his side of the truck, I realized the enormity of the mistake I'd made. I'd just stormed out of a restaurant, crying—something I would *never* have done without Ryker's provocation. Then I got into his truck, of my own volition, because why? He has nice eyes? Give me a break. I was becoming exactly like those other girls who fell for his charm and forgot myself. Not tonight. Not anymore.

He got into the driver's side and said, "Can I at least take you through a drive-thru?"

"Really?" I said harshly. "After everything, the first thing you're offering me is food?"

He sighed and pulled onto the road.

"Do you need directions to my house?" I asked.

"I remember the way," was all he said.

I folded my arms over my chest and looked out the window as he took every turn the right way toward my house. If the clock was any indication, we still had an hour left until we *had* to be back, but I couldn't wait for this "date" to end.

Instead of stopping in front of my house, he parked along the curb at the end of my street.

"My house is that way," I said, sounding snootier than I wanted to. It was like Ryker brought out the worst in me by simply existing.

"I know," he said lightly.

I looked at him, trying to understand what he was playing at, but yet again, I couldn't see his angle. I was tired—tired of the games, tired of the manipulation, and tired of feeling like I had to fight for my space in the world as a curvy girl.

"What do you want, Ryker?" I finally asked, the exhaustion leaking into my voice.

"I want a truce."

I rolled my eyes, because that was the last thing he wanted. "You just want my friends and me to lie down so you can keep living your fantastic life. Never mind the fact that you made my sister afraid to walk into school every morning or that Faith *sobbed* over what you did."

"That's not it at all!" he said, his voice rising.

"Then what is it?" I demanded. "You're saying one thing and doing another, and none of it makes sense!"

He raked his fingers through his hair and scrubbed his face, letting out a frustrated sigh. I'd never seen him less composed. "Can you just shut up for a second?"

My eyebrows rose, but I waited. "This has got to be good."

He rolled his eyes at me, then took a deep breath, squaring his shoulders toward me. "I met someone."

"Oh my gosh!" I cried, reaching for the door, ready to just walk the rest of the way.

"Wait!" he said, placing his hand on my thigh. It was big, covering a large expanse of jean and making heat shoot straight to my bones. I froze, out of surprise if nothing else.

"I met this girl," he said, "and she's the most annoying person I've ever laid eyes on. She's demanding and forceful and cocky and damn if she doesn't have a special talent for getting under my skin." His eyes held mine. "And for the first time..." He blinked and cleared his throat, then clenched the steering wheel with his free hand. "I feel lost."

The small phrase said through gritted teeth hung between us, and I clung to the meaning behind his words. Had we changed his mind?

"So," he said, businesslike again, "truce?"

A soft snort came through my nose, and then I leaned across the console, using a move of his own against him. I was inches from his face, and the second I watched his eyes flick to my lips, I knew I'd won.

"You want me to call a truce?" I breathed.

His Adam's apple bobbed, and he nodded.

"Then leave my friends alone." I broke the spell and got out of the car.

His headlights didn't leave my back until I was inside my house.

THIRTY-FOUR

WHEN I MET my friends in the Academy parking lot the next morning, they each seemed lighter, laughing and joking in a way I hadn't seen them do before. After I told them about my conversation with Ryker and his change of heart, the tension seemed to have fallen off of them like raindrops off flowers. But I knew better.

Just because Ryker said he wanted a truce didn't mean he would actually follow through. If all my years playing basketball taught me one important lesson, it was this: don't assume you've won the game until the final buzzer sounds.

I held on tightly to the straps of my backpack as I listened to Adriel talk about nailing one of her moves for an upcoming dance competition. She said if she placed well, she'd qualify to dance on the national stage. Which was awesome, but I couldn't really focus, not with Ryker and all of his friends standing around his pickup just a few yards away. There were a couple of girls standing with the group, but Ryker wasn't touching any of them. Why?

Had the world really shifted off its axis the night before?

As we got closer, nerves danced over my skin and landed in my stomach. One of the guys standing around Ryker's truck started oinking like a pig, and then another gestured at his crotch and yelled, "Want to eat my slops?"

My lips curled in disgust. I opened my mouth to put him in his place, but Ryker said, "*Enough.*"

His low voice cut through the chatter instantly, and a silence fell over the entire parking lot, like even the students walking around us knew they shouldn't speak.

My eyes widened as I took in Ryker. Was he...defending us? My friends and I stood still, like deer caught in the headlights of their bullying. Of Ryker's defense.

"Man, it was just a joke," the guy said.

"Wasn't funny," Ryker said simply. He bent and

picked up the backpack by his feet and turned to walk inside.

Each of the guys around him seemed just as confused as I did, but they slowly stopped leaning against his pickup and followed him into the building. Once all their backs were to us, Des hit my arm. "What was *that*?"

Adriel nodded fervently. "You said he asked for a truce, not that he'd get everyone else to shut up too!"

"I don't know," I answered honestly, watching Ryker easily take the stairs to the school. I bit my bottom lip. What had happened?

On my other side, Faith rubbed my shoulder. "I can't believe you did it! You beat the bully!"

Nadira readjusted her backpack. "And she's going to get a tardy if we don't get inside." She started walking toward the door.

With a small smile, I shook my head and followed her. "You have to admit, I just made being a mathlete a lot easier."

Her smile matched my own. "I'll just be happy not to be called a firehouse dog." She rolled her eyes.

My lips fell as I realized that the win was flawed. Getting Ryker and his goons to stop wouldn't cure all the hurts they'd inflicted on my friends, not just in the last month, but for all the years leading up to this. None of us had escaped our first three years of high school without scars, and I shuddered at the memories of middle school.

What good was having Ryker stop bullying these five girls when his heart was still the same? When he hadn't actually changed or made amends?

The victory felt hollow as I made my way to my locker. Ryker stood at his, and I knew a conversation was coming at the way his shoulders were turned toward me. For the first time, I actually wanted to have it—to talk to him—but Mrs. Bardot caught up to me.

"Cori! I just got a request I want to talk to you about," she said. "Can you come to my office with me? I'll get you a note for first period."

I nodded and gave Ryker a last look before following her to her office down the hall. What kind of request could she have gotten that would be so urgent? My heart clenched—what if something bad had happened to one of my parents? My sisters?

"Is everything okay?" I asked her.

"I think so," she answered cryptically, slowing in front of her office.

Unlike the rest of the teachers, her name plate

only said BIRDIE on it. I followed her through the wooden door, and my eyes automatically landed on her white bird, Ralphie.

He sat happily on his swing, moving forward and backward. His orange beak almost looked like he was smiling.

"He's having fun," Mrs. Bardot said, following my eyes. She took a seat at her desk and gestured that I should do the same.

Letting my backpack slide down my arm, I settled into one of the wooden chairs opposite her. "What's going on?" I couldn't imagine what kind of positive request she'd gotten that might warrant a first-hour meeting.

She tapped on her keyboard, logging in to what looked like an email account. "I just got a message from a basketball coach in Hawaii asking about your academics and wanting me to put him in touch with your basketball coach."

My eyes widened. "What?" I'd only applied to that college on a whim, not thinking I'd actually get in. "That's amazing!"

She smiled and went to her file cabinet, pulling open the top drawer. "I need to add that college to your list of options. Have you applied to any others already?"

I nodded and ticked them off on my fingers.

She took the pencil from behind her ear and wrote them down. "Great. I love that you've taken initiative this early. That's quite uncommon for our students who want to pursue collegiate athletics."

The first person that came to mind was Ryker. What was he doing for college? He'd said he wanted to play football, but where? I didn't know. I hardly knew him at all.

Maybe that was part of the problem? I didn't know him beyond the hard, beautiful, bullying exterior. And maybe that was why he bullied people like me—because he didn't know, really know, anyone like me either.

"Now that I know this is the plan," Birdie continued, placing my file back in the drawer, "I'll start looking out for potential scholarships for you to apply for and alumni who may be living in those areas." She shut the drawer and rubbed her hands together. "I'm excited for you, Cori! It will be so great for you to get out and see the world."

"Thank you." I smiled, but it wasn't the kind that made me feel any lighter. The truth was, I didn't know anything outside of Emerson, not really. Would the rest of the world be any better?

Or would I just find more people like Ryker? More people like my parents? "Anything else?"

She sat across from me and folded her hands on the desk. Today, she was wearing a burnt orange dress and had a big leaf ring on her finger. "It was an interesting game Friday, yes?"

My throat got tight, and I felt like a deer in headlights all over again. I couldn't speak, so I nodded.

"Unfortunate, what happened to Ryker." She regretfully shook her head. "His parents are quite upset, as is he. Rightly so." Resting her chin on her hand, she pinned her brown eyes on me.

The fighter within me that had caused me to declare war on Ryker rose up, and I looked right back at her, not wavering at all. "You're right. It does hurt to be humiliated in front of your classmates and friends."

Her head tilted, and she said, "It sure does." She glanced at the watch on her wrist with a big maple leaf on the face. "Ryker and his parents should be here any minute. They want whoever was behind this to be punished, and I'll be reminding them of Emerson Academy's zero-tolerance bullying policy that requires us to expel anyone who is found bullying, unless they were to come forward and apologize of their own accord." She arched an eyebrow. "Is there anything you want to tell me, Cori?"

The edge of my fingernails dug into my palms as I clenched my hands under the table. This was it. My chance to choose. Should I back down, or should I stand up for what was right? I knew my answer. "Yes, there is something I want to tell you," I said, my voice full of emotion. "I hope you can help Ryker recover from some of the *torment* of that night. He's never humiliated someone because of the way they looked, so I can't imagine why anyone would do that to him." I stood and put my backpack over my shoulder. "Yes to the college in Hawaii. I want to get as far away from here as possible."

I pulled the door open hard, the gust of air making Ralphie tweet angrily in his cage.

As I stepped into the hallway, I came face to face with Ryker's older twin. The man who had to be his dad with broad shoulders, deeply tanned skin, and emotionless, pale green eyes. Just the set of his mouth emanated power. His presence was so intimidating, I almost didn't see the slight blond beside him. Or Ryker standing behind them.

Ryker's dad gave me a look that told me I was

nothing but a fly buzzing around him, a slight inconvenience. "Excuse me, little girl."

Little girl? My eyebrows drew together as he brushed past me, his rich suit rubbing past my shoulder. His wife walked behind him, six-inch heels pounding evenly on the floor.

"Stay out here, Ryker," the man demanded harshly, and the door slammed shut with even more force than I'd used to open it just seconds ago.

Ryker folded his arms across his chest, tucking his hands into his armpits. "What are you doing here, Red?" He'd used his old nickname for me, but his voice didn't have the usual bite. His eyes didn't hold the usual ice. He just seemed... tired.

"Talking about college." I realized Mrs. Bardot had forgotten my pass to first hour, so I either had to wait for her to finish with his parents or go to first hour and be berated by Mr. Aris for my tardiness.

Ryker took me in, and I wondered how differently he thought of me from how I'd looked the night before. Instead of the perfect waves Adriel had put in my hair, I had my red curls in a loose braid, and I'd worn about half the amount of makeup.

Inside the office, his father's voice rose, clearly audible in the hallway. "That young man is not just a high school student. He is the future CEO of Dugan Industries!"

Ryker sat on the bench along the wall and leaned his head back against the wall, closing his eyes. I glanced between him, the direction of Mr. Aris's class, and the office.

He opened one eye and said, "I can feel you staring, Red. Sit down."

My cheeks felt hot as I sat on the bench beside him, leaving about a foot separating us.

"You wanna know why I'm so messed up?" he said.

But I didn't need to ask. Inside the office, I heard Ryker's father yelling at Birdie, who may have been eccentric, but had her heart in the right place.

His harsh voice seeped under the door, and I could feel the hatred just as surely as if it had been aimed at me. "You know just as well as I do that money talks at this school. If this isn't solved and the person responsible isn't punished, I *will* pull my donations, and you *will* lose your job."

Ryker met my eyes for a moment, and in them I saw something different... pleading. "You and all your friends will get the chance to live your lives someday. And I'll have to live *his*."

The door opened, and Ryker's dad snapped,

"There is no need for Ryker to have a word with you. If he needs help, we'll hire a real professional. Come on, son."

Ryker stood with his parents and walked away, seeming a little less tall than before. Mrs. Bardot sat beside me on the bench, rubbing her temples.

Her tension seemed so palpable it rested on my chest like a fifty-pound weight, making it impossible to speak.

With a heavy sigh, she stood and said, "Let me get your note."

THIRTY-FIVE

I COULDN'T GET Ryker and what I'd overheard out of my mind for the rest of the week. Not when Adriel told us her dance studio would be performing during halftime at an upcoming football game. Not when the Curvy Girl Club 2.0 ate lobster on Thursday and toasted our victory with sparkling grape juice. Not when my mom let us know the twins should wrap up filming in only a few weeks, which meant they'd be back home. And not on Friday when I walked from the high school to the elementary school in my gym uniform.

So much of how I saw Ryker had changed in a week, and I'd only overheard a couple of sentences. How had I been so blind not to consider that Ryker had been made that way? That his actions hadn't come from a sense of entitlement but very real pain?

It made me think of him differently. Made forgiveness just a little bit easier. Of course he would be a bully—it was all he'd experienced in his life.

I reached the elementary building and pushed the buzzer. As I waited, I realized the breeze was chilly, even though the sun was warm. Even the wind knew things were changing.

"Cold?" a voice asked from behind me.

I nearly jumped out of my skin to find Ryker standing just a few feet away. "God, warn a girl next time."

"Okay." He smirked. "But while we're talking about next time, I prefer to go by Ryker."

I rolled my eyes, biting back a smile. "Noted."

He began shrugging off his navy-blue jacket and extended it my way. The luxurious material practically stared at me, and I stared right back. "What is this?"

"A jacket," he said, shaking it. "Take it."

I eyed it, too confused to make a move. Was this...a peace offering? Or something else entirely?

With a sigh, he spread it out and draped it over my shoulders. "It's not poisonous."

As he stepped back, warmth and his scent on the jacket flooded my senses. I gripped the edges and pulled them tighter around me. "Thank you."

His gray eyes stayed on me as he nodded. "It looks better on you than it does on me."

Whether he meant it or not, my body didn't care. Nervous little butterflies stirred in my stomach, and I felt the warmth from his jacket reach my cheeks. Even though he was fit, his broad, muscular build meant the jacket was still big on me, and I sank into it.

The lock in the door clicked, signifying we'd finally been let inside. He held the door open, and I began shrugging off the jacket to give it back. His hands brushed over my shoulders, and he helped it back on. "Keep it. We still have to walk back."

Awkwardly, I nodded and continued through the open door. Mrs. O'Haire stepped out of the office, looking frazzled.

"I'm so sorry. Some kid just puked on a teacher's desk, so it's all hands on deck," she said. Without waiting for a response, she rushed back away, and Ryker and I gave each other a look.

His nose crinkled. "That's disgusting."

I tended to agree. "I swear my little sisters throw up way more than is humanly possible." I shuddered, thinking of last Christmas when they'd eaten too much of the green and red dessert Aunt Rosie brought over. The bathroom had not been a pretty sight with both of them sick at the same time.

"Do you miss them?"

I nodded, talking softly in the empty hallways. "They'd be in this class if they weren't in LA."

"How much longer are they there?"

"For the next few weeks. Which means I'm basically invisible here."

He snorted. "You? Invisible? It doesn't seem possible."

"You haven't met my family under normal circumstances. Invisible is my middle name." We reached the door to the gym and stalled outside.

"What do you mean?" he asked, a crease forming between his eyebrows.

I had an urge to press my thumb to it, to smooth it out. Instead, I pushed open the door and said. "If I wasn't helping my dad at the store until suppertime every night, I wouldn't see him until we said goodnight."

"I get that," he said, and then Ms. Anaheim greeted us, putting a halt to our conversation.

"Ryker," she said. "You're wearing pants today."

Was that a blush I saw? The hint of color on his tanned cheeks made me smile.

"Yes, ma'am."

"Great," she said. "Let's set up the court. We're playing hockey today."

I left his jacket on the bottom row of bleachers and followed Ms. Anaheim's instructions to put one of the goals together while Ryker prepared the other one. She had us play as goalies, and for the next couple of hours, I had way more fun than I thought would be possible with a direct view of Ryker across the gym and pucks flying at my face.

I was still smiling when we walked out of the building. "I really think we would have won if Ms. Anaheim had given us another minute."

He smirked. "Sounds like something a loser would say."

My mouth fell open, and I hit his arm. "Rude!"

Laughing, he shook his head. "More like honest."

Holding back the smile on my lips was impossible. Exasperated, I looked away, over our empty campus. In minutes, it would be filled with students leaving school, but for now, it was a bubble, just Ryker and me. And for once, I didn't want it to burst.

As we approached the steps, Ryker said, "Are you working with your dad on Saturday?"

I nodded.

"Come to my house afterward." He reached into his shorts pocket and got out his phone. "Type in your number."

I looked from the phone to his eyes, waiting for the punchline. Or maybe just the punch. But I couldn't find any. "Ryker?" I breathed.

"Yeah?"

"Are you asking me out?"

His full lips curved into a smile. "I think technically I'm asking you in."

Shaking my head, I took his phone and did something crazy: I typed in my number. When I handed it back, he typed something into the phone. Reading upside down, I saw he saved me as Nash. And then he sent me a text.

"I'll see you tomorrow?"

Slowly, I nodded, and as we walked up the stairs, I wondered why I'd said yes. Or more realistically, why I couldn't say no.

THIRTY-SIX

KNOX and I stood at the cash register, him running the checkout and me bagging. Or, I *would* be bagging if there was anyone coming through. The afternoon before a football game always got a little slow for the store, and Janet had taken advantage of the downtime to grab dinner with one of her children.

Knox turned around and leaned back against the counter. "I never thought I'd say this, but I'd rather be cleaning out the fish bins."

I laughed. "Miss Harry, do you?"

Knox made the sign of the cross. "May he rest in peace."

Shaking my head at him, I said, "How was your week?"

"Lots of tests and studying. You?"

"Interesting," I answered. "I got to hear Ryker's dad go crazy on our guidance counselor."

Knox's eyebrows slid up his forehead. "What?"

I told him a little of what had happened at the game the week before, and Knox scrubbed his hand over his clean-shaven chin. "I told you, didn't I? The guy's a nightmare."

I nodded, folding my arms over my chest. I couldn't help but think maybe Ryker could be different from his father. Or at least that he was becoming different. "Can I ask you something?"

"Sure," he answered easily.

"How did you know you wanted to date Courtney? That you could trust her with your heart?"

His lips turned into a knowing smile. "Any particular reason—or person—for your question?"

My cheeks warmed, so I turned away. "No worries, you don't have to answer."

"I'm just teasing, Cor." He reached under the register and got a roll of paper towels and a cleaning spray. Absently wiping the register, he said, "I don't know. Courtney and I have been friends forever, and at some point, it just seemed dumb not to let it be more."

Well there went any reassurance I had about

saving Ryker's number in my phone, much less showing up at the address he'd texted me. "So that's it?" I asked. "Try not to be dumb?"

"Kind of." Smiling, Knox hit the button to run the conveyor belt and ran the damp paper towel over its whirring surface. "No one has it figured out, Cori. There are a million kinds of relationships, and the best part of being in high school and dating is figuring out what kind *you* want. And then, when you eventually find someone worth holding on to, you put your heart out there and hope like hell they'll catch it."

Slowly, I nodded. Maybe he was right. I was acting like going to Ryker's house for an afternoon was a matter of life and death, when in reality we were just spending time together. Was that a crime? He'd seen something special in me, stood up to his friends for me.

A customer approached us with an entire cartload of groceries, and I began bagging as the items came toward me. Still, a twinge of guilt remained, settling in the pit of my stomach. Ryker had called Nadira a firehouse dog. He'd led his crew in corralling Faith. The people he spent most of his time with had oinked at us this morning and made super lewd comments. I might have seen him changing, but how would my friends ever forgive me if they knew?

How would Ginger forgive me?

A devil on my shoulder whispered that Ginger didn't need to know.

After all, hadn't Knox just said dating didn't need to be a big deal? I was just going to Ryker's house, for crying out loud. Not marrying him. Maybe he wanted to talk more about what he'd done wrong—find ways to be better. Wouldn't I be doing him and my friends a disservice if I didn't hear him out?

Maybe Ryker was right—I had a Jesus complex, thinking the whole world was resting on my shoulders. I decided then I was only going to take responsibility for me. Do what *I* wanted for once instead of worrying about how it would impact everyone else. And what I wanted was to hear what Ryker had to say.

As I finished bagging the customer's groceries, Janet walked in, her giant purse over her shoulder.

"Hi, you two!" she said smiling brightly. "Thanks for covering the register."

"Of course," Knox said, stepping out of the space behind the checkout stand. "Cori here struggled, but I was a natural." He brushed off his chest.

Janet giggled. "Oh hush, you. This girl's been some of the best help here since she was fourteen!" She took her spot behind the register and set her purse down. "And I also hear she's amazing with kids."

My eyebrows drew together. "Huh?"

Janet nodded. "My granddaughter Anna is in the gym class you aid for on Fridays. Between you and that boy you're with, she has only amazing things to say."

My lips immediately turned up. "Anna is the sweetest."

At the same time, Knox said, "Boy?"

Janet tapped her chin. "He had a funny name. Robinson? Rine?"

Knox's eyes widened with realization, but before he could draw any more conclusions, I waved at them both and said, "I better get to the football game! Have a great shift!"

I hustled toward the back of the store where my locker had a shirt that was not bright yellow with a banana on it. Unfortunately, Knox's legs were much longer than mine. He caught up to me quickly and said, "The boy you're talking about is *Ryker*, isn't it?"

I picked up speed and pressed my lips together.

"Isn't it?"

I couldn't go any faster, so I kept the pace, hoping to dodge this conversation all together.

"Cori, stop." He put his hand on my shoulder, and I slowed down. "Why would you be interested in *him*? Cori, he's a bully! You of all people should know to stay away."

The insinuation behind his words made my anger swell. "Me of all people? What are you saying, Knox? That because I'm fat I can't date someone like him?"

Knox recoiled at the force of my words. "No, no. It's just... I thought you had more self-respect than that."

"Self-respect?" I spat. "Have you ever considered that maybe Ryker *isn't* like his dad?"

He narrowed his eyes. "Cori, you know better. You put a fish under his car, for god's sake!"

My cheeks burned because he was right, and I knew I sounded pathetic saying Ryker had changed when we'd really only had one good conversation after a gym class. But it wasn't something I could logic through. It was something I felt. Turning away from Knox, I shrugged and said, "Sometimes you put your heart out there and hope like hell they'll catch it."

THIRTY-SEVEN

DESIRAE ABSOLUTELY KILLED the national anthem. Like, brought-tears-to-my-eyes good. I clapped loudly as she ended the final haunting note, and on my right, Faith whistled loudly. On my left, Adriel said, "That was incredible!"

I nodded in agreement. "You got that, right, Nadira?"

She nodded, tapping on her phone screen. "Sending it to her right now."

"Perfect," I said, sitting back down in the bleachers. "By the way, when does Mathletes start?"

Nadira stuck her phone in her pocket, leaving her hand in there with it. "First meet is next week." She smiled. "I'm actually pretty excited. I think we have a good team this year."

Faith frowned. "I'm awful at math. I don't know how you do it with an audience."

Nadira snorted. "I mean, it's usually just a mom or two watching, but I'm happy to help with homework any time."

"Take her up on it," I said emphatically. "I'm pretty sure Nadira's the only reason I passed trig last year."

Giving me a look, Nadira said, "That and your mom's homework schedule *and* the fact that your sister drove you to school." She explained to our friends, "This girl is notorious for leaving her homework to the last minute. I don't know how you're keeping up with it with your mom in LA."

I rolled my eyes, not wanting to give my mom any credit. "There's no way I'm giving her a reason to hover even more. Mom was so uptight last year. It's been kind of nice having some more freedom lately."

Adriel sipped from her cocoa and held it in her hands. "How long will she be in LA?"

"Just a few more weeks, then back to lockdown." I sighed, not wanting to think about how much life would change. Even if I had felt lonely at times, it had been nice to see how it would be living on my own. "Can someone change the subject?"

"Sure," Faith said. "I just found out my parents are getting a foreign exchange student this spring."

Nadira raised her eyebrows. "The last semester of your senior year? Why?"

Faith shrugged. "Apparently Headmaster Bradford asked a few parents to take whoever it is and mine said yes."

"You don't even know who it is?" I asked.

"Nope." She popped her lips. "Not a clue."

Adriel cringed and said, "Can we keep our fingers crossed he's hot at least?"

I laughed. "That would be cool, right?"

Faith shook her head. "My parents would never let a guy get within ten feet of me, much less in a bedroom down the hall."

Shrugging, Adriel said, "Well, if it's a she, maybe she'll have some hot foreign friends come visit."

Faith crossed her fingers. "One can hope."

Des walked toward us, smiling and thanking the multiple people who were stopping her along the way, gushing about her performance. The bright red lipstick she wore made her grin stand out that much more. She looked absolutely beautiful and vibrant.

As she drew nearer, I lifted my hands and pretended to bow down to her.

"Oh, stop it," she said with a smile and scooted past me to sit next to Nadira.

Cheering sounded around us, and I looked to the field just in time to see Ryker's powerful form carrying the ball down the field. An opponent grabbed at his waist, but he easily spun out from their grasp.

My heart rate picked up speed as he headed toward another opponent, this one aiming for Ryker's ankles. Ryker soared into the air, lifting his knees to his chest and dodging the guy altogether.

He continued down the field, gaining so much distance there was no chance of anyone getting him before...

"TOUCHDOWN!" Mr. Davis called from the announcer stand.

Ryker dumped the football on the ground, lifted his hands in the air, and spun in a circle like a dainty ballerina.

I couldn't help but laugh as the crowd around me shouted, "RYKERINA! RYKERINA!"

"Of course," Nadira muttered. "He'd find a way to make an embarrassing hashtag his own."

Adriel put her arms around Faith and me. "Maybe that's the secret?"

"What do you mean?" Nadira asked.

"We've spent all this time being ashamed of our curves, worrying about people bullying us for them," Adriel said. "What if we owned them like he owned that stupid hashtag?"

Des smiled over at us. "We'd rule the world."

Grinning, I said, "Don't we already?"

They laughed, but sitting with them at the game, I couldn't help but feel like we were actually crushing this high school thing. We had good friends. Great seats for the games. An entire world full of opportunities for romance. And our futures lay ahead of us like gold waiting to be mined. What was there not to love?

The game passed quickly, and before long, we were on our way to Waldo's with the rest of the school. When we arrived, I noticed Betty standing by our usual booth. Despite the large number of people in the diner, the seats were blissfully clear.

She grinned at us, the lines around her eyes crinkling happily. "Saved your seat! I'll grab your shakes."

We thanked her profusely, and as we slid into the booth, Des said, "God, I love her."

"Same," I agreed, reaching for a menu. I'd just grabbed something quick from a drive-thru on the way to the game, and I was hungry.

Faith said, "I feel like royalty."

"You are a queen," Adriel said with a grin.

Nadira shook her head at us, always the serious one. "We're spoiled is more like it. We need to leave her a good tip."

"Here, here," I said.

The restaurant got louder, and I looked over my shoulder to see Ryker and his crew walking inside. They each wore letterman jackets like suits of armor and sauntered forward like time stood still around them.

My eyes landed on Ryker first. On his gray stare and strong jaw and full lips. His eyes collided with mine, and for a moment, all the air left the restaurant. My lips curved into a smile I couldn't control, and I turned away from him, hiding my face behind my menu.

Their group walked past us and to the only other empty booth in the place.

My phone vibrated in my pocket, and I was glad to have the distraction. Until I saw who the text was from.

Ryker: You look beautiful tonight.

Without thinking, I glanced at him, and he looked at me over the top of his phone, his lips slightly quirked.

My cheeks heated, and I glanced down at my phone.

Cori: You looked better in the uniform.

I almost couldn't believe myself as I hit send. I tried to focus on what Nadira was saying about Mathletes, but my thoughts were stuck on the guy across the diner, full-on smiling at his phone. I'd hardly ever seen him so carefree.

My phone vibrated again.

Ryker: I'll show you better tomorrow.

Ryker: Bring your swimsuit.

THIRTY-EIGHT

MY SATURDAY SHIFT at the store was both the longest and shortest shift I'd ever worked. Eight hours had flown by, despite my usual work partner being off duty. I missed working with Knox, but I didn't need him getting in my head before my "date" with Ryker.

As I changed out of my work shirt and into a graphic tee that clung to my curves, I couldn't help but wonder what Ryker had in store for us. Of course there was the niggling doubt that wanted me to believe this was all a setup. But there was also a small piece of me that hoped for more.

When Ryker wasn't being a complete jerk, he was...nice. Easy to talk to. And surprisingly, we had a lot in common with sports and our invisibility to our parents. For example, Dad never even asked me what I did after I got off work at the store. As long as I was home when he got there, he never even worried. Never bothered to ask how I felt about being alone every evening of the week.

Today would be no different. Except instead of video-chatting with the girls or watching TV, I'd be with Ryker. Somewhere that required a swimsuit.

My cheeks heated at the suit I'd put in a small beach bag in my car. I'd opted for a bikini, if only to test him. If he couldn't handle seeing my stretch marks and dimples on full display, he didn't deserve me. I might have been willing to put my heart out there, but I wasn't going to dangle it forever.

I said goodbye to Dad on my way out of the store and then went to the minivan in the parking lot. After getting in, I sent Ryker a quick text and typed his address in my map.

My jaw fell open at the location.

He lived on the coast, not half a mile from Des. Why had she failed to mention her almost-neighbor? She had to know where he lived, right?

But how could I bring it up to her without divulging how I'd happened on his address? Maybe some mysteries were meant to be unsolved.

I followed my phone's directions to Ryker's

house, my heart beating faster and my nerves stringing tighter the closer I got.

Would today's trip bring memories I'd cherish or ones I'd rather forget? As I pulled into the expansive driveway in front of the massive, modern home, I knew I'd find out soon.

No sooner than I'd turned off the minivan, a garage door opened, revealing Ryker in dark blue boardshorts and a tight white T-shirt.

I reminded myself to keep my mouth closed. If I couldn't handle him in a shirt, how on earth would I handle him without one? Feigning confidence I certainly didn't feel, I grabbed my beach bag and got out of the car.

"Hey," he said, his eyes tracing lines up and down my body. He inclined his head over his shoulder. "Come on." He extended his hand for mine, and I stared at his fingers for a fraction of a second.

Was he wanting me to take his hand? Was I ready for that? Then I mentally kicked myself for getting so worked up over a simple touch. I was nearly eighteen years old. I could hold a hand if I wanted.

But Ryker said, "I'll carry your bag."

I closed my eyes for a moment, feeling even sillier than I had before, and extended the bag his way. It was light, but the gesture was nice. Until he started walking through the garage, digging through the contents.

"Hey!" I cried, reaching for the bag.

He turned away, saying, "I want to see what swimsuit you brought!"

I reached around him, brushing my arm over his firm core, and grabbed the bag. "You'll have to see it on."

His eyes heated as he said, "I'd rather see it off."

The double entendre sent heat to my stomach and flames to my cheeks. Judging by the smirk on his face, Ryker noticed.

I rolled my eyes and said, "So are we just going to hang out in your garage all day?" To be fair, it had fancy checkerboard flooring, was sparkling clean, had three shining cars inside, and was the size of my house, but it wasn't my idea of the perfect date.

"Of course not." He scoffed. "I have something better in store."

If he took me to his bedroom, I swore I'd punch him in the face.

But no, he led me out the back door of his garage, which opened to a patio and an unimpeded view of the ocean. The private beach had chairs and umbrellas out just like Des's, but his home had a big infinity pool in the back, along with a jacuzzi.

"I thought we could swim and maybe have a little fire." He gestured toward the firepit covered in glass beads, and I took it all in. Including Ryker, who was pulling off his shirt and...

There went my jaw on the ground again.

Each of his muscles rippled as he lifted the shirt over his head, revealing tan skin and a toned body.

If the ocean breeze wouldn't have been rolling over us, I would have fanned myself.

As it was, he dropped his shirt on a lounge chair, and I tried to act like there hadn't just been drool dribbling down my chin. Wasn't I supposed to be a strong, independent woman, immune to his charm?

But just like Des loved shoes, abs were my weakness. I just hadn't seen any this up close and personal. What would it feel like to run my fingers over the ridges?

With a smile, he pointed over his shoulder to a door on the house. "That's the bathroom if you want to change."

Slowly, I nodded and stutter-stepped that way. The problem was, did I really want to change into a swimsuit when I'd be standing across from all of *that*?

I didn't want to be that girl, the insecure one. But I couldn't help thinking that the girls he brought here most of the time probably wore a lot less than I planned to—and had a lot less to show. My stomach wasn't toned, and even though my breasts were large, I had dimples covering my thighs.

But as I put on my swimsuit, I decided to be proud of the body I had. This body had helped me play basketball on an elite team. It carried me everywhere I went. Why bother hating it when I could love it instead?

I looked at myself in the mirror, the black fabric showing my cleavage and the stretch marks on the pale skin of my stomach. I looked at my thighs and the bit of extra fat that always rubbed together when I walked.

And I loved myself, truly, just as I was. There was no one else like me, and I was going to be completely, unapologetically, me, whether Ryker liked it or not.

I flipped a curl over my shoulder, smiled at myself in the mirror, then walked out of the bathroom. Ryker leaned against the edge of the infinity pool, and his lips parted as I walked closer. No matter how insecure I might have felt, I held my head high and strutted my stuff just like any one of his size-two girls would have.

"Co—" His voice broke and he cleared his throat. "Cori, you look amazing."

I smiled, crossing my arms over my chest. "Wait until you see my cannonball."

A laugh came through his parted lips, and I could tell he was surprised by my response. "Cannonball?" he asked.

"Oh yeah." I dipped my toes into the water, finding it perfectly warm, like bath water.

He leveled his hands over the water, gliding his fingertips over its surface. "Well, I have to see this."

I lifted an eyebrow. "I don't know. How would you feel about having the weakest cannonball at this party?"

He laughed. "No way yours is better than mine."

"Show me," I challenged

With a grin, he lifted himself out of the water, and it glistened as it slid over his muscles. Holy hotness.

"Ready?" he asked.

I barely managed a nod.

He took a few steps back and, with a running

leap, landed in the middle of the pool with his knees held tightly to his chest.

Water lifted from where he landed and splashed over my waist, beading and sliding down my legs. As he came out of the water, he shook the moisture from his hair and beat his chest. "How was that?"

"Cute," I said, examining my nails. "But I'll show you how it's done."

"I'd like to see you try."

With his eyes on me, I stood and backed up a few steps, following his wet footprints on the concrete. Taking a deep breath, I ran toward the water and launched myself into a cannonball.

The saltwater rushed up around me, and I could feel how big of a splash it was. As I came out of the water, I imitated his hair flip and lowered my voice. "How was that?"

He lifted his hands and bowed to me. "Queen Cori reigns again."

I laughed, shaking my head. "Told you I was good."

Chuckling, he said, "You know, I don't think I've ever had a girl do a cannonball on a date before."

I shrugged. "You've never dated a girl like me before."

"Maybe that's a good thing." He came closer, heat rolling off his body, intensity flaring from his dark gray eyes.

My breath caught at his proximity. He had to be inches away now. His eyes flicked to my lips, and I could feel the pull inside me wanting to close my eyes and put my lips to his.

There was only one thing I could do.

I cupped my hand and splashed water all over his face.

"What was that for?" he sputtered, wiping at his eyes.

Laughing, I said, "You better buy me dinner first."

His lips curled into an attractive smile. "I'll do better than that."

THIRTY-NINE

RYKER GOT out of the pool, water dripping from his shorts and down his body. Then he walked toward the refrigerator under the patio. From the pool, I saw several packaged trays of food.

"What is that?" I asked.

"For our campfire," he answered with a grin. "I even had Margaret get us stuff for s'mores."

"Margaret?"

"Yeah." He closed the fridge and walked back toward me. "She's my nanny."

I snorted. "You have a nanny?"

"Oh yeah I do." He waggled his eyebrows.

"Ew."

Laughing, he said, "I don't know. She's been with us forever, and now she just kind of runs errands for all of us when we need it." He sat down on the edge of the pool and dangled his feet in the water while I rested along the pool's edge.

I couldn't believe the kind of life he lived. Sure, my parents were well-off, and there were plenty of wealthy people at the Academy, but this was another level entirely.

"You're judging me," he said quietly.

I wanted to deny him, but I couldn't. "It's just different is all."

"Look, it's not like I hired her."

"I know."

"And I didn't ask my parents to keep her on."

"I know," I said lightly.

He took a deep breath.

"Why does it matter what I think anyway?" I asked. "It's not like you need to defend how your family spends their money to me."

His gray gaze held mine, and his voice was rough as he said, "I think you know why it matters."

"Why is that?" My voice came out a whisper, but I needed to hear him say it. See what all of this was about.

"My dad always told me you shouldn't put all your chips on the table," he said.

But I shook my head. "My heart isn't a game."

His lashes fluttered against his cheeks as he closed his eyes, and when he opened them, I swore his gaze was deeper than the ocean. "I like you, Cori. And I want to be the kind of guy you'd like back."

The way he said it sent butterflies to flight in my stomach and a smile to my lips. "Ryker has a crush?"

He kicked some water toward me. "Don't tease. I'm serious."

I lifted my eyebrows. "You really want to be someone I could like?"

He nodded.

"Why?" I asked. "Why now?"

He glanced at the pool, the water reflecting over his eyes. "Because I can't take another day of looking at you and knowing that I did everything I could to mess things up and nothing to make things right. Because I feel like, with you..." He reached out and touched my cheek. "I could live the life I want to and not the one everyone expects me to. With you, I can be me. The me I actually want to be." His lips quirked as he tucked a curl behind my ear and met my eyes.

Then all teasing was over. I realized I wanted this to work, the way we were now, but love didn't exist in a vacuum. "Then you need to apologize to my sister. And to my friends." His eyes grew dark, but I continued anyway. "What you did to them wasn't right," I said, "and it's not going away just because you're ready to move on." I took a breath and tried to get him to see just how much this meant to me. "You want a chance with me, then you need to make things right with them."

He got up, lifting his feet out of the water, and walked toward the house. My heart constricted, confused. "Ryker, what are you doing?" Was he done with this date already? I pulled myself out of the water, following him.

"I'm getting my phone," he said over his shoulder.

"You're what?" I asked. What message could possibly be so important he needed his phone right this second? Was he calling security on me to have me leave or something?

"You heard me." He reached for the handle of the garage door and opened it. "And I heard you. If I want a chance, I need to right my wrongs." He approached his car and reached through the open driver's side window, retrieving his phone with the Emerson Academy case.

He strode past me, back toward the exit, toward

the patio, tapping on his phone. "What's Ginger's number?"

I followed him, stammering, "You want her number?"

"How else am I supposed to call her and apologize?" He sat in a lounge chair, waiting for my answer.

A breeze made goosebumps rise on my skin, and I folded my arms across my chest. "Are you really doing this?"

He nodded and stood, gently taking my hands. "I know I was a jerk, but you're right. I need to fix it. I should have done this a long time ago. Or at least when we all had dinner together, but now is better than never."

I hesitated, having trouble focusing with his warm skin on mine.

"I promise I won't hurt her," he said softly, mistaking the reason for my hesitation.

With my eyes closed, I recited her number by heart. When I opened them, I watched him put the phone on speaker and set it on a small side table. As it rang, he held his finger to his lips. He didn't want her to know I was there.

I held my breath as Ginger's voice came across the speaker. "Hi, this is Ginger."

I smiled softly. She was always so professional when she didn't know the number—just in case it would be someone important to her career.

Ryker took a deep breath. "Ginger? It's Ryker. Dugan."

The phone was silent for a long moment as we waited for her response. If the phone wouldn't have been ticking off the seconds, I would have thought she'd hung up. However, a moment or two later, she said, "To what do I owe the *pleasure*?"

I cringed. She was doing her cold, formal thing, where she got super particular about her words because she didn't want anyone to be able to use them against her.

"Ginger, I'm calling to apologize." Ryker enunciated each word like it was important she understood.

Still, she stuttered, "What?"

He looked at me for a moment and then back at the screen. "I was a bully to you. I called you names I shouldn't have, said things I'm ashamed of, and never thought about how it made you feel. You never should have been afraid to walk into school, and the fact that I contributed to that—" His voice got tight, and he cleared his throat. "I'm sorry. You deserved so much better."

My eyes stung and I blinked quickly. Ginger must have been crying too because a soft sniffle came from her end of the phone.

"Why are you doing this?" she asked.

Ryker looked straight at me. "Your sister showed me how much my words affected other people. I can't change the past, but I'm making damn sure I don't hurt anyone in the future like I did to you. When you know better, you do better."

My heart swelled at his words and the earnestness in his expression.

"Thank you," Ginger said quietly.

"It was long overdue."

She chuckled softly. "It was right on time."

FORTY

RYKER CALLED and apologized to each of my friends in the Curvy Girl Club 2.0, saving Faith for last. He and his friends been the harshest with her, and I didn't know how he'd repair it. Maybe he couldn't. But it meant a lot that he was willing to try.

Faith's number stayed on the screen and rang and rang until finally her cautious voice sounded on the phone. "Hello?"

"Faith?" Ryker asked.

"Who is this?" In the background, I could hear the TV, but it was becoming quieter.

"This is Ryker Dugan." As if he needed his last name.

"Oh," Faith said, confusion clear in her timid voice.

Ryker closed his eyes. "Faith, I'd like to apologize to you."

"You want to *what?*" She sounded just as shocked as Ginger.

"I wanted to say I'm sorry." The words hung in the air between them for a moment, and then Ryker raked his hand through his still-damp hair. "It sounds so weak though, after what we did to you the first day of school." He groaned, clearly disgusted. "Faith, we were assholes. I'm sorry for cussing, but there's just not another word for it. Jerk doesn't come close enough. And if you hate me forever, that'd be totally fair. But either way, I just want to let you know that you don't need to worry about something like that ever happening at the Academy again. I swear it."

Tears budded in my eyes as Faith began speaking thoughtfully. "You know I used to dream about this day. When you'd realize what you did wrong and apologized."

"And?" Ryker asked.

"It's better than I imagined." The smile was clear in her voice. "I forgive you."

Ryker looked at me, shocked, then back to the phone. "Just like that?"

"If someone wrongs you seven times, you forgive them seven times," she said softly, then chuckled. "Just, don't make me forgive you again, okay?"

Ryker managed a smile. "I promise."

"Thanks for calling," Faith said.

"You're welcome," Ryker said softly and pressed the red button on the phone.

As he sat back in the chair, I stared at him, wondering who this was sitting across from me and what he'd done with the Ryker Dugan I knew. Because this guy wasn't him. He'd made phone call after phone call, apology after apology, and he was still standing. I couldn't believe it.

"You're really different now?" I breathed.

He nodded forcefully. "I told you, Cori. I want to be better. For you."

I couldn't hold back my smile as I said, "You already are." And then I decided I wasn't going to hold back anything. Not my smile. Not my feelings. And definitely not the urge building within me to kiss the guy sitting across from me.

I walked around the table and sat on the chair next to him. He wet his lips as I drew closer, close enough for my bare thigh to touch his, to feel the heat in our shoulders brushing.

His eyes flicked from mine to my lips, and there was no holding back. There was no waiting. There was no doubt.

Only the distance closing between us and my lips falling on his. Electricity tingled throughout my body as he wrapped his arms around me and deepened the kiss. The breeze might have been cool, but his hands were hot on my body. Toying with the edge. The edge of my bikini strings. The edge of my hair. The edge of temptation.

My breathing quickened as I ran my hands over the firm ridges of his shoulders and worked my fingers into the base of his hair. I'd been kissed before, but now I thought maybe I hadn't after all, because that felt nothing like *this*.

Everything seemed to fall away except for him and me and the ragged pace of our breathing.

His hand cupped my cheek, and he held my stare, his intoxicating lips mere inches from mine. And then they did something almost as good as kissing me. They curled into a smile. He gave me another too-short kiss, making my stomach swoop, and pulled back again. "What happened to wanting dinner first?"

"Forget it," I said breathily. My cheeks were hot, from the kiss or bashfulness I didn't know. Maybe both. No one had ever set my skin on fire like that or made me want more, more, more like Ryker had.

But instead of leaning in for another kiss, he stood up, taking a deep breath.

Was it possible he'd felt even a portion of what I had? Was I crazy to hope?

He walked to the refrigerator by the house and said, "S'mores?"

"What about the other food?" I asked.

He shrugged, grabbing a bag, then gave me a smile that made me melt like the marshmallows were about to eat. "Life's too short to save the sweet stuff for last."

I couldn't help but agree.

We walked to the firepit, which was formed from raised stone. Ryker pushed a button, and yellow and blue flames rose from glass beads, crackling against the dwindling sunset. Lighting this fire was way easier than the last time my sisters and I made a fire in our backyard. Ginger's eyebrows may or may not have survived the ordeal.

"You're smiling," Ryker said.

I nodded. "Just remembering making s'mores with my sisters."

He settled into the chair next to me and began opening the bag. "Margaret used to make s'mores with me. She always teased me though because I'd eat all the chocolate before the marshmallows were even roasted."

"Obviously," I said, enjoying the warmth from the fire. "Everyone knows chocolate is the best part of a s'more."

"That's what I tried to tell her." His smile heated my cheeks just as the fire did my hands. "She eventually gave up and just started leaving bags of chocolate chips around the house."

My mouth fell open. "You're kidding."

"No way. Do you know how hard it was to crunch those cookies?"

"That was a jerk move, by the way," I said.

Chuckling, he scratched the back of his neck. "Yeah, sorry about that. But to be fair, you did tape a fish to my pickup."

I sniffed. "Allegedly."

His smile was contagious. "I'd take a thousand fish taped to my truck if it meant another kiss like that."

The butterflies in my stomach fluttered happily as I bit my bottom lip. "That can be arranged."

"Or we could skip the fish pranks and get straight to the kissing?"

A soft laugh fell through my lips, and I nodded. I'd expected him to rush, to close the gap and kiss me like we had seconds left, but he didn't. He took his time, his hand gently pushing back my hair and cupping the nape of my neck. His eyes closed slowly, thick lashes brushing together. And then there were inches between us. Millimeters.

My move.

I made it, pressing my lips to his yet again in a kiss that was less of a fire and more of the embers left behind. His touch was gentle and mine was curious. As we discovered more of each other, more of the ways we were the same, all of the hate that had been there fell away.

Our lips parted, and his gaze flicked cautiously to my eyes. "Sorry, I keep distracting us from our food."

"Hey," I said, leaning in for another kiss. "Life's too short to save the sweet stuff for last."

FORTY-ONE

I CHECKED my phone at a stoplight on the way home. My text messages had completely blown up, especially in the Curvy Girl Club 2.0 group chat.

Nadira: Hell just froze over. I got a call from Ryker.

Des: NO WAY. I just got one too. Did he apologize to you?

Nadira: Yes! And it was actually... nice?

Faith: No fair. I want an apology.

Adriel: Holy crap. I just got off the phone with him. He apologized to me too!

Nadira: What is he up to?

Faith: Maybe he's had a change in heart? He did stop those guys from picking on us yesterday...

Nadira: Maybe...

Des: You should just enjoy it, Dir. Who cares why he apologized as long as he did.

A car honked behind me, and I jerked, realizing the light was green. I really shouldn't look at my phone while on the road. But it just continued dinging, so I pulled into the parking lot of a fast food place and put the van into park.

Faith: OMG HE CALLED ME TOO.

Adriel: What did he say?

Faith: He apologized. I forgave him.

Nadira: You did?!

Faith: It was the right thing to do. He sounded like he really meant it.

My lips formed a soft smile. I thought the same thing.

Des: Cori, where are you? Did you get a call? Why aren't you doing a victory dance or something?

My smile grew at her text, but was immediately dimmed by the fact that I didn't get a call—and the reason why. How could I tell them I'd just spent the entire afternoon with the very person we were talking about? That I'd enjoyed it? That I was hoping there was more to come?

I let out a sigh and typed a message back.

Cori: Too busy victory dancing to reply. ;) I got

an apology, and he called my sister too. Looks like we won!

And speaking of my sister. I went to the text she'd sent me.

Ginger: CALL ME AS SOON AS YOU GET THIS. (Everything's okay, but hurry up!)

I pressed the button to call her, connected her to the van's speaker system, and started down the road.

"Hello?" she answered.

"Hey," I said, not wanting to ask her what the news was.

"So I got an interesting call earlier..."

My lips tugged into a smile. "Yeah?"

"Yeah." She paused. "Ryker called me." Her voice sounded conflicted.

"Is that a bad thing?" I asked.

A sigh came through the speakers. "He apologized to me, you know, for being a horrible human being last year."

Her words made me cringe. Maybe because I'd thought the same thing about him, and I'd learned how wrong I was. "That's good, right?"

"I think so? I just can't help but wonder why. It was so out of the blue."

"It wasn't. He called all of my friends to apologize."

"Seriously? Why?" She almost sounded mad.

"Maybe the leotard worked," I offered. "Or maybe he'd seen how much his words were hurting other people and wanted to change. Why question it?" No matter how it had come about, Ryker had apologized, and that meant something. A lot, actually.

"True," Ginger agreed. "I just can't help but feel like the other shoe's about to fall, you know?"

As I turned onto the road toward home, I tried to fight the doubt her words brought with them. Still, I couldn't deny the way Ryker had been for as long as I'd known him. "It wouldn't be the first time, would it?"

"Nope," she agreed. "Hey, I was also going to ask you if you wanted me to come home for homecoming? I could have one of my friends help with your hair?"

Homecoming. It was only a month away, and I didn't want to think about it. Not in the slightest. "I don't know," I said. Dances were always fun, but lone-wolfing it was getting old. And there was no way Ryker would ask me to go with him, so I'd just get to see him and one of the IT girls win royalty while I sat like a peasant on the sidelines.

"Do you have a date?" she asked. "Or will you be too busy making paint fall from the sky on Ryker's head?"

I chuckled. "He apologized. I think I'm done with that war. No," I let out a sigh, "I'll probably be rolling with the girls. If they don't get asked." Which was entirely possible.

"I know it feels sad to be the only one without a boyfriend, but try not to let it get to you. Before I met Ray, I was always wishing for a boyfriend, and I wish I'd just enjoyed my time with the girls while I waited for him to find me."

"Easy for you to say," I retorted, pulling into the driveway and parking the van in the second garage spot. "I just got home. Let me switch you from the van to my phone."

"That's okay. I have to get homework done anyway. I'm just so relieved you won't have anything to do with Ryker anymore. Now you can get to enjoying your senior year."

My hand faltered on the key. "Right. Thank goodness for that." I would get to enjoying my senior year, just not the way she, nor I, had ever imagined. "Talk to you later."

Once I got inside the house, I took a shower to help with the tangles in my curly hair and maybe even remove the heat that stained my cheeks from Ryker's kiss. Dad got home around the time I was getting out of the shower and set about making supper for us.

It was another one of Mom's frozen casseroles, and as we ate it, he asked me all the arbitrary questions parents had to. How was your week? Did you finish your homework? What are your plans for the rest of the weekend?

I answered each of them and tried my best to engage, but my mind was on Ryker. On what I'd done.

I'd *kissed* the school bully, the same one I'd promised to take down. He'd apologized to the people I loved, turned over a new leaf.

Things were looking up. Or upside down.

Mom called and told us goodnight, then we went to bed. As I lay against my pillow, going over the day's event, I thought it couldn't have gone any better.

That was, until I got a goodnight text.

Ryker: Good night, beautiful.

FORTY-TWO

THE GIRLS and I agreed we didn't need to walk to school together anymore, not since Ryker had called off the attack and apologized. So when I rolled into the parking lot a minute too late and hurried toward the school, I was relieved no one had to wait on me.

Of course, the football guys and IT girls were standing around Grant's Jeep like they owned the place. Heck, with how much their parents gave to the school, they probably did. I held my breath as I passed them, waiting for the comments about a fat girl running, but nothing came.

My chest felt even lighter as I took the front steps two at a time and made it inside just as the warning bell rang. I waved hello to a few girls from the basketball team and called to Nadira that I'd see her in calculus.

As I neared my locker, I slowed, trying to even my breath. The last thing I wanted Ryker to see was me red-faced and winded from a walk inside.

But when I got close enough to see through the people in the hallway, I realized I hadn't needed to worry at all. Ryker wasn't there. The disappointment I felt was much too strong.

The warning bell rang, giving me a chance to snap out of it while everyone around me started toward class. I hurriedly put my combination in and turned the locker open. Inside, there was a clear plastic bag wrapped with a curled blue ribbon. Inside were chocolate chip cookies.

My lips formed a smile as I lifted the card attached to the ribbon.

I think I owe you one. Or twelve. -R

My smile wouldn't go away as I loaded my books into my bag and started toward first hour. Now I was lamenting the fact that Ryker and I didn't have any classes together so I could thank him for the cookies. Or ask him what they meant.

I kept looking for him in the hallways but didn't see him until lunchtime when I was sitting in the cafeteria with the girls.

He sat at a round table with his friends across from where we were. His head was turned toward his friend Grant, but I could tell his attention was elsewhere. As if he felt me staring, Ryker turned toward me, and a slow smile spread on his lips.

I smiled back and focused my attention on my friends. Nadira said her first Mathlete competition was Thursday afternoon and our teachers should be making the announcement soon.

While the team usually traveled to other competitions, the one hosted at the Academy was all hands on deck. The Academy used us students to help with scoring, running papers from one room to another, and helping the visiting teams navigate our circuitous home.

"Cori?" Nadira said.

"Sorry." I perked up. "What's up?"

"Do you want to come to my house after school that day? My mom has to work, but she said we could rent a movie and order a pizza."

"You know I'm in," I said immediately. "Anything other than another one of my mom's frozen organic lasagnas."

Adriel chuckled. "That has to be better than the keto diet my mom has me on."

"You're on a diet?" I asked, looking at her plate filled with meats and cheeses.

She frowned and nodded. "I have to try and lose at least two sizes to fit the dance costume."

My heart ached, but I didn't press, and neither did the other girls. It was obviously a sore subject for her.

"I can order you something special," Nadira offered.

That seemed to cheer Adriel up. "That would be amazing."

"So it's set?" Des asked, looking up from her phone.

Nadira nodded.

"Okay, on to something juicy," Des said.

As if we knew it would be good, we all leaned in closer.

Des glanced around, and once she seemed satisfied no one was listening, she said, "Rumor has it that Tatiana asked Ryker to come over to her place Sunday for a hook-up."

The ache in my chest was too big. Too real.

"And?" Nadira said. "Doesn't that happen every weekend?"

Des's eyebrow quirked. "It does. But this weekend, he turned her down."

My lips parted, half from relief and half from shock. Ryker had turned down a hook-up? "Did they say why?" I couldn't help but hope it had something to do with me.

Des shrugged. "Said he's seeing someone."

Adriel's mouth fell open. "So hell has frozen over? First an apology and now he's off the market? Who's the mystery girl?"

My cheeks felt hot, and I was seconds from giving in and telling them about Saturday evening when Nadira said, "Whoever it is, I feel sorry for her. It's just a matter of time before he goes back to his old ways and leaves her heart broken."

Faith frowned. "You don't think he could change?"

"No way," Nadira said. "Guys like that don't change. They just get better at hiding their real selves."

Des sipped Diet Coke through her straw. "Dir has a point."

The ache in my chest was back, but ten times as strong. I wanted to believe in Ryker, to defend him, but how could I? They had a point, and furthermore, they wouldn't understand where I was coming from. Standing up for him would be like a betrayal to them, and I just couldn't do it. Not after all we'd been through together.

No, best to see how it worked and once things became serious—if they did—I would tell my friends how it all went down and beg forgiveness for not asking permission.

FORTY-THREE

AS I WALKED out to my car after school, my phone went off with a text message.

Ryker: How were the cookies?

I weaved between a Bugatti and a Porsche on the way to my van and typed back a response.

Cori: Almost as good as the ones I gave you. Where did you buy them?

Ryker: I'm hurt. Those were homemade.

Cori: In who's kitchen?

Ryker: Mine.

Cori: ...

Ryker: I got the dough out of the package, put it in the oven and everything.

I laughed out loud and came to a stop by my

van. Leaning against it, I basked in the warm fall sunlight. I loved this time of year.

Cori: I'm impressed. But you know 12 cookies is too many for me.

Ryker: Yeah?

Cori: It's unfortunate really. I don't have anyone to share them with.

Ryker: Well, you know, I happen to be a great cookie eater.

Cori: Is that an official title?

Ryker: It could be. Should we put it to the test?

Cori: When?

Ryker: After practice? There's this coffee place I think you'll like.

Was Ryker asking me on a date? A *second* date? I tried to calm my giddiness as I got into the car, but it was hard. I bit back a smile as I typed back the most nonchalant reply I could muster.

Cori: Sure. Send me the address?

Within a few seconds, he sent me a map pin to Seaton Bakery.

Ryker: Can't wait.

I locked my phone screen and pulled out of the parking lot, grinning like a maniac. Ryker had asked me out, and not only that, he'd asked me to the best bakery in the tri-city area. I'd only learned about Seaton Bakery because of Ginger and her friends, and ever since then, I'd stopped by whenever I was in the area to grab a coffee or a cupcake.

Once I got to the store for my shift, Janet greeted me with her usual cheery grin. I waved to her before going to find Dad. He was back by the butcher counter, helping to package meat.

"Hey," I said to him and the butcher, Diego. "It's been a while since I've seen you, Di. Why are you working so late?"

He grinned. "You know your dad. Relentless."

I chuckled, because I was supposed to, but Diego wasn't entirely wrong.

"Just about finished," Dad said, wrapping up a cut of beef.

"Is that from Ray's ranch?" I asked.

He nodded. "Customers are loving it."

That brought a smile to my face. Dad didn't give compliments freely, so the fact that he acknowledged Ray's beef at all was huge.

"It's good stuff," Diego said, walking back to the sink to wash his hands.

Dad continued wrapping meat and asked, "How was school?"

"Good," I said honestly. "I was actually

wondering if I could grab some coffee with a friend after this shift is over?"

Dad's eyes narrowed suspiciously. "A friend?"

My cheeks heated, and I realized I had no reason to hide. Ryker was officially father approved. What kind of world was I living in that I could tell my dad before my best friends? Rather than think on it, I admitted, "Ryker asked me out."

Dad's lips twisted into a smug grin under his thick mustache. "Ryker? The one you didn't like?"

My cheeks heated more, and I turned away. "Forget I asked!"

Chuckling, he said, "Be home by nine."

I smiled to myself as I walked back to the lockers in the employee break room. Knox was working in the back, breaking down boxes, and he barely gave me a second glance as I passed him.

My smile quickly faded at his snub. We'd been friends at work for months, and now he wanted to turn against me? Why? Because I had a different opinion than him?

I shut my locker a little too hard and got to work. But instead of helping him with the boxes like I usually would have, I grabbed a bucket of water and disinfectant and went to the opposite end of the store.

Dad wanted the shelves regularly wiped down, but no one ever wanted to do it. I'd tackle the chore for now, just to get away from Knox and his judgement. He probably hadn't ever had so much as a conversation with Ryker. Just because Ryker's dad had done awful things, that didn't mean Ryker would follow down the same path.

I scrubbed the shelves, angrily moving items aside and then placing them back. By the time six o'clock rolled around, I had made my way down three aisles. I marked it off on the cleaning sheet Dad kept in the back and then went to my locker.

It was either my academy uniform or jeans and a Ripe T-shirt. I'd never dated like this before, but I was starting to realize how much effort went into getting ready for a date. Maybe I should keep a cute outfit around just in case?

For today, I decided on my work outfit—at least the jeans looked good—and left the store. Dad called behind me, "Have fun on your *date!*"

Blushing, I waved goodbye and walked through the parking lot to the van. Seaton Bakery was about a twenty-minute drive away, which meant I had plenty of time to overthink how this date would go. How I wanted to walk into the bakery—whether he'd be there first or not. If I should wear my jacket zipped all the way up to cover my banana-yellow shirt or casually open to show how relaxed I was pretending to be.

Turned out I didn't even have time to decide how to wear my jacket because Ryker was already there. Exhaust rolled out his pickup's tailpipe, but as I drew closer, he turned off the engine.

Before I could open my door, he was there, opening it for me.

"Hey." I smiled up at him, taking in his still-damp hair and the sweet cologne coming from his freshly showered body. I was already drooling, and I wasn't anywhere near the desserts.

"Hey," he said softly, his voice husky. He leaned in easily and gave me a short kiss that stole my breath and made my heart beat faster. I was coming to realize how comfortable Ryker was with kissing. Did it mean as much to him as it did to me?

I shoved back the insecure thought and smiled at him. "I love this place. I'm glad you picked it."

"Yeah?" He stepped back from my van so I could get out, and as we walked toward the door, he slipped his fingers through mine.

My skin tingled under his touch. Kissing was one thing, but hand-holding? I'd never seen him do something so sweet and innocent with another girl.

He held the door open and kept ahold of my hand as we walked inside. A woman stood at the register, grinning at us. "Aren't you two just the cutest couple?"

Ryker easily grinned. "She makes me look good."

The woman nodded. "You have the most beautiful red hair. Actually... do you know a girl named Ginger Nash? Your hair is just like hers."

I grinned. "That's my sister! I'm Cori."

"Gayle." The woman extended her hand, and I shook it. "What can I get you two?" she asked.

Ryker waited for me, and I ordered a flat white with a croissant sandwich while he got the same.

"It'll be right out," Gayle promised. "Sit anywhere you like."

There were a few people spread about the bakery, but Ryker led me to a booth in the corner. It felt cozy and intimate, and I loved the idea that I would get him all to myself, just like I had on Saturday.

Sitting across from each other, it would have been awkward to hold hands, but we were tall enough that our knees brushed under the table. I liked it, the subtle reminder of his touch, his presence.

Ryker leaned forward, his elbows on the table. "Can I tell you a secret?"

I nodded.

"I haven't been able to stop thinking about you."

My cheeks warmed, but I wasn't quite so ready to give in. "I heard you got a call from Tatiana on Sunday."

He straightened slightly. "Yeah?"

"I heard you told her you were seeing someone."

A crooked grin spread on his face. "I am."

"And who would that be?" I couldn't handle this jealous feeling in my chest, the worry that he would say this meant nothing to him.

He looked over his shoulder for a moment and said, "I'm really bad at this."

The change in tone took me off guard. "What do you mean?" I asked worriedly.

"This." He gestured between the two of us. "I'm great at keeping girls at arm's length. At taking what I want and walking away. And I know that makes me sound like a terrible person."

"It does," I agreed.

"But I'm trying to be better, trying to prove to

you that I'm better. And—" He swore under his breath. "I am really bad at this."

I couldn't help but chuckle at his distress.

"Why are you laughing?"

"I'm not used to seeing you like this," I said. "You act like ruling the whole school is as easy as breathing."

He rolled his eyes. "Clearly you've never met yourself."

My eyebrows drew together. "What does that mean?"

"Come on. You show up the first day of senior year and walk in like you own the place. But you've always been like that."

"What do you mean?" I asked again.

He raised his eyebrows at me like I was being coy. "You've always been unafraid to just go for it. You're a beast on the basketball court, and everyone wants to be your friend. They're never scared of you or worried about what your parents will do to them. They want to be your friend because of who you are. And, okay, maybe I do too."

My heart fluttered at the compliment, but I couldn't help but say, "I'm pretty sure we're past being friends."

"I hope so," he breathed.

A soft smile tugged at my lips. "Where has this Ryker been the last four years?"

"I don't know." He reached across the table and took my hand. "But I'm glad he's here now."

My heart agreed with him, and my smile from earlier turned into a full-on grin. "I thought you said you were bad at this."

"I am." He stroked his thumb over the back of my hand, leaving a trail of tingling skin. "I haven't even asked you the question I wanted to yet."

"And what would that be?" I asked.

"Cori Nash you are a special girl. And I want you to be mine."

The air left my lungs as I tried to comprehend what he was saying. "Wh-what?"

Like it pained him, he said, "I want you to be my girlfriend. And I want to be your boyfriend. And you're going to figure out how new this is for me, but I want to try it with you." His hands gripped mine firmly. "I know I'm terrible at this, but please don't make my first time asking a girl to be exclusive a complete failure."

A light laugh bubbled out of my chest. "Seven out of ten. But I'll accept."

From behind me, Gayle said, "Did I just hear what I think I heard!?" She set our drinks and food on the table. "Congratulations, you two!" She folded her hands over her heart. "So adorable!"

Ryker chuckled in a happy, carefree way I'd never heard before. "I was worried I'd mess it up."

"You did great," Gayle reaffirmed and said, "I'll let you enjoy your date."

As I looked at the guy across from me, my *boyfriend*, I realized that was exactly what I was doing. Enjoying myself in a way I hadn't ever expected.

"This is crazy," I said.

"I know," he agreed, taking a sip of his drink.

He chuckled, and I couldn't help but giggle along.

"You know what's crazy?" I said.

"What?"

I swirled my drink, watching the foam transform from white to the palest of browns. "That people like you can just ask someone out without your parents having to be all over the decision, you know? I bet that's nice."

"Nice," he repeated, a bitter hint to his tone. "I guess it's just that some decisions matter to them more than others."

"What do you mean?" I asked.

He shook his head, looking out the windows at

the parking lot. "You know my dad has had my major decided since before I started high school?"

My eyebrows drew together. "What?"

He nodded. "Or that my mom's stylist picks clothes for my wardrobe?"

"Seriously?"

"You know that most of the time I talk to my parents through Margaret?" He scoffed and took a sip from his coffee before looking at me again. "She knows my school schedule better than either of my parents do." He tried to be nonchalant, joking about it, but the ache in his voice was clear.

"Don't worry, I understand all about absent parents," I said.

"But the other day—"

"The other day was the first time anything my family has done has been about me," I said. "Ginger almost died when I was in seventh grade. She had really bad pneumonia and had to be in the hospital for weeks. I never saw my parents while she was there—just my aunt Rosie."

I took a deep breath, trying to dislodge the lump in my throat. I didn't talk about this much. The people who knew about that time in my life went through it with me.

"The twins took it really bad. They started

throwing tantrums in school, making scenes anywhere we went, picking fights with other kids. Mom felt so guilty she took them to therapy, and the therapist recommended role play as an outlet to get their feelings out. And they were good. They've been in acting lessons ever since."

Ryker met my eyes. "And what about you?"

"What about me?" I asked, blinking back the stinging in my eyes and trying to smile.

With a soft expression, he reached across the table and cupped my cheek with his hand, then lowered it to the table. "That was when you started playing basketball, right? Eighth grade?"

"Yeah, I..." My lips parted as I took him in. "Wait. How did you know?"

His lips quirked. "I pay more attention than you think, Nash."

Shaking my head, I said, "Well, it was a lifesaver. I could get out my anger on the court and still be the good girl my parents wanted me to be."

"Let's be real," he said with a smirk. "You've never been the good girl."

I tried to hold back a smile and said, "Really, what kind of girl am I?"

"Right now?" he asked. "Mine."

FORTY-FOUR

THE BUBBLE of the bakery only lasted so long before it was back to my car, back home. I was only minutes from the bakery, but the happy, light-hearted feeling I'd had only moments ago had been replaced with a ball of nerves.

Why?

A cute guy who actually had a lot in common with me had asked me to be his girlfriend. He'd promised exclusivity. He'd realized how wrong bullying was. And then he kissed me goodnight so right I forgot my name. Why was I so on edge?

My phone began ringing, and for a moment I hoped it was Ryker, but instead I saw my mom's name on the screen.

I swiped to answer and held it to my ear. "Hello?" In the background, I could hear the sounds of the set. "Are you still at the studio?" I asked.

"Yes, but that's not why I called. How was your date?" Mom asked. "Dad said you went out with Ryker again tonight."

My cheeks felt hot even though she couldn't see me. Had Dad seriously called Mom to tell her about my date? Did that mean they actually cared? A happy feeling lifted my lips into a smile, but then a sinking feeling filled my gut.

Who else had he told?

"Mom, you haven't told Ginger yet, right?"

"No, why?"

Um, maybe because I was dating her archenemy and that would be just a step below dating Ray in terms of the sister code. "Because it's still early," I said instead. "I don't want to make it into something it's not."

"Sure," Mom said lightly. "So it didn't go well?"

I replied quickly, needing her to know that it had. "No, it was good. Great, actually."

"What did you do?"

My eyebrows rose. Mom was actually asking me about how my date went—and listening? Not lecturing? This couldn't be real life.

"Cori?" she said.

I slowed at a yellow light, venturing into these new waters with my mom. "We went to a bakery and had coffee and sandwiches. He was really sweet."

"He seemed sweet at the dinner we had." Someone yelled in the background, but Mom continued. "Do you think he'll ask you to homecoming?"

The light turned green, and I continued down the road. How hadn't I thought of homecoming? But he was my boyfriend now. Did he still have to ask or was going together just implied? I tried to remember whether or not Ray asked Ginger to prom. "I don't know," I said finally.

"I'm sure he will. Your father and I both agreed he seemed smitten with you. Your dad said he'd never seen a guy so nervous as when Ryker asked him for a date with you and Dad told him a family dinner was required!"

Ryker? Nervous? "That's crazy." It didn't jive, but my heart couldn't help hoping that maybe this had been more to Ryker long before our truce. What would that mean about him? About me?

"Your dad said he couldn't stand still the entire time, bouncing from one foot to another." She chuckled. "I remember how your father was on our first date. We were seventeen, and his hands were sweating so bad he didn't even hold my hand in the movie theater."

I laughed at the thought of my big, burly father as a nervous teenager. "That's cute." Sometimes it was hard to remember that my parents were people too. That even though their main roles were parenting and store ownership, they were a couple too.

I turned the corner to the house and pulled the van into the garage. Mom made me promise to call her before our Thursday night video chat, and then we said goodbye. As I walked inside, I realized it was one of our first conversations that had been about me and my life... It felt good.

I went to the kitchen and got myself a glass of water and the last of the cookies Ryker had baked for me, then sat down at the island to work on homework. I could hardly focus though, because I knew I needed to ask Ryker the impossible: to keep our relationship a secret.

I looked from my eighteenth-century history textbook to my phone sitting innocuously on the counter. The longer I waited, the more likely it would be for news of our relationship to show up on social media or spread in his circle of friends...

My phone started vibrating, and I nearly fell out of my chair. With my heart racing from surprise, I looked at the screen and saw Ryker's name along with the photo I saved with his contact information. He did look good in a leo.

Then I realized I was staring and swiped the screen to answer. "Hello?"

"Hey." His voice was the perfect mix of smooth and husky, and I was beyond glad I could fully appreciate it now that I was his...girlfriend. Holy crap. I was Ryker Dugan's girlfriend! I'd pinch myself if I wasn't worried it was a dream. No way was I waking up from this.

"How are you?" I asked, trying not to be nervous for my impossible ask.

"Great. I'll be better when I see you tomorrow."

My stomach fluttered, and my lips formed an effortless smile. "I was thinking the same thing."

A pause hung between us, and I could hear the soft sound of waves rolling against the shore. I pictured him outside, sitting on one of the lounge chairs where we shared our first kiss.

"Hey, so I have something to ask you," he said awkwardly.

"Me too, actually," I said, "but you go first."

"I'm going to sound like a jerk, but..."

My stomach immediately clenched. I should have pinched myself when I had a chance—before this dream turned into a nightmare. "What?"

"After what happened last year with Beckett, Coach has been super uptight about anyone on the football team starting a new relationship during the season. I know it's a lot to ask, but can we keep our relationship quiet? At least until season's over?"

His words were like finding out you landed on free parking in Monopoly only to discover there wasn't any money left on the board. Sure, you were safe, but what good was being safe when you could have gained so much more? Had a part of me wanted him to be disappointed about keeping things secret?

"Sure," I said quietly. This was fine, right? The girls and I had even planned for me to date him and break Coach's rule... before he apologized. Before I fell for him.

"I know it sucks with homecoming, but I promise I'll make it up to you at the winter dance." His words were earnest, and I had to admit it brought a smile to my face, the idea that Ryker was planning so far in the future for us. None of his other "relationships" had lasted more than a night.

Still, my pride was working full force. "We don't

have to do this, Ryker. Maybe it's just not a good time. We can call it until you're ready—"

"Cori, of course I'm not ready!" he cried. "Did you see me in the restaurant? I nearly passed out just asking you to be my girlfriend. But there's not a chance I'm backing out now. My life has felt empty for so long until you stepped into it this year. I may not be ready, but damn it, I can't go back to my life before you. I've wasted so much time on things that were expected of me to give up on the unexpectedness of us."

"So you're okay with this?" I asked meekly, almost afraid to believe his words. "Dating in secret and dating only me? You've never done this before. Especially not with someone like me."

There it was, all my vulnerabilities and fears out there on the table for him to see and use against me. But like Knox said, sometimes you put your heart on the line and hoped like hell they would catch it.

"I'm not okay with it," he said flatly. "I'm not okay with you walking around school and having other guys look at you like you could be theirs. I'm not okay with seeing you at the homecoming dance without being on my arm. I'm not okay with seeing you after a game and not being able to kiss you in front of every damn person so they know exactly whose I am." His voice rose with passion as he said the words until finally, he breathed, "and I'm hoping you're not okay with it either."

My heart swelled and ached with each of his words. I wanted those things too. To fully enjoy my first real relationship with the support of my friends and family. But that's where this would lead, right? "So we'll tell everyone?" I asked. "The day after football season?"

"And not a second later," he promised. "And then I'll give you the biggest, most ridiculous winter dance proposal this school has ever seen."

I giggled at the thought. "That doesn't seem like your style."

"Cori, *you* are my style."

I couldn't help the giddy grin or the way he made my heart melt. "It's a date then. The day after football season."

"The second the last game is over," he breathed. "I'll see you tomorrow, girlfriend."

I smiled and shook my head at the words. "I'll see you tomorrow, boyfriend."

As the call ended, I held my phone to my chest, imagining the day after football season and wishing it would come soon.

FORTY-FIVE

THE NEXT DAY AT SCHOOL, everything felt different. Or maybe it was just me. As I parked, I looked around for my friends. Of course Nadira and Faith's cars were already there, and Des was her typical late self. Not that I could tell them what had happened the day before.

Adriel drove past me in her beautiful tan Mercedes G-Class, and I tried to keep from drooling.

"Hey!" I called, waving to her, and walked over to her parking spot. "Have I ever told you I love your car?" I eyed it longingly.

Smiling, she shut her door and clicked the lock button. "My mom's choice."

"She has good taste." I hitched my bag over my

shoulder and walked toward school with her. "How was your weekend? What did you do?"

"Hmm. Well, I danced, danced, and..." She tapped her chin. "Oh yeah, danced."

I chuckled. "Training getting a little intense?"

She nodded. "Half the girls in the studio homeschool so they can be there more. Isabella, Tatiana, and I are the only ones who actually go to school full-time."

"And I thought two hours a day for basketball practice was a lot," I said.

"There's just a lot of money involved," she explained, a tinge of bitterness to her voice. "People have mortgaged their homes to keep practicing at the studio."

"Why?" I asked, shocked.

"Because anyone who dances at nationals with Liliana is practically guaranteed a spot with the New York City Ballet. From there, the sky's the limit. Broadway, music videos, acting..."

"Wow," I breathed.

She slowed and muttered, "Great."

"What?" I followed her gaze and caught the crowd of popular kids hanging around Ryker's truck. He sat on the tailgate, his slacks lifted to show a peep of navy-blue socks, his eyes hidden behind mirrored glasses. Adriel's reaction and mine were *not* the same.

Even though I couldn't see his eyes, I watched the corner of his mouth quirk as he caught me staring, smiling, because there wasn't a girl within five feet of him. Isabella had curled against Grant, and Tatiana was making out with Josue, a foreign exchange student who'd been recruited to the football team for his prowess in rugby.

Still, my eyes were on Ryker and those lips that I now knew could kiss me breathless.

"Think they'll mess with us?" Adriel asked. "Should we try another direction?"

I lifted my chin. "I think we're good. He's a changed man, right?"

She huffed. "Sure." Still, I could feel her holding her breath as we passed only feet away from the group.

Maybe I held my own too.

But they didn't bother us, not a single muttered insult, not one farm animal sound. Only the feeling of Ryker's eyes on my back as we walked by.

When we were out of earshot, Adriel said, "Okay, that was crazy."

I had to agree. "Senior year's looking up, right?"

"Definitely," she said.

We reached the bottom of the stairs, and a big commotion ahead of us caused me to look up. Someone had unfurled a massive banner that said BE MY HOMECOMING DATE, DES?

"Des?" I muttered, looking around. She was several feet behind us, her phone held limply in her hand and her jaw slack.

"Will you get down from there?" she yelled at the guy standing atop one of the pillars.

My eyes pinballed between the two of them. Was that...

"Not until you say yes!" he yelled.

"Is that Faith's brother?" Adriel asked.

I nodded. Faith's brother Ken was a junior, and really hot if I was being honest, but Des did not date younger guys. Also, part of me wanted to kick him for potentially weirding out the vibes in our group.

Adriel put her palm to her forehead. "This is painful."

"Sure," Des yelled, catching up with us. "But only if you bring my friends with us in a limo." Under her breath, she said, "Might as well get a good ride out of the deal."

"Anything!" he called.

With an exasperated smile, I shook my head. "Put the guy out of his misery."

"Yes!" Des said. Then she continued up the stairs as if it were just another day.

Behind her, Adriel and I gave each other a look.

"And so the danceposals begin," she muttered.

I couldn't help but smile, thinking in just a couple months I'd be getting my own.

As we walked up the stairs, I could hear Mrs. Bardot calling to Ken, telling him to get that banner down before the other schools started arriving for the mathlete competition. Not that Ken could possibly hide such a massive banner. A dumpster might not even be big enough.

The first bell went off as soon as we walked in the doors, and Headmaster Bradford's voice came over the PA system.

"Please drop off your homework and then leave your bags in your lockers. That includes your cell phones. You will not be needing them today. Once you are done, report to your first-hour class for further instruction. Good luck to our Emerson Academy mathletes! Although our mascot was named for a writer, we're sure your skills in arithmetic will do us proud."

The speaker cut out, and Adriel said, "You heard the man."

I laughed. "See you at lunch."

She waved goodbye, and we parted ways. The halls were a mess as everyone tried to turn in their homework. As I walked to my locker, I couldn't help but think that a school this prestigious should have come up with a better system.

I entered the combination and began putting my books in when I heard Ryker say softly, "Hi, girlfriend."

I turned to find him behind me, holding a single red rose. He'd hidden it with his body, and I quickly took it, smiling down at it.

"It made me think of you," he said.

That was good because I'd been thinking of him nonstop. But of course I'd never admit that out loud. "Thank you," I said instead.

He went to his locker, lifting up on the handle. He must have jammed it so he didn't need to enter the code. I made a mental note so I could leave a gift of my own sometime.

"Excited for the game against Beaver's Bend?" I asked. The game was two hours out of town this Friday, and I couldn't help but feel sad I wouldn't be able to go.

He shrugged, lifting books into his own locker. "It's the last game before homecoming, and then we have a couple more before the playoffs." He shut his locker and leaned against it. "I'm supposed to be leading my team to state, and all I'm thinking about is a girl with red hair and a personality to match."

My cheeks heated. "Some people bring it out in me more than others," I teased, trying to regain my footing, my poise. Because inside, someone had just thrown a bunch of confetti and was blowing an air horn. It was a downright rave in there.

With a chuckle, he leaned close and whispered. "Come to my house Saturday?"

My mouth was dry, so I swallowed. Nodded.

He dropped his lips so swiftly on my cheek, his touch was almost like the ghost of a feather. But my smile, and the feeling inside, were real.

FORTY-SIX

MY JOB throughout the day was to write tallies on a whiteboard to keep score. Again, not very sophisticated. It would have been the easiest job in the world... if Ryker hadn't been assigned to the same room. He had to bring the final scores from the classroom to the office where the official results would be tabulated.

And damn if I couldn't stop looking at him. He was having the same problem. I almost missed writing a tally mark twice in the first round alone, so much so that the teacher in the room, Mr. Sullivan, had to ask me if I needed a cup of coffee.

No, I wasn't tired, just infatuated with the hottie across the room who shook with silent laugher every time I missed a mark. Luckily, no teams from our school had competed in the room yet, so it was just the teachers seeing what an idiot I was around Ryker. I needed to get my act together.

At lunchtime, Mr. Sullivan ushered me out of the room, saying, "And for the love of all things holy, wake yourself up, Nash."

As the door shut behind us and we entered the hallway full of students, Ryker burst out into laughter. "Need some coffee?"

"More like a new boyfriend," I muttered. "One who isn't so distractingly good-looking."

"Oh, well in that case." He held up a golden key. "I guess I'll just have to put this baby away."

"What is it?" I asked, my curiosity piqued.

"Just a key to a little time with my girlfriend without anyone solving for X."

My eyes sparked. "Um, yes please? Why didn't you say anything sooner?"

He stopped outside the gym's storage closet and looked around. When it seemed like no one was watching, he hurriedly unlocked the door and rushed me inside. The room was dark, but a string hung from the ceiling and Ryker pulled it, flooding us in light and revealing dusty shelves of football pads and helmets.

I giggled breathlessly. "I must say, I love a man with connections."

Stepping closer to me, he breathed, "I must say, I love a girl with curves." His hands slid over my hips, pulling me close to him, and if I was having a hard time breathing before, it was impossible now with my heart pounding in my throat and my lips begging him to close the final distance between us.

But first, his gray eyes held mine, captivating me in their beauty and depth. I couldn't decide whether my favorite thing about Ryker was his eyes or his lips. But as his mouth pressed against mine, I made my decision.

A low moan rose in his throat, and knowing how I affected him made me want to deepen the kiss all the more. I wound my arms around his neck, playing with his hair, and made the most of this stolen moment.

He bit my lip and pulled slowly away, making shivers run up my spine, then alternated kisses and nips along my jaw to the base of my neck. The sensation was pure pleasure that made me want his lips on me that much more.

I gently pulled on his hair, angling his mouth back to mine, and he stumbled a few steps forward, bracing me against the shelves of discarded football gear. It hadn't felt that hard, but soon helmets began falling to the ground around us, and just like that, the moment was gone as we stared wide-eyed at the very loud mess forming on the floor.

Ryker cursed and immediately leapt to action, catching what he could and stopping the rolling helmets from the shelf we'd dislodged.

But then we heard a new, more dangerous sound: a key in the lock.

Ryker waved me with his hand to stand behind the door, and just as soon as I'd gotten to the corner, it came open.

"Ryker?" Mrs. Bardot said. "What are you doing in here?"

Pressed into the corner behind the heavy wooden door, I couldn't see him, but I could hear him casually say, "Just needed a minute away from all that math."

I rolled my eyes. That was the best he could do?

Mrs. Bardot was quiet for a moment before saying, "Your cheeks are flushed."

"It's warm in here."

I closed my eyes, trying to keep my breathing as shallow and quiet as possible. If she caught us, our relationship would be so far from a secret it might as well be pasted across the front page of the *Everyday Emerson.*

"Just get to class," she said, stepping into the closet. Someone pulled the string, and I was plunged into darkness.

The door shut, leaving me completely alone. A room that had just moments ago held so much heat felt downright cold, and I had no idea what to do. People were still out in the hallway, and without my phone, I had no idea how much longer there was left of lunch before I'd be late to the mathlete competition and in serious trouble.

I put my palm to my forehead. What an idiot I'd been. Of course something like this would happen. It was just Ryker. He was like magic, intoxicating me any second I was around him, once with a heady rush of anger and now with the desire of possibility.

I let out a sigh and resolved to wait a few minutes until Ryker and Mrs. Bardot got far enough away for me to leave. Surely no one was just hanging out in the hallway by the gym. They'd be out on the quad enjoying the last of the good fall weather or in the cafeteria, scarfing down a catered meal.

I walked to the crack in the door where a thin

sliver of light was shining and pressed my eye to the gap.

The hallway seemed empty—at least I couldn't hear anyone outside. I counted to sixty five times in my head, then slowly opened the door, peeking out to see an empty hallway.

Feeling relieved, I let out the breath I'd been holding and stepped outside, quietly closing the door behind me, but when I looked up, I was staring straight into the eyes of Mrs. Bardot.

She looked oddly intimidating for a woman who had her arms folded over her vest covered in algebraic symbols.

"Coriander Nash," she said, and her tone and the use of my full name was enough.

Tears sprang to my eyes, and I said, "Please don't tell my mom."

God, I was a baby.

Her frowned deepened, and she said, "I won't tell your mother, but I do want to speak to you. My office. Now."

Swallowing, I followed the clacking of her bright blue shoes down the hallway, around the corner, and into her office. The second I stepped inside, she shut the door behind me and said, "Sit down."

I followed her directions, but didn't meet her eyes when she sat across from me. Humiliated didn't even come close to the way I was feeling. Not with my eyes stinging with tears, my cheeks red, and my chest hollowed. Ryker and I had been caught in the worst possible way.

"Cori, over the last several years, I've become fond of your family. I watched Ginger go from a shy freshman to a confident senior making major life decisions. I watched you play your first junior varsity basketball game and get so excited to make a buzzer-beater shot, you threw the basketball all the way over the backboard and missed the hoop completely."

As if I needed more humiliation.

"I've seen you become a steadfast friend and an excellent teammate. I've *never* seen you behave the way you have this year." She crossed her hands on her desk and said, "I need you to look at me. I need you to *hear* this."

Slowly, I lifted my gaze to her murky brown eyes behind golden-framed glasses.

She held my stare and said, "Footballs might be fun to toss around, but hearts aren't made for games."

The tears threatened to spill, and I blinked quickly. "Is that all?" I asked, my voice hoarse.

She only nodded.

As I walked back to the room where I was stationed for the rest of the day, her words echoed in my mind.

Hearts aren't made for games.

FORTY-SEVEN

THE FIVE OF us girls sprawled around the den in Nadira's basement. Her parents had set it up with massive leather couches and a projector that displayed a giant picture on a white sheet. Her dad and brothers always hogged the room during basketball season, but I couldn't count how many romcoms she, Des, and I had watched down here throughout the years.

"What do you want to watch?" Nadira asked, flicking through streaming services. They had it all—Netflix, Hulu, Prime Video...

"Um," Adriel said, "I want to watch Des explain her homecoming date!"

I leaned forward, looking between Des and Faith.

Des frowned, "Faith, is it okay that I told him yes?"

Faith shrugged. "It means he'll stop asking me for strategies to get you to say yes."

I laughed. "He's been asking you?"

Faith rolled her eyes. "Yes, for the first time ever, my brothers are coming to me for relationship advice."

"That's sweet," Des said, "but I don't like your brother that way."

Faith shrugged. "That's okay." She paused. "Just...be honest with him? I don't want him getting hurt."

"Of course," Des said. "I was actually planning on going by myself, you know? With you guys."

Nadira lifted an eyebrow. "Who says we didn't have dates?"

"Your mathlete jacket?" Des teased.

Nadira patted her leather jacket with a big plus sign on the front and whispered into her collar, "She didn't mean that."

Laughing, I said, "I think it will be fun to go in a group. And now we're riding in a limo."

Faith groaned. "Riding along with my little brother on his date. This has to be a peak in my life."

Not as much as the excitement and then scare I'd had earlier with Ryker. I wanted to tell them about it, but I was so humiliated I couldn't even bring myself to repeat the story out loud.

"Speaking of peaks," Des said, "did you hear Mrs. Bardot caught Ryker in an equipment closet?"

My heart froze, along with the rest of my body.

Adriel pursed her lips. "Who's the poor girl this time?"

Des shrugged. "Said he was alone." She winked at us. "Do you think all that math work got him...worked up."

"Ew!" Nadira threw a pillow at her. Faith blushed so red she could have blended into a tomato. And me? Well, I had to laugh a little. The math *had* gotten us worked up.

"You were with him," Nadira said, pointing the remote at me. "Did he say he had a secret hook-up?"

For a girl who always talked, I was having a hard time coming up with anything believable to say. Because if I was bad at keeping secrets, I was even worse at lying.

"Yeah," Adriel said sarcastically, "because he and Cori are *so* close."

"Right?" Faith laughed. "I'm pretty sure Cori's earned herself an enemy for life."

I picked at a ragged edge of my thumbnail, wishing this conversation would be over and desperately searching for a way to end it.

Luckily, Nadira's brother did it for me. Terrell shouted down the stairs, "Pizza's here!"

"Bring it down!" Nadira said.

"No way!" he yelled back.

"I'll give you a slice!" she yelled.

"I already have some! Mom ordered us one too," he shouted.

Nadira rolled her eyes and began pushing herself off the couch, but I said, "I'll get it."

"Fine by me," she replied, relaxing back into her seat and continuing her channel surfing.

I started up their stairs out of the basement and saw both of Nadira's brothers, Terrell and Carver, and her dad digging into a box of pizza at their kitchen island.

"Hey," I said, walking toward them.

"Cori with the jump shot!" her dad said, lifting his hand for a high five.

I laughed and high-fived him. "Getting ready for the season?"

"Oh yeah," he replied, shimmying his shoulders. "It's my favorite time of year."

I grinned back. "I can relate."

"Same," Nadira's younger brother, Carver, said through a mouthful of pizza.

Coach Harris popped him on the back of the head and said, "Manners." He gestured his pizza at me. "We have company."

I laughed. "I think we're a little past that." I put my arm around Terrell, who was now bigger and taller than me, by far. "Ever since Dir and I got this one in a dress."

Terrell glared at me and said, "I never should have sold out so easily."

"Three gummy bears was definitely worth it," I said.

Coach Harris chuckled. "Cori, I've been meaning to ask you. Do you want me to put in a good word with the women's' coach at Brentwood U? She's gearing up for recruitment, and I think you'd be a great fit for the team."

His words flattered me, honestly, but I said, "I don't know. I've been thinking about trying to get out of state somewhere."

He nodded. "Makes sense, but keep in mind, college is a different world. You'll be so busy with practice and school you won't have time to go home all that often."

"I'm not worried about going home," I admitted. "Just looking for a change in scenery."

"Fair enough, just give it some thought," he said, passing me the unopened box of pizza. "Okay?"

"Okay," I promised and started toward the stairs.

Each of us girls took a couple slices of pizza and sat back to watch *Sierra Burgess is a Loser*. The film was a little cringey—with the main character catfishing some guy who thought she was one of the school's popular girls. But it was cute, too.

When it was over, Faith said, "I couldn't imagine being dishonest with someone like that."

Nadira frowned. "Haven't you ever wanted to be someone else?"

I looked at her, my eyebrows drawn together. "What do you mean?"

Tucking her legs underneath her, Nadira said, "Come on." She gestured at the screen. "Who wouldn't want to be looked at—or, talked to, I guess—like they were that pretty, popular girl? I'd give anything for a guy to see my personality first, before he saw all of this." She gestured at her face and then body.

"Nadira," Des said, "you're beautiful and completely original. There's no one else like you. Why waste time trying to be someone else?"

Nadira sat back and sighed. "It's easy for you to say. Your YouTube channel already has fifty thousand subscribers, and half of them are guys begging you for a date." She jabbed her hand at me. "Cori's a freaking goddess who brought down THE Ryker Dugan, Adriel's an incredible dancer, and Faith is the nicest person I've ever met." She let out a heavy sigh. "I guess I don't blame you for not understanding."

The pain coming through her voice was almost too much to bear. "Dir," I said, "you've been my best friend since we were kids! You singlehandedly brought me through four years of math at the Academy, and you crushed it at the competition today. You can't tell me you don't see how special you are."

"So what?" she asked. "I'm good at math and that's it? When's the last time you've ever watched a romcom where a guy said, 'Oh baby, do some more math for me.'"

I chuckled, even though I knew it wasn't funny. Not really. "Just wait," I said. "You'll see."

"Sure," she said skeptically. "What I want to see is another movie."

Adriel reached over and took the remote. "Fine, but I'm picking the next one."

Laughing, Nadira said, "Okay."

As we watched the next film, I thought how lucky I was to have found someone who saw me for me, and I hoped someday, my friends would be able to experience it too.

FORTY-EIGHT

I DIDN'T SEE Ryker the next morning, but when I walked out of the locker room, dressed in gym clothes for our volunteer period, he was there.

I jumped backward, my hand over my heart. "You scared me!"

He chuckled. "That's not usually the reaction I get from women."

I rolled my eyes at him. "How you walk around with a head that big, I'll never know."

"Don't worry, my confidence has been knocked down a few pegs. Have you heard the rumor going around school?"

"About what you were doing in the equipment closet alone?" I laughed, a little, but it was quickly overshadowed by the talk Mrs. Bardot had with me in her office. As I looked at the attractive guy next to me, I had to wonder if I was making a mistake. Sure, I liked him, and he made me laugh, and talking to him was really easy...but had I forgiven him too easily?

He groaned. "You should hear the things the guys said in the locker room before practice yesterday."

I couldn't help but laugh. "I'm assuming it didn't stroke your ego?"

He gave me a look. "What about you? Did you get out okay?"

"Yeah," I said lightly. He held the door open for me, and we stepped into the cool breeze. I found myself wishing for his warm navy jacket. Or simply that he could put his arm around me out in public.

"Good," he said. "I'm still bummed you can't come to the game tonight."

"Same. My mom told my dad this morning that the twins should be done filming by next Friday. We're going there tonight for their last weekend in Hollywood."

He frowned. "So no Saturday date?"

"Nope." I found myself just as disappointed as he looked. How had I gone from hating him to hating the time I couldn't spend with him? "But I'll see you Monday?" I asked.

He nodded. "And you'll kiss me good luck before the homecoming game?"

Butterflies lifted in my stomach. "Of course."

"It's a date," he said.

That night, I loaded into the car with Dad, and we drove to Hollywood. He tried to make small talk with me, but I couldn't focus. I just wanted football season to be over so Ryker and I could stop all the secrets.

So what if our guidance counselor thought our relationship was a bad idea? I didn't need to take advice from someone who wore math on their clothes. And if my friends were really my friends, they'd forgive me. Maybe even support me.

But there was one person I was really worried about: Ginger. She might just be the person he'd hurt worst of all, but she'd never seen his good side. The real Ryker who was just himself when no one was around. I realized I wanted her to get to know him just as bad as I wanted him to know her and how amazing she was.

I couldn't wait to see her. With her so busy at college and me wrapped up in my senior year, we'd hardly had a chance to talk lately. I missed her.

When we got to the apartment, Mom came and gave me a big hug. It caught me off guard. As I hugged her back, I realized maybe she was trying harder to be there for me. I only wished she hadn't waited for my last year in high school to take an interest in my life.

Feeling conflicted, I said, "Why don't you and Dad go on a date? I can watch the twins."

Tarra frowned at me. "I don't need a babysitter!"

"Yeah," Cara agreed. "I'm a working woman!"

Mom chuckled. "Are you sure, Cori?"

I nodded. "Absolutely. We can have some girl time."

Tarra perked up, but Cara eyed me suspiciously.

Dad put his arm around Mom and said, "Don't question it. Let's go."

Her smile, along with the color on her cheeks, was priceless. "Want to grab a hand towel to dry off your sweaty hands?" I teased.

Dad looked confused. "What do you mean?"

Chuckling, Mom grabbed her purse from the hook by the door and said, "Let's get to our date."

The second the door shut, I rubbed my hands together. "What do you want to do?"

"Netflix?" Tarra suggested.

"Dream bigger," Cara said.

I looked more closely at her. "Are you wearing eyeliner?"

"Yeah? So?"

"You're eight years old!" I said.

"I've worked more than you," she mouthed back.

I rolled my eyes and walked to the couch. "Great, they've gone Hollywood on me." To be fair though, they did have a leg up on me in some ways. They definitely would when their movie aired. But after dealing with an eighteen-year-old guy who had daddy issues, I could handle their nonsense.

Cara stood by the door, getting a glittery backpack from the hook. "Aren't we going out?"

"You can drive, working woman," I said, grabbing the remote from the coffee table and flicking on the TV. "Or order an Uber. Oh wait, you have to be eighteen to get a cab. Shoot."

Tarra whispered something to our sister.

"Sorry," I said loudly. "I can't hear you over all the not-working I'm doing." To make matters even better, I changed the TV to the game show channel. "I'm just a dried-up, talentless senior."

"Fine," Cara said harshly. "We don't want to hang out with a boyfriendless loser anyway."

Her words rubbed me the wrong way, and I said, "No boyfriend? Huh? How about the school's wide receiver?"

Their eyes widened in surprise, and I immediately regretted my outburst. The twins could keep a secret about as well as a news anchor.

"What?" Tarra squealed. "Are you dating Ryker? I thought you didn't like him!" She jumped on one side of the couch, and Cara landed on the other. "Is that what Mom was talking to you about earlier this week? I overheard her say something about a date, and I thought it was Ginger. No way did I think it could be you."

I glared at my little sister. "I thought you were better than this."

She glared at me, but Tarra said, "We're happy for you! Now can we go do something fun? Please? We've been working nonstop, and Mom got the craft table guy to start serving things from Ripe, and I just want some fast food, *please*."

My heart melted, just a little. It had to be hard working all the time as an eight-year-old, living in a new city surrounded by adults who demanded adult work of you. "Fine," I said. "But you're both riding in the back."

I texted Mom and Dad and told them we were going out to get food, and then we went downstairs to the car. I found the greasiest burger chain I could, and at the last minute, I decided to get an extra meal for Ginger. This would be a fun way to surprise her.

I put in the directions to her dorm, and while the twins ravenously ate their dinner, I navigated the roads to UCLA. Once we got out of the car in the parking lot, Tarra said, "Do you think she'll be here?"

I shrugged. "If she's not, more for us, right?"

"True," Cara said.

I started toward the towering dorm building, and they followed behind me. We rode up the elevator to the top floor, and I couldn't help but realize how uninterested I was in all the college guys we passed. They were cute, sure, but none of them held a candle to Ryker.

I was falling, hard, and still waiting to see if he'd catch my heart or not.

"Which dorm is hers?" Cara asked.

"This one." I stopped in front of the door with

809 on the front and knocked.

"One second!" Ginger called.

I grinned at my other two sisters and held up the bag of fast food.

The second she saw us, Ginger squealed, bypassing the food altogether to give us each a big hug. "Come in!" she said. "Rachel went home, so it's just us."

I walked into their room, which looked so cute with the lofted beds and twinkle lights strung around. The twins looked around as Ginger grabbed the bag of food and sat on the floor to eat it.

"You guys are a godsend," Ginger said. "I was about to order food because I couldn't make it to the dining hall in time—they close early on the weekends."

I made a mental note to check the dining hall times at whatever college I went to. The twins climbed on her bed, and I sat at her desk. She had books on a video-editing software open in front of her monitor.

"How was your week?" she asked all of us.

Cara folded her arms over her chest. "Apparently Cori's was better than all of ours."

Ginger's brows drew together while I silently

begged Cara to shut her fat mouth.

"We hosted the mathletes this week. Catered lunch," I said quickly.

"I meant your boyfriend," Cara said. "Apparently she's dating Ryker!"

I closed my eyes in frustration. Why did Cara have to go diva on us now? Couldn't she have waited until *after* I moved out of the house?

"What?" Ginger said. "Is that a joke?"

I glared at Cara, and Ginger said, "Oh my gosh, it's not a joke." She set her burger down, looking absolutely horrified. "Cori, you're not...dating him, are you? Please say no."

I couldn't lie. Not to the sister I'd shared a bedroom with my entire life. So I decided to go with the truth, to beg forgiveness instead of permission. I lifted my chin and said, "He's my boyfriend."

The line between her eyebrows grew even deeper. "Cori, I thought you were smarter than that."

I was prepared to beg forgiveness, to defend my character, but Ginger's words cut me deeper than I could have prepared for. "What?" I asked. "I fall for a guy you don't like and all of a sudden I'm stupid?"

Ginger shook her head. "Just because everyone

else falls for his game didn't mean you had to!"

"It's not a game, Ginger." I drew up all my strength to explain. To stay calm. I knew she wouldn't react well, right? I just had to help her understand what I saw in him. She had to know that he wasn't the same person who had taunted her all those days. "He's different now."

"Please." She rolled her eyes. "People don't change."

"Well Ryker has," I argued. "He called and apologized to you, and he's kept the other guys from picking on my friends and me."

"Yeah, until he gets what he wants from you," Ginger said bitterly.

My mouth fell open. "You think *that's* all he wants from me? That's all I have to offer?" I hadn't meant to cry, but now my eyes were stinging, and I was standing up from her chair. I knew Ginger would have a hard time coming around, but for her to suggest what she had...

"I'll be in the parking lot when the twins are ready to go." I wiped my eyes and walked toward the door.

"Cori, come on," Ginger said. "You can't honestly believe he cares about you."

"I do." I sniffed. "Why can't you?"

FORTY-NINE

THAT NIGHT, I lay on the couch in the apartment, staring at the ceiling and wondering why Ginger's words had bothered me so much. I'd known she'd react poorly, right? Wasn't that the whole reason for keeping the secret?

A part of me had been holding out hope that she'd support me—that she'd trust my judgement. And now, a part of me worried that what she'd said was true.

My phone vibrated, and I held it up, the bright light making me squint. I dimmed the screen and read the text from Ryker.

Ryker: We won! I keep looking around Waldo's for you. I wish you were here.

My lips turned into an easy smile as his words smoothed the jagged edges of my heart.

Cori: That's a coincidence because I wish you were here too.

Ryker: Can I see you when you get back?

Cori: Please?

Ryker: It's a date.

Cori: Tell me how you played. I want to imagine you in those football pants.

Ryker: I just laughed out loud and now all my friends want to know who I'm texting. Thanks for that.

Cori: My pleasure.

Ryker: I scored three TDs. Ran for 177 yards.

Cori: That's a lot, right?

Ryker: Not shabby.

Ryker: How's your family?

Cori: They've been better. Cara has been a complete prima donna all weekend. And Ginger's mad at me.

Ryker: Why?

I closed my eyes, not wanting to make him feel bad. I knew how it felt to not be good enough, and I didn't want to give him that feeling, not when it was so far from the truth.

Ryker: You can tell me.

I let out a sigh. I wanted to be open with him, share the fears Ginger's words had stirred up in me. And then, I realized, I had to. I didn't want a relationship built on a card tower of lies and secrets.

Cori: She found out we're together and she thinks you don't really like me.

Now that I typed it, the whole thing seemed ridiculous. Ryker hadn't done anything since we started dating to make me feel like he wasn't all in.

Ryker: Why wouldn't I like you?

Cori: That's what I said!

Ryker: That's my girl.

My cheeks warmed at the casual way he called me his. It made me feel better, more secure.

Ryker: I know it will take time, but I'll show her how much you mean to me.

Cori: And how much is that?

I bit my lip, waiting for his answer. I wasn't sure what I was expecting, but Ryker's next message wasn't it.

Ryker: I'll show you. Sunday night.

Butterflies gently fluttered their wings in my stomach as I imagined how he might show me. What that would mean for us, for our future. We only had a week until the homecoming game and then three weeks until the end of the season if they made it past the playoffs. Two if they didn't.

Cori: I can't wait.

The rest of the weekend was...awkward. Ginger was mad at me and hardly said two words as we checked out the stars on Hollywood Boulevard. Cara spent most of her time on a phone the producer had given her to grow a social media following. Mom and Dad held hands like I wished I was doing with Ryker.

And me? I tried not to think of Ryker every second of the day or what we'd be doing later.

Finally, finally, it was time for us to go home on Sunday, and Dad agreed to drop me off at Brentwood Marina for my date with Ryker. I'd only been here once before with Dad to pick up a shipment of seafood for the store, but it looked bigger than I remembered. Had they been expanding?

My phone told us to make a right, and as Dad turned the car, Ryker came into view wearing white sneakers, navy pants, and a sweater that hugged his muscled shoulders like I wanted to.

His hair was spiked haphazardly, and I realized

how much it had grown since the beginning of the year. I liked it like this—it seemed less severe than the close-cropped cut he'd worn before.

Dad glanced from Ryker to me and said, "Do you know what he has planned?"

"Not a clue," I said.

He chuckled as he pulled alongside Ryker and rolled down the window. "You better take care of our girl."

Ryker saluted. "Yes, sir."

I shook my head at the pair of them and opened the door. "I can take care of myself."

"Of course," Dad said. "That's how I raised you. See you home by ten."

Ten o'clock, on a school night? I smiled big. "See you then."

As Dad drove away, Ryker slipped his fingers through mine, and I couldn't help but soak in the moment, the smell of his cologne mingling with the salty air coming off the ocean.

He leaned over and kissed the top of my head. "How's my girl?"

I held his arm and rested my chin on his shoulder. "Better now. I missed you."

He kissed my forehead. "Me too."

"Where are we going?" I asked, glancing

around the rows of boats around us, ranging from small ships to massive yachts.

He pointed toward the end of the dock to a large yacht. "I thought we could watch the sunset on the water. How does dinner with a view sound?"

My heart swelled. "Incredible," I breathed. I'd imagined having a boyfriend before—someone I could go to prom with or hang out with at the movies. Never had I imagined him planning something so romantic, or enjoying it quite this much.

His smile lit up the entire marina as he gripped my hand tighter and led me down the dock. The planks creaked under our feet until we reached the gleaming white boat. Ryker held my hand as I walked up the steps to the boat's deck, and he led me to the head of the boat where a table with flickering votive candles waited.

As I sat, he lifted the cover off of a charcuterie board and popped the cork on a bottle of champagne. The bubbles spilled over the edge as he tipped it, filling two glasses for us.

I stared in awe at the setup. How much time had gone into planning this? I decided to appreciate it. I mean, how could I not with the lowering sun casting warm rays over his skin, making his eyes shine.

"This is amazing," I said, taking a sip of champagne. The bubbles fizzed over my tongue, instantly warming and lifting me from the inside out.

He held out his glass. "It's all for you, Cori."

I clinked my glass to his and drank again. "I can't wait for football season to be over," I admitted.

"Me neither." He glanced down at the table, the flames flickering in his eyes as he looked back to me. "It feels like every second I'm not with you is fantasy."

"What do you mean?" I asked, tilting my head.

His hand covered mine on the table. "I mean I never feel more myself than I do when I'm with you."

I could understand what he meant. "I've never felt more seen than I do with you."

He reached up and tucked a loose strand of hair behind my ear. "I see you."

My heart warmed, fuller than it had ever been. I glanced over the water, watching the sun sink even lower. Its light hit the clouds just right, creating a beautiful cascade of orange, yellows, pinks, and purples. The scene reflected on the rolling water, surrounding us with such pure beauty it brought tears to my eyes.

I'd never been happier than I was in that

moment, and I hadn't even shared it with my friends. I couldn't wait to share this with them, to show them how beautifully Ryker had treated me when given the chance.

I glanced to him, seeing the sunset reflected in his eyes, and I realized... I loved him. I loved this rough-around-the-edges guy across from me because he'd given me a glimpse of his heart of gold.

"You're beautiful," he breathed.

With a smile, I wholeheartedly said, "So are you."

FIFTY

ON MONDAY AT SCHOOL, I walked to my locker feeling on top of the world. Ryker hadn't been in the parking lot with his friends, so I hoped I'd see him at his locker. But when I reached mine, he was nowhere to be seen. Feeling disappointed, I entered my combination and opened my door to see a glass container filled with chocolate chips on the top shelf.

There was a folded piece of paper in front of the jar, and I picked it up.

In case you couldn't find your chocolate chips at home. – R

The note left a dopey grin on my face, and I set it back, reaching for the jar. It easily came open, and I popped a few pieces of chocolate in my mouth, savoring the rich flavor.

"Are you seriously that obsessed with chocolate?" Nadira asked beside me.

I nearly jumped out of my skin, then when I realized it was just her, I extended the glass container. "Want one?"

"Sure." She reached for a few pieces, and I put it back in my locker. "How was your weekend?" she asked.

I shrugged, wishing I could tell her about Ginger's reaction. But I couldn't without bringing up everything else, and that day wouldn't come until football season was over. "It was fine. I still haven't gotten a homecoming dress."

"My mom ordered mine online," Nadira said. "I'm pretty sure she had a calendar reminder set so she wouldn't forget."

I laughed; that was so like Nadira's mom. "Do you like it at least?"

Even though Nadira usually didn't like dressing up, she seemed genuinely excited. "She got it off this vintage site. It's this beautiful deep red with off-the-shoulder straps, and it fades to black at the bottom of the dress."

"It sounds gorgeous," I said. "Can she order me one?"

Dir laughed. "That's more up Des's alley. Maybe you can get her to go shopping with you?"

I nodded, about to reply when I caught sight of Ryker out of the corner of my eye. He was walking into Mrs. Hutton's health class, and he looked...incredible. I loved the way his expression just relaxed when he thought no one was looking, when he didn't have anything to prove.

"Stare much?" Nadira said, hitting my arm.

My cheeks flushed bright red as I hurriedly looked away. "Just zoned out."

"Uh huh." She bumped my shoulder. "He's good-looking, but he's a jerk, remember?"

Because I couldn't speak, couldn't agree, I simply nodded.

"This is me," she said, pointing toward current events. "See you at lunch?"

"Yeah," I said. "See you later."

Focusing on my homework all day proved almost impossible, but when I asked Des if she'd help me shop for homecoming dresses, she gave me a fair reason to be distracted.

"Be thinking about what style you want," she said. "We've got to hustle!"

With that order in place, and Faith agreeing to come with us, I focused on my "assignment." Although Ryker wouldn't be my date, maybe we could dance together? Or at least sneak a kiss before the night was over. I wanted him to see me in my dress and wish he could be with me just as much as I wanted to be with him.

Finally, the last bell rang, and I immediately met Des and Faith by Des's locker. She held up a pair of football cleats.

"For my dress?" I teased.

She rolled her eyes. "Mom brought them for me. I need to give them to Diego."

I didn't need an excuse to go hangout by the boys' locker room and maybe catch a glimpse of Ryker in his practice gear. "I'm not in any rush," I said. "My dad actually gave me the evening off."

"Yay," Faith said. "Maybe we can grab dinner at Waldo's when we get done dress shopping?"

"I'm in," Des said, and I agreed.

The crowd in the halls thinned the closer we got to the gym and the locker rooms. How had it been only a month ago that I'd caught Aiden outside and asked for his help in a prank that changed everything? It felt like forever.

We drew closer to the locker room and stood

outside the door, but the boys' voices were carrying from downstairs.

Faith creased her brows. "Isn't locker room talk private?" she asked. "Should we stand somewhere else?"

"Shh," Des said, leaning closer. "This is going to be good."

I felt the same as her, leaning closer. Grant's voice carried up the stairs. "Come on, man, when are you going to tap that cow?"

Another guy said, "Why would Ryker have sex with Red? I wouldn't go near her with a ten-foot pole. And you know I have one."

The sound of snapping towels and laughter sounded up the stairs, but I felt like I was hearing them through a tunnel.

"I dunno," another guy said. "I've heard redheads are good in bed."

A sinking feeling filled my gut. They weren't talking about me. They couldn't be...

"Shut up," Ryker said, but not with enough force to silence them.

"Come on," Grant said. "I hate watching those cows walk around like they own the place."

"Right?" another guy said. "Unless...you *do* like her."

A hush fell over the locker room like they were all waiting for what Ryker said next. My stomach was tight, churning, as I did the same.

Ryker's voice rose above the silence, cutting straight to my heart. "Mark my words. Cori Nash will know where she belongs by the end of the football season. And me? I'll enjoy every second."

A din erupted in the locker room, but I couldn't hear anymore. I spun on my heel and ran across the gym despite Coach Ripley's shouts about no street shoes on the court. I didn't care. I had to get as far away from the ugliness I'd heard as I could. As far away from the ripping in my chest as possible.

I stopped, gasping for breath, on the front steps of the school. Burning tears streamed down my cheeks. Each inhale hurt, and each exhale ripped me apart. What had I just heard?

This was all a game to Ryker? I'd been falling in love, and he was playing a joke? It made my vision grow blurry and my head feel hot. How could this happen? How could the guy I'd been with the night before be the same guy I'd heard only seconds ago?

"Cori!" Des said, hurriedly coming to a stop beside me. "What was that about?"

I tried to talk, but a wail escaped my lips instead. "How could he say that?" I asked.

Faith sat on my left and put her arms around me. "It was awful."

I gasped for breath, wiping at my eyes, and Des put her hand on my cheek. She turned my face toward her and said, "Cori, what is going on?"

"I love him, okay?" I said so loudly my words echoed off the concrete. "I love him, and I kept it a secret, and it was all a *game* to him."

Des's full lips parted. "You what?"

I stood, feeling claustrophobic under my friends' stares. "I dated him! I've *been* dating him."

"For how long?" she asked.

I shook my head, unable to reason what I'd experienced with Ryker with what I'd heard coming out of his mouth. "Weeks. A month, I don't know."

I'd expected the surprise on Des's face, but the hurt was even worse. "Why didn't you tell us?"

I shook my head, biting back more angry tears. Of course now I wasn't only the butt of a joke that everyone was in on but me, but I was also a bad friend. I stood and said, "I've got to go."

I ran the rest of the way to my van and peeled out of the parking lot. As I paused at the stop sign, I saw Ryker leaving the locker room, his fingers hooked through the face mask on his helmet.

As if he felt me looking, he turned to me and

gave me a heartbreakingly wide smile and lifted his fingers in a wave.

Before a fresh round of sobs could come, I turned and drove away from him and every single lie I'd fallen for.

That night, message after message came through my phone, first from Des and Faith, and then from Adriel and Nadira. They were worried about me. Wanted to understand what was happening. But how could I tell them when I didn't understand it myself?

The worst message was from Ryker.

Ryker: Did you get the chocolate chips?

I didn't respond, just stared at the latest message, not wanting to see all the ones that had come before. The ones where I'd admitted how much I cared for him. How much I missed him.

How stupid I had been to fall head over heels for him.

Another message filled the bottom of the screen.

Ryker: I special ordered them from Germany. I hope you liked them.

I closed my eyes, not able to reconcile this Ryker with the one I'd heard earlier. How could those people say those things about me—call me fat, untouchable—with no reaction from Ryker? The guy I'd fallen for would have stood up for me. Would have told them exactly how he felt about me instead of letting them disparage me in front of the entire football team.

But that was the only explanation. Ryker wasn't the guy I had fallen for. I'd fallen for a fantasy, something that didn't exist in the real world. No matter how much I wanted it to.

FIFTY-ONE

I KNEW I was being a crappy friend. I knew it when I ignored all my friends text messages the night before. I knew it when I pulled into my parking spot at school, hoping I could make it to first hour without talking to anyone.

But all I could see was the guy standing with his friends around his ridiculous black truck.

He met my gaze and smiled, but tears immediately flooded my eyes and I looked away. Why I hadn't just pretended to be sick, I didn't know. But I was here now, and no way was I running away or backing down.

But while I was trying to look anywhere but at Ryker, my eyes landed on my four friends standing by the base of the stairs.

My chest tightened and my feet slowed. How could I approach them when I'd lied to them? Kept secrets? We were supposed to be in this together, and I'd gone off on my own. And for what? Some guy who clearly didn't care about me at all.

Slowly, I reached them, and they stared at me like I was a stranger. Nadira especially looked at me through guarded eyes.

I stood in front of them, clenching my backpack straps like they were my last hope. Maybe they were, because I had nothing left to hold on to.

"Hey," Faith said softly, breaking the silence.

I looked at her, thinking that maybe I had betrayed her most of all. The person I took up the ax for had just been a pawn in my own demise.

"I'm sorry," I said finally and turned to walk away.

"Wait," Des said, grabbing my hand.

"What else is there to say?" I asked, turning back toward them. "I lied to you. I've been seeing Ryker for weeks without telling you. The same guy we all fought to take down! I'm just as pathetic as all those other girls who throw themselves at him."

Nadira tilted her head. "Cori..."

My eyes stung, and I blinked them quickly. "I

wouldn't blame you if you never wanted to talk to me again."

"Hey," Adriel said, "we're here for you. I mean, come on, I could see why you'd want to keep something like that a secret. It's not like he's a jerk or anything," she added sarcastically.

I laughed despite myself and wiped at my eyes. "Maybe I just didn't want to hear what I knew you all would say."

Des sighed, pressing her lips together. "We would have told you he's a chauvinistic pig who is constantly directing blood flow to the wrong part of his body....which, I can't blame you for not wanting to hear."

I shook my head, laughing again, but the laugh quickly transformed to a sob. "Stop making me laugh. I'm heartbroken, remember?"

Nadira reached out and pulled me into a hug. "But you're also Cori. And you don't stay down for long."

I hugged her tight, wanting to believe her words, even though they felt the farthest thing from true.

"Come on," Des said. "We need to get into school. I have a meeting with Birdie this morning.

Maybe I can get her to call in an order for an emergency Curvy Girl Club meeting."

"Please," I said, walking up the stairs with Nadira's arm around my shoulders. I couldn't bear the thought of seeing Ryker in the lunchroom, surrounded by all the people who had made it their goal to humiliate me and break my heart.

As I went through each of my classes, I felt like I was seeing my classmates through different eyes. How many of them were as innocent as they looked? How many of them had known? How many would cheer when I was taken down?

The thought made my heart break even more, and I swore if this pain grew any bigger, I wouldn't be able to move.

One breath at a time, one painful heartbeat at a time, I made it until lunchtime without falling apart. When the bell rang and I went to the AV room, I was absolutely exhausted. But my friends were there, with an all-dessert meal, ready to hold me while I cried and dry every tear.

I held on to them, thankful I had anything to hold on to at all.

After school, I hid out in a bathroom to make sure I wouldn't see Ryker at my locker. A good ten minutes of scrolling social media later, I went to my locker to get my homework. But when I saw who was standing next to it, I turned right back around.

The hallways were empty, which meant I could hurry away as fast as I pleased. Unfortunately, it also meant Ryker didn't have people to dodge around as he followed me. He easily caught up to me and skidded to a stop in front of me.

"Cori, what's going on?" he asked, his eyes full of concern I now knew was fake.

I glared at him, all my hurt, all my anger, coming out in my words. "I guess I finally figured out *where I belong.*"

His eyebrows drew together. "What are you talking about?"

My hands clenched at my side, my nails digging into my palms. "I heard you in the locker room yesterday." My voice echoed off the empty hallway around us, but I didn't care. This pain was too much to hold inside.

Part of me wanted him to tell me it was a misunderstanding. That where I belonged was with him, but his lips only parted and he stood before me, speechless.

I had been right.

Tears stung my eyes, and I didn't even bother blinking them back. "You're a pig." I pushed past him, but he caught my arm and said, "Cori, wait!"

I glared at him, all the pain in my body coming through my gaze. "Don't touch me. Don't *ever* touch me again."

Without waiting for his response, I tore my hand from his grip and walked away with my head held high, just like I should have all those weeks ago.

FIFTY-TWO

I CHANGED into my jeans and Ripe T-shirt in the store's back bathroom. Knox was there in the back, breaking down boxes again, but I couldn't meet his eyes. I was so ashamed—by how I'd treated him, by how I'd ignored his advice.

He'd been right. Just like Ginger. And I couldn't stand the idea of hearing it. But Dad told me that Knox and I needed to work together to get the latest shipment out on the shelves, so I had no choice.

I pulled a box cutter down from the shelf and started on the boxes on the opposite end of the storage room. For the better part of an hour, we worked in silence, but soon we were only a few feet away from each other, and the tension in the air was so thick even a box cutter couldn't have put a dent in it.

"Cori," Knox said finally. "We've got to talk."

I looked down at my box, at my dry skin from working with the cardboard. "We don't have to," I said, still not meeting his eyes.

"*I* do. Will you listen?"

Slowly, I turned to him, the care in his expression almost too much to bear.

He looked down at the box cutter in his own hands and then back at me. "I just wanted to apologize to you for...what I said. I thought I was being a good friend, but I talked to Courtney about it and she helped me see that sometimes being a friend means letting someone make their own choices and celebrating them if they fly but catching them if they fall."

My heart hurt, but in a good way this time. "You talked to Courtney about me?"

His bashful smile was adorable. "Obviously I needed to call in backups. I lost my best work friend."

I chuckled tearfully and shook my head. "You didn't lose your best work friend. I just...lost myself for a while."

"What happened?" he asked, genuine concern clear on his face.

I let out a sigh and blinked quickly, not ready for the flood of tears to come back. It seemed like I had an endless supply of them lately. "I just finally learned who he really is."

Knox outstretched his arms, and I fell into them just as easily as I had fallen for Ryker. But this time, I knew Knox would catch me. I knew he was my friend.

After a moment, Knox pulled back and looked me in the eye. "Cori, you are an amazing girl. And I promise someday you'll meet a guy who will treat you like you deserve. You won't have to guess where you stand or whether he's who he says he is."

I barely managed a smile. That idea seemed as far off as a complete fantasy. It would be a long time before I trusted anyone with my heart, let alone all of me, but I appreciated the gesture. "Thanks, Knox."

He patted my back, and we walked our carts out to the aisles, unloading the shipment like Dad had asked in a quiet companionship. After a couple of hours of solid work, Dad came by and said, "Nice work, you two."

"Thanks, sir," Knox said.

I smiled at Dad. "Thanks."

"Cori," Dad said, "I was wondering if you wanted to get supper?"

"Um, sure?" I said. Dad hardly ever took off work early, much less to spend time with me.

"Meet you outside?" he said. "We can take my car."

I nodded, and as Dad walked away, I said goodbye to Knox.

"See you," he said, "and remember, keep your chin up. Good things are coming."

I managed a smile before walking to the back. I changed back into my school uniform and went to the parking lot where Dad had his car running. I hoped he had the heater on because this fall chill was starting to get to me.

I got into the car, enveloped in warm air, and said, "Where are we going?"

"I thought La Belle?" he said.

My eyes widened. "Italian food? Yes please."

With a chuckle, he put the car in reverse and pulled out of the parking lot.

"What's the special occasion?" I asked. "I'm assuming it has to be for us to get gluten."

"Just wanted to talk to you about something."

His eyes stayed on the road, but I noticed the lines around them. They seemed deeper than usual.

"Is everything okay?" I asked.

"I think so."

We rode in silence for the rest of the short trip, and when we got into the restaurant, he was too busy talking with the waitstaff to say much. But finally when we got seated and ordered our food, I asked, "Dad, what's going on?"

He reached into an inner pocket on his jacket and pulled out an envelope. "I got this today, along with a call from the basketball coach asking if you'd commit to the team."

I looked at the letter, addressed from Chaminade University of Honolulu, and my mouth fell open. "*What?*"

Dad looked at me, his blue eyes full of emotion. "You applied for college in Hawaii?"

I swallowed, realizing that, for once, he understood what I wanted. "I did."

"Why?" he asked, even though I could tell we both knew.

"I needed somewhere I could be me. Not Ginger's little sister or Paul's daughter." My voice cracked. "Somewhere I wouldn't be constantly reminded how little I mattered to the people I love most." I hadn't meant to, but I broke down, sobbing over the table, right there in the middle of La Belle, surrounded by fancy businesspeople and couples dressed up for dates. And there I was in my little school uniform feeling every bit of the helpless child I was.

Dad scooted out of his side of the booth and came to my side, holding me tight. "Oh, honey. Honey, honey, honey," he soothed.

I cried in his shoulder for everything I thought I had and everything I lost. Everything I'd been so careless to wish for.

When I finally caught my breath, I wiped at my eyes with the white cloth napkin, rubbing away dark spots of makeup and my endless supply of tears. I felt vulnerable, like Dad had seen every piece of me, and it was too late to bother retreating now.

He held my hand between us and said, "I know it's been hard, having the sisters you do. You know how your mom reacted to Ginger's illness, and I know she's felt like the twins need her. You've always been our constant. Our Coriander. The one we can depend on to do what's right."

"But I don't want to be depended on," I sobbed, my throat raw. "I want my *parents*."

The ache in my chest felt hollow, like it had

been there so long it was just as much a part of me as my red hair or the freckles that dusted my nose and cheeks.

Dad rubbed his hand over his beard, letting out a deep breath. "What can I do?"

His words hit my heart in a way nothing had before, because for the first time I felt like he really cared to hear my answer. But the problem was, I'd gone so long fading into the background, asking for what I really wanted sounded pathetic.

I shook my head.

"Tell me," he said.

I looked into his eyes, which were so much like my own. "Pay attention? And then care?"

His nod was quick. "I promise, Cor. Tonight's about you. Tell me about this college."

As our appetizers arrived, I told him about applying for all those colleges, which felt like so long ago. And then I told him about what Nadira's dad had offered for Brentwood U.

"Wow." Dad sat back in his chair, rubbing his beard. "That's incredible, Cori."

I smiled. "It is. And I know basketball won't last forever, but I'm happy it's here for now."

"It doesn't matter if it lasts for a day or a year. A memory lasts a lifetime."

He was right. I pulled a piece of a breadstick apart, thinking it over.

"And Cori?"

I looked up at him. "Yeah?"

"If you go to Brentwood U, I promise I'll be at every damn home game and half of the ones away."

My hands stalled, leaving my bread soaking in the oil. "What about the store?"

"The store will always be here, and I'm starting to realize you will not." His voice cracked, and he said, "Come here, kid."

I leaned into his hug, realizing that for once, I felt seen by the most important man in my life. And maybe that's what I'd needed all along.

FIFTY-THREE

IN THE MORNING, I got to school early, hoping to get to my locker before Ryker. The problem? He and his friends acted like old men in a coffee shop, shooting the bull every dang morning.

I kept my eyes forward as I walked by, but I could hear a commotion as someone parted from the group. Only seconds later, Ryker came to walk beside me.

"You didn't answer my calls last night," he said.

I kept walking, picking up my pace. "Nope."

"All seven of them."

"So you *can* count."

"I guess I deserved that."

We reached the stairs, and I turned on him. "What are you doing here?" I demanded. "Embarrassed you lost and now you're showing all your friends you still have a chance?"

"No, Cori, if you'd just let me explain—"

"No!" I cried. "Why can't you understand, Ryker? I don't want to hear anything from you! It was all a game..." My eyes watered, and I blinked quickly before looking back to him. "Footballs might be fun to toss around, but my heart is not a game."

He held his hand to his chest. "I didn't say it was."

"You didn't need to. You showed me just fine." I started up the stairs. "Don't call me anymore."

A few kids around us oohed, and I was sure our argument would be all over the school and at least half the tri-city area within the hour, but I didn't care. Ryker had already made me a laughingstock —what was a little more humiliation?

"Shut up," Ryker barked at them, but I just rolled my eyes and kept walking away. He could fight all he wanted, but no amount of begging or cajoling would change anything. This was over.

We were over.

Nadira offered to ask for us to sit in the AV room again for lunch the next day, but I was done. No more hiding. No more falling into Ryker's games. Any of them. I held my head high as I walked through the serving line and picked items from the hEAlthy menu. Then I went straight to the table with my girls, not worrying whether he was looking at me. Trying not to worry about whether or not he cared.

I sat in the open chair between Faith and Adriel and said, "Let's start planning. What's going to be the ultimate prank?"

"What do you mean?" Des asked.

"Ryker," I said, trying not to choke over his name. "We're obviously not done teaching him a lesson. What's our next move?"

Faith and Nadira gave each other a look, and Faith said, "Cori, don't you think we should just let it go?"

My mouth opened and closed. "L-let it go?"

After giving Nadira another look, she nodded. "If you pull a prank on Ryker, you might hurt him. You might humiliate him, but then what? You'll be doing exactly the same thing to him that he's done to you. You're better than that."

I scoffed, wiping at my watering eyes. "Knox,

Ginger, you guys. Everyone seems to think I'm better than I am."

Adriel put her hand over mine. "If we can all see it, why can't you?"

I blinked quickly, shaking my head. "I don't know. But I can't just sit back and let him win."

Faith leaned forward. "What if... what if that's how you win?"

"What do you mean?" I asked.

"Bullies want to tear you down so you feel just as bad as they do on the inside," Faith said. "The *ultimate* failure to them is watching you thrive. Watching you *live your life* the way you want to, regardless of the bullying, regardless of the games."

Des clapped her hands. "Amen."

"But she forgot one thing," I said, looking at each of them. "That he'll never have friends as good as you." I shook my head, trying to steady my quivering jaw. "Ones who hold you accountable when you mess up and love you even harder after you fall."

Adriel put her arm around me. "You've done the same for us."

I smiled now, taking in the Curvy Girl Club 2.0. "Ugh, I hate it though."

"What?" Nadira asked, alarmed.

"Because, this means Birdie was *right*."

My friends started laughing.

"Only you," Des said.

I couldn't help but agree. Only me. I'd be the only one dumb enough to fall for a bully. But I'd be the one to pick myself up and find the best revenge of all. The ability to see myself through my own eyes. It was about damn time.

FIFTY-FOUR

AFTER SCHOOL, I found Des and Faith waiting for me at the top of the stairs. I knew they'd been waiting for me because the second I walked out the doors, they stood up from leaning against the bannister.

"What are you two doing?" I asked.

Des looped her arm through mine and walked down the stairs with me. "Taking you dress shopping, obviously."

I shook my head. "I'm not going to the dance."

"Why not?" Faith asked.

"Yeah," Des said. "Faith's brother got us a limo and everything."

We reached the bottom of the stairs, and I shook my head. "Well, first, I have to work tonight.

And second, why would I want to go and watch the *IT* girls be all over Ryker all night?"

Des rolled her eyes. "So what about Ryker? There are other hot guys in our school and you know it."

I raised my eyebrows. "The same guys I've been in school with for at least four years and have *never made a move* on me?"

"And," Faith said, "you can just ask your dad for an hour or two off, right? It shouldn't take too long to find something that will look amazing on you."

"Exactly," Des agreed. "And besides, it's not all about guys. What about the CGC 2.0? We'll be there too, and if you haven't noticed, I'm the only one with a date, so it's not like you'll be alone all night."

"Right," Faith said. "So it's settled?"

I looked at Faith. "You've been spending way too much time with Des. You're getting pushy."

Faith laughed. "So that's a yes?"

I sighed. "Let me text my dad."

Des squealed excitedly and clicked her key fob so it honked. "We're taking my car."

We walked to her car, and I climbed into the back seat, which was honestly as much a feat of athleticism as scoring a basket. As soon as Dad texted me it was okay, she cranked her music and peeled out of the parking lot. I couldn't help but glance back at the football field where the team practiced. Ryker was somewhere among them, living his life.

I needed to live my own.

Des took us to Emerson Shoppes and walked into Vestito, a formal dress shop that ordered custom designs from all over the world. Ginger had gotten her prom dress from here the year before, so at least I knew they had some selection off the rack.

An associate dressed in a slick black dress offered to help us search, but Des promised her she had it covered. Honestly, I trusted my friends more than the size-two saleswoman. Most smaller girls just didn't get what would look good on bigger bodies.

"Let's head over here," Des said, walking toward one end of the store that had more of the plus-sized designs.

As we followed her, Faith asked, "What color are you looking for?"

"Anything but red or orange," I said. "It clashes with my hair." I fingered a green dress. "Or green. It would make me look like a leprechaun."

"Oh hush," Des said. "Green is beautiful on you."

Shaking my head, I picked through the rack, looking for a dress that spoke to me.

"What about this?" Faith held up a royal-blue gown with an asymmetrical hemline.

"Maybe," I said, and I swear the sales associate from earlier swooped in like she'd been listening the entire time.

"Let me get a fitting room ready," she said.

As the saleswoman walked away, Des leaned in and muttered, "She's so getting paid on commission."

"Mhmm," Faith agreed, and back to work we went. In less than half an hour, we had a pile full of dresses for me to try on. While they sat on fancy white couches with fizzing glasses of soda, I got to work in the dressing room.

Some people wanted to see everything, but I only left the dressing room if it was something really good. Which the first five weren't.

As a curvy girl, it was so hard to look at something on the hanger and see if it would fit right. With the way my body was shaped, it either fit everywhere but the chest was too tight, or it hugged my chest and left me drowning in fabric everywhere else.

Finally, I felt one that slid over my body like a glove. I stared in the mirror, surrounded by a soft light bar, and took in the view. The deep green sheath dress clung to my curves and accented my chest in a sweetheart neckline. Beading of the same color added texture to the dress without making it gaudy. I stood on my tiptoes, imagining how good my legs and butt would look with an extra lift.

I stepped out of the dressing room, tiptoeing to the platform so my friends could see me.

Faith sat up, her eyes widening, and clapped her hands together. Des gave me a pleased look.

"This is the one," Des said, nodding.

"Yes!" the saleswoman agreed. "And you so don't look like a leprechaun."

We each gave her a look, and she scurried away. I glanced back at myself in the mirror and ran my hands over the fabric, smiling at my reflection. I couldn't wait to wear this dress to homecoming, regardless of who would or wouldn't see me. As long as I could see myself.

FIFTY-FIVE

ON MY WAY to the elementary school on Friday, I clutched Ryker's navy-blue jacket to my chest. I needed to give it back to him. Even if it smelled like him. Even if holding it made me feel like that happily ever after I'd been hoping for wasn't so far away. Maybe that was exactly why I had to return it. Because hoping for something that would never come only increased the heartbreak.

As I reached the halfway point to the elementary school, I got the feeling someone was watching me, and I had an idea who.

After taking a deep breath, I turned to see Ryker walking toward me. He wore the school-issued sweatpants and a tight gym T-shirt. No jacket, even though it was cold outside. I could help change that.

His walk changed as our eyes collided. He slowed, then moved with more purpose. His gray eyes flicked from mine to his jacket in my arms. No matter how much I wanted to hold on to it, I had to give it back.

Using all my willpower, I extended it toward him. "Sorry I haven't given it back sooner."

His hands hung limply at his sides. "Keep it." He continued walking past me, and my eyebrows drew together.

I followed him, having to walk quickly to keep pace with his long strides. "It's your jacket, Ryker, just take it."

"No."

"Why not?" I demanded.

He pressed the buzzer for the office to let us into the elementary school.

"*Why?*" I repeated.

"Because! I don't want another reminder of how much I messed up!" The door clicked, and he pushed inside, leaving me shocked, frozen.

No matter what I'd heard him say in the locker room, the pain in his voice seemed real. I recognized it in my own.

I rode home from school with Ryker's jacket sitting in my lap, the faded scent of his cologne rising to my nose. And I cried.

Why couldn't healing be linear?

Why couldn't I just hear what he said about me and move on with my life?

Why did each breath still hurt?

I folded my free hand in the navy fabric and let out a shaky breath. Maybe that was how it was with first love. It changed you forever and made you see what a risk it really was, handing over your heart.

My fingers itched to call Ginger, to ask her for advice, and if she didn't have any advice to give, at least some comfort. But I knew I wouldn't be getting that.

I'd betrayed her in one of the worst possible ways. I'd betrayed myself. Was still betraying myself, because if I was honest, I still wished Ryker and I could be together. That he would be the person I thought he was.

I drove down the street to our house, taking in the white brick and lawn gnomes out front, and seeing something I hadn't seen in a long time: Ginger's car parked in the driveway.

My mouth fell open, and I nearly slammed on the brakes. What was she doing here? She had told me she'd come back to help me get ready for the homecoming dance, but I thought that had fallen through.

I parked beside her car and left Ryker's jacket in the passenger seat. I didn't need her knowing how absolutely pathetic I was. Part of me wanted to stay in the car with the jacket. Not face her and let her know she'd been right. But not having her was worse than being embarrassed.

So I grabbed my backpack and walked to the front door. It was unlocked, so I pushed it open, and my eyes absolutely bugged out.

There in the living room were my mom, my dad, and all of my sisters.

"Surprise!" they yelled.

My mouth fell open. "What's going on? I thought you wouldn't be here until late!"

"We're done filming!" the twins cheered in unison.

Ginger came and put her arms around me, hugging me tight. "No way I'd miss your senior homecoming."

Mom came and hugged me next, whispering in

my ear, "Congratulations on your acceptance, Cori. We're so proud of you."

I hugged her that much tighter. "Thanks, Mom."

I still wasn't sure whether or not I'd go to Hawaii, but it felt nice to know I had the option. That I could go anywhere and be anything I wanted to be with my family's support.

Mom stepped back, and I hugged the twins. "Welcome home... even though we have to share the bathroom again."

We laughed together, and for a while, everything felt the same but different. We were all home together, but over the last few months, we'd all become different people. Ginger was a college student now, living on her own. The twins had starred in an actual movie. Mom had lived apart from Dad for the first time in twenty years. And Dad? He'd put the store second for the first time in his life.

Ginger wrapped her arm around my shoulders. "Want to get ready for the game together?"

"Are you going?" I asked. "Or is that too high school?"

She chuckled. "My friends are all going to be there. It's going to be a curvy girl reunion."

I smiled, hoping this time next year everyone in my Curvy Girl Club would be as close as they were. "Sure. But don't get mad about your desk."

She narrowed her eyes at me playfully. "Can't believe you took it over."

Mom looked at her watch. "You girls better hurry. It's supposed to start in an hour."

I looked at her in surprise. How did she know?

"What?" Mom said. "I read the *Emerson Essay*!"

I tried not to be pleased that Mom read the parents' newsletter even when she was away. Maybe she cared more about me than I thought.

"Okay," Ginger said, "we'll get going."

Ginger and I walked back to our room. As I walked to my closet to hang up my dress and pick out an outfit for the game, she sat at her desk, not commenting on all my stuff that sat atop its surface.

"So..." she said quietly.

"Can we just forget Ryker?" I asked, pulling out a pair of jeans and a baggy EA sweater. "I hate that he came between us."

Ginger nodded and pretended to zip her lips, then unzipped them slightly. "But can I say one thing?"

I closed my eyes, so not ready for another lecture. "Fine."

"I talked to my friends about what happened."

"Great," I muttered, unbuttoning my uniform top. "So they know what an idiot I am too?"

"Let me finish."

"Okay." I turned away from her to finish undressing.

"Zara had heard what happened between you two, and she reminded me how bad it felt to have my family be against the guy I loved. So whatever happens, if you break up forever or get back together tonight or ten years from now...I trust you. I trust you the way I always wanted Mom and Dad to trust me. And if that means you make a few mistakes—or forget to refill your inhaler and almost die in the middle of nowhere—I'll still be here for you."

I blinked, turning to her. Even though Ginger had messed up last year and gotten stuck in the country with an empty inhaler, I still looked up to her. She had found the love of her life, was accepted into her dream school, and was living each day on her own terms. What she thought of me mattered more than I cared to admit. "You mean it?" My voice came out small.

"Of course," she said softly. "That's what sisters are for."

FIFTY-SIX

WHILE DAD STAYED home and helped Mom and the twins settle in, Ginger and I took her car to the school. Riding in her passenger seat took me back to last year.

"Can you believe I've kept up with homework without doing it on the ride to school in the morning?" I asked.

Laughing, she said, "Honestly, no. What's it been like without having Mom looking over your shoulder every day?"

I shrugged. "Easier actually. When she was always telling me what to do, I wanted to do the opposite."

She snorted. "I get that."

"Are you excited to see your friends?" I asked.

With a big smile, she nodded. "I haven't seen Rory and Beckett in months. I've managed to catch up with everyone else at least once so far."

"Have Callie and Carson gotten married yet?" I asked, only half-joking. Each of her friends were in a relationship, but something about Callie and Carson felt special. Maybe because they'd been friends for so long before getting together.

Ginger chuckled. "Not yet, but I have a feeling the second they graduate, they'll be walking down the aisle."

"And you?" I teased.

"Don't even start. Mom's supersonic ears will overhear."

I laughed, but the second Emerson Academy's football stadium came into view, everything seemed a little less funny. Like my surroundings had been doused in shades of gray somehow.

I tried to act like everything was okay, because it was, in a way. I knew no matter what, I would be okay. But what had happened—my heartbreak, the lies, the humiliation—was not. It made me afraid to trust anyone else. Afraid to trust myself.

Ginger parked in the guest lot behind the

stadium and said, "Want to grab some concessions before we go in?"

I nodded and got out of the car. "You know I love the popcorn here. I can't eat as much of it when I'm playing basketball."

"Trying to stay in shape?"

"No," I said. "I can't eat it while I'm playing."

She giggled and walked beside me, glancing at her phone every so often.

"Are they here yet?" I asked.

Knowing I was talking about her friends, she said, "Zara's late, as usual. But Rory and Beckett saved me a seat."

I smiled. "That's exciting." We fell into line behind the other people who knew football went best with snacks. Along the concession stand, the booster club had hung posters of each football player, including their name and jersey number.

My eyes fell on the poster with Ryker's name. His picture, the one where he stared down the camera, faced off at me. There wasn't a hint of the guy I thought I knew in the photo. The one whose gray eyes sparkled when he laughed and caught the sunlight so beautifully at sunset.

Ginger followed my eyes. "Are you okay?"

I wrapped my arms around myself and gave what I hoped was a reassuring smile. "I will be."

"You're right," she agreed. "It's wild how quickly things change. Remember last year at football games Mom always forced us to bring quilts and earmuffs?"

I shivered a little in the cold. The sun hadn't even set, and I was already longing for the warmth of Waldo's Diner after the game. "Honestly, maybe we should have brought them tonight."

"There's hot chocolate for that," she said with a smile. "Besides, we can't admit our mom was right about something."

"True." I stepped up to the counter and put in an order for popcorn and a hot chocolate, then Ginger did the same, and we paid.

When we reached the bleachers, Ginger waved at her friends, then turned to me. "I'm going to go say hi to Mr. Davis. Can you catch a ride home tonight?"

"Sure," I said.

She smiled and gave me a hug. "See you in the morning, sis."

"Love you," I replied and started up the steps. I found Adriel, Faith, and Nadira a few rows back and went to sit with them.

"Hey," Adriel said gently, scooting over to give me a little more room on the edge of the bleacher.

"Hey." I forced a smile, trying to prove to them, and maybe even myself, just how fine I was. How easy it was to ignore the guy on the field who'd completely decimated my heart.

"Um, Cori?" Faith said.

"What?"

She pointed in the exact direction I was trying to avoid, and I saw Ryker standing on the sidelines, the football in his hands, staring at me. Even at this distance, I could see his eyes clearly, the conflict on his face.

He lifted one of his hands in a wave, but I turned away. I'd meant what I said to him. To myself.

"What is he doing?" Nadira asked. "You told him to leave you alone, right?"

I nodded. "Maybe we need to send a stronger message... Is it too late to stage a coup?"

Adriel chuckled. "Knowing you, you could pull it off."

"I'll take that as a compliment," I said, taking a sip of my cocoa.

"It was," Adriel affirmed.

I leaned my head against her shoulder for a

moment. Maybe this was the love story of my senior year—how a five-nine, plus-sized redhead came to love herself, exactly as she was. How she fell for four amazing girls and discovered just how fulfilling female friendship could be. How fulfilling life could be without a guy. Even one as incredible as Ryker had appeared to be.

Over the speaker system, Mr. Davis began announcing the players, announcing the homecoming game. I guarded my heart as Ryker caught the ball and the defense worked to tackle him. I guarded my gaze as I felt him looking at me from the sidelines. And finally, I guarded my heart as the homecoming royalty took the field.

Mr. Davis introduced each of the candidates, and my heart clenched at the mention of Ryker's name. He looked just as incredible in his football uniform as Isabella and Tatiana did in their shimmering dresses.

My lip trembled, thinking of all the possibilities I'd missed out on with the Ryker I'd known. No matter how the lie had come to light, I still missed the guy who acted like the sun rose and set with me.

"Our homecoming queen is Tatiana Robinson!" the cheer coach, Pam Alexander, announced over her microphone at the field. The crowd went wild, their cheers echoing in my mind.

I blinked quickly. I had thought I could handle this, the homecoming game, but I couldn't. The longer I sat here, the more I gave into wishes that couldn't possibly come true.

"Guys, I've got to go," I said.

"Want us to come with you?" Des asked.

I shook my head. "I'll see you tomorrow." I stood and began walking down the bleacher steps.

"And our king is Ryker Dugan," Pam said, making the entire crowd go into a frenzy. They began chanting his name.

I kept my eyes on the steps in front of me, my hand firmly on the railing, trying not to imagine the crown being placed on his head. Him leaning in to give Tatiana the customary kiss.

I finally reached the landing and turned to hear the speaker system breaking through the crowd.

"Cori, wait!" Ryker's voice caught me off guard, and I froze, my eyes snapping to the field. To his.

He held the microphone tightly in his hand, stepping toward me, shrugging off the red velvet cape. "Wait."

My mind didn't want to listen, but my heart had

control of my feet. They stayed firmly in place as the crowd fell silent, as Ryker swallowed and looked right at me, then to the entire audience taking him in.

He spun in a slow circle, seeing the home crowd and the opposite bleachers filled with visitors. Then he looked at me again. "I don't deserve this crown. And I don't deserve a second chance. But you, Cori, you deserve an apology."

My heart caught in my throat, and I covered my chest as if the presence of my hand would help resume its beating.

"The first day of school, I did what I always did. I made my friends laugh...at the expense of someone else. And Cori, she saw through the show and called me on it."

I closed my eyes, wishing more than anything that I hadn't spoken up that day. That I'd run for Mrs. Bardot and comforted Faith later, rather than sooner.

"And me, being the arrogant jerk I was, thought it a challenge," he continued. "I told my friends I was going to make her life miserable. Starting with her walk to school and ending with breaking her heart."

The aching in my chest told me that he'd won by scores.

Feedback squealed through the PA system, and I covered my ears, looking to the press box to see Ryker's father wrestling over the microphone with Mr. Davis. My mouth fell open as I watched two teachers hold him back and walk him out of the box.

The feedback stopped, and Ryker spoke into the microphone again, his voice surrounding me. "The problem was I had no idea who I was dealing with."

I snorted, tears flooding my eyes.

"Cori Nash is a stubborn, persistent, cunning...incredible, beautiful, *wonderful* woman."

The tears flowed freely now as I ached to believe each of his words.

"She showed me how cruel I'd been." He took a deep, shaky breath. "She showed me how good I could become."

My vision blurred until I blinked it clear.

"Cori, I'd apologize for everything, but if I hadn't gone through with it, I never would have known you the way I do now. What I am sorry for is ever hurting you. And I know I don't deserve a second chance; you've already given me more than

I deserved once. But I promise, I won't ruin it ever again."

My lips trembled as I took him in, his words, his eyes on me, hopefully waiting for my answer. But it couldn't be yes, because if it hurt this bad after one mistake, a second would surely break me.

I turned then and ran away from the field, away from the bleachers, away from the boy who held the microphone, and most of all, my heart.

FIFTY-SEVEN

THE AIR HAD FELT cold before, but now it was absolutely frigid compared to the hot tears streaming down my cheeks.

Ryker had said everything I'd wanted to hear, but I couldn't just forget what he'd done. I was hurt.

I was *scared*.

"Cori, wait!" he yelled, but this time it wasn't over the speaker system. He was only feet behind me, and I turned to see just him and me surrounded by cars in the parking lot.

I stared at him, still wearing his football uniform, his hair damp from sweat. "What are you doing here?" I asked, looking over his shoulder toward the field. "What about the game?"

Ryker stepped forward, each movement

purposeful until he was only a foot away. His head tilted as he took me in, those soulful gray eyes seeing through me like no one else did. "Footballs are fun to toss around." He reached up and brushed his thumbs over the tears on my cheeks. "But hearts aren't made for games."

My lips parted, but no words came out. I didn't even know where to start.

"Please, Cori," he breathed. "Give me a second chance."

"I..." I looked up at him, my heart and brain in a bigger battle than Ryker and I had ever been. "I don't know if I can."

I stepped back, and his hands hung limply in the air before he lowered them to his sides. "Why not?"

"Why not?" I let out an incredulous laugh and gestured between us. "Look at us! We're a mess."

"And?"

I rubbed my temples. "And you broke my heart."

He took a tentative step forward. "Mine's not feeling so great either."

"And you embarrassed me. I was the butt of everyone's joke."

He slowly stepped closer. "I don't know if you

saw what happened back there, but I kind of set the record straight."

I let out a frustrated groan. "How are you joking right now? Is this really just a game to you?"

"No!" he cried, raking his fingers through his hair. "Cori, I'm joking because if I showed you how much you meant to me, I'd be a damn puddle on the ground. I wouldn't be able to get up and keep walking after what I did to you. After what I lost." He beat at the pads covering his chest. "I'm here because I can't give up on us, Cori." Tears shone in his eyes, and his voice broke with emotion. "Not now that I know what I have to lose."

I stared at him, my heart begging me to just give in, to accept his apology and live the happily ever after I so desperately wanted. But I couldn't put my heart at risk, not so easily. "So what I heard in the locker room? I'm just supposed to forget it?"

"I was trying to be honest without getting kicked off the football team. I was going to tell them—tell everyone—when the season was over that where you belonged was with me."

"And now?" I asked.

"They know." He shrugged, stepping closer again. This time, I didn't back away. His right hand wound around my waist, pulling me ever so gently toward him. "Everyone knows, and I'm not wasting another second pretending to be the guy I was. I'm *yours*, Cori. Only yours."

My lips quivered, and tears flowed even more freely.

"Cori," he breathed, eyes full of concern as he wiped at my cheeks. "Baby, please don't cry. If you don't want this, I'll leave," he said desperately. "I'll go and never bother you again. Okay?"

The sobs came harder, and he held me to his own shaking chest. "Please don't cry."

So overwhelmed with emotions, I held him tightly, clinging to everything I'd wanted so badly. Letting myself realize that the nightmare was over. That maybe I hadn't been wrong about Ryker. That believing him now could be worth the risk.

I stepped back, sniffing and wiping at my eyes with the heels of my hands. "Ryker James Dugan."

He looked at me, desperation in his gray eyes.

I let out another mix of a sob and a laugh. "I know I shouldn't, but I love you. I love you with everything I have."

His lips split into a watery, tearful grin, and he hugged me again, his football pads crackling as I held him right back.

"I love you, Cori. I love you so, so much."

I lifted my chin and pressed my lips to his in the most tender kiss we'd ever shared. His hands weaved into the back of my hair, holding me so delicately like one wrong move could shatter this newfound love. But if I knew anything, it was that this feeling wasn't going away. I smiled against his lips, realizing I never wanted it to.

Cheering erupted around us. What seemed like half the school filled the parking lot, had followed us to watch the outcome.

"Great! They're in love!" Coach Ripley shouted. "NOW CAN YOU GET YOUR EVER-LOVING HEAD BACK IN THE GAME?"

Ryker laughed against my lips and said, "I guess this has to wait."

"Go," I said, smiling even bigger.

"I'll see you after the game?" he asked.

"Right in the end zone," I promised.

He gave me a final kiss and jogged away.

While everyone walked back to the stands, my friends walked toward me. Des was grinning ear to ear while Adriel had a permanently shocked look on her face. Faith seemed genuinely happy for me, but my eyes were on Nadira. If it was going to work with Ryker and me, my friends *had* to be on board.

Nadira folded her arms over her chest and chewed on her bottom lip.

"Dir," I begged. "Say you're happy for me."

"I have to tell you the truth..." She looked from her folded arms to my eyes and sighed. "He has me converted." A slow grin spread across her face.

I squealed, my feet dancing on the pavement I was so excited. "Yes!" I cried and went to hug her. My other friends joined in, hugging and cheering, and I couldn't help but think this was exactly what happily ever after was supposed to be.

FIFTY-EIGHT

DES'S HOUSE was a flurry of hair spray, glitter, dresses, and of course Mama De Leon's famous cooking. Between my friends, the moms hanging out with Mama De Leon, and all of Ginger's friend, the house was completely full as we got ready for the homecoming dance.

Adriel had just finished my hair, and I walked in my comfy robe to sit by Ginger in front of the nachos on the kitchen island.

"These look so good," I said.

Ginger glanced around and then said, "I think I even saw Mom eating some."

My eyes widened. "No way! Mom ate something with GMO corn?"

Ginger nodded, grinning wide. "Wish she could

have loosened up this much before I went to college."

I laughed. "Yeah, but then you would have missed out on all the fun of a forbidden romance."

"True," Ginger said, taking another bite of a chip.

On the other side of Ginger, Zara grinned at me. "Girl, you are on fire. Ryker's going to lose his mind."

My cheeks blushed under the elaborate makeup Des had done for me. She'd even added thick eyeliner and a smoky eye. "You don't think it's too much?"

"No way," Callie said from across the counter. "You look amazing."

I smiled back at them. "Thank you. I never got to ask how college was going. Is it as good as everyone makes it out to be?"

My sister and her friends exchanged a glance until Jordan finally said, "It's better."

I laughed softly.

"But," Ginger said, "enjoy the rest of your senior year."

"Yes," Zara agreed. "It goes by too fast."

"I will," I promised. It would be easy, especially

since I'd be attending the homecoming dance with royalty.

"Cori!" Nadira shouted at me, coming over to us. "You have to get your dress on! We have fifteen minutes until our ride gets here, and my mom will kill me if I don't get any pictures." Of course Nadira's mom was the only one who had to work on a Saturday night.

"I'm going, I'm going," I said, waving goodbye to my sister and the original Curvy Girl Club. I followed Nadira back to Des's room that overlooked the ocean. It was beautiful today with the sunset just cresting over the waves. It reminded me of the night I knew I loved Ryker, when I'd seen the sun reflected in his eyes.

I couldn't wait to spend the evening with him, to dance with him close, not worrying who knew about us, but loving him out loud just like I had wanted to.

I turned away from the window and got my dress from Des's closet. The five of us got dressed, helping to zip each other up or adjust the straps on our heels. Eventually we were all ready, and we just took each other in for a moment.

We were all so different. Des in her bright red dress with a slit high up her thigh. Adriel in a soft pink gown. Nadira in her vintage cocktail dress and Faith in a baby-blue dress that cascaded over her hips, rippling to the floor.

"We look good," Des said, grinning into the mirror above her dresser.

I put my arm around her shoulders. "We do." I hardly recognized the girl staring back at me, but at the same time, I'd never felt more like myself. My lips were full and pouty, my eyes dark and intense, my skin stark white, and my curves sultry. I would never shy away from who I was or let someone else determine what I thought of myself ever again.

"How about a picture?" Adriel asked. "Before our parents assault us?"

I laughed and nodded in agreement. Adriel's mom could have given my mom a run for her money in the overbearing parent department.

I reached for my phone on Des's bed and held it out for us to take a selfie. We grinned into the camera, five parts of a perfect whole, and froze this wonderful moment, our friendship, forever.

A few knocks sounded on the door, and Mama De Leon called, "*Sus novios estan aqui!*"

"What did she say?" Faith asked.

I grinned at the same time Des groaned. "She said, 'Our boyfriends are here.'"

I hurriedly sent the picture to our group chat so we could all have it and then tucked my phone into my beaded clutch. Des walked forward and opened the door, showing everyone on the other side, but my eyes landed on Ryker.

First on his eyes, those beautiful gray eyes that widened at the sight of me. Then his lips, their fullness as they curved into a smile that he covered with his hand. I walked straight toward him and wrapped my arms around his shoulders.

He kissed me quickly before holding me tight. "You look *beautiful*," he breathed.

I smiled as I stepped back and took him in. The crisp white shirt he wore fit almost as well as his navy-blue pants, secured with a worn leather belt that matched his shoes. "I'm going to have the hottest date at the dance, if I do say so myself."

Chuckling, he said, "Second only to you." His eyes flicked away from me, and I followed his gaze to Ginger, who stood off to the side. My nerves ratcheted up. I knew she wasn't his biggest fan, but she wouldn't say anything hurtful, would she?

"Hey, Ginger," Ryker said, extending his hand.

Ginger looked at his hand. "You can put that away."

I felt like all the air in the room got sucked away

until Ginger's lips pulled into a smile. "After what you did for my sister last night, I think a hug is in order," she said.

I stared in awe as two of the people I cared most about hugged each other for a moment. Ginger stepped back and put a hand on his cheek. "Take care of my sister, or I'll bury you."

Behind us, Mom chuckled. "She's just joking. Right, Ginger?"

"Of course," Ginger said. Once Mom turned away, she made the I'm-watching-you gesture at Ryker and whispered, "Totally not joking."

Ryker tugged at his collar, and I took his hand in mine. "You don't need to be nervous. I think we're both pretty good at holding our own."

"Well," he replied, "I want to get even better at holding on to you."

As I smiled up at him, I said, "Good, because I'm never letting go."

We kept our promise as we all took pictures as a group and even as we rode to the dance in the limo Faith's brother promised. It was everything I dreamed a dance could be with Ryker as my date. We had fun dancing to the fast songs, and during the slow songs, he held me close to him, making me feel like I was the only girl on the dance floor.

"So who do you think won?" he asked, trailing his fingers down my spine until he laced them at my waist.

"What do you mean?" I asked, looking up at him. His eyes looked stunning in the lights.

His lips quirked into a smile. "The war? Who do you think won?"

I couldn't help but laugh. "Me, of course."

"That's funny," he said, "Because I thought the exact same thing."

EPILOGUE
ADRIEL

I took a deep breath before taking to the football field with the rest of my dance team. Tonight, we wore glittering navy jerseys and long black pants. My false eyelashes fluttered in the wind, flapping in front of my view, but maybe that was a good thing because after what Ryker did the week before, even more people than usual were at tonight's game, looking for a show.

My heart thrummed quickly, and the stadium lights made my skin hum with heat despite the chill in the air.

Mr. Davis's voice boomed over the loudspeaker. "Tonight, we welcome to the field Emerson Dance Studio, five-time national competitors with their sights set on the championship this year!"

Electricity buzzed over my skin at the thought of the national stage—what could be at stake for my final year in the dance studio. I couldn't wait to compete, to prove that I belonged onstage, regardless of my size.

Mr. Davis announced each of us dancers, and I grinned and waved at the crowd, trying not to throw up. The nerves were back yet again. But the second we lined up and took a deep breath in unison, all the worries, all the fear, were gone.

Music played over the speaker system and my body took over, giving my overactive mind a rest. I moved in unison, performing the way we had practiced time and time again in the studio. As if outside myself, I watched us nail each of the moves, heard the crowd gasp and cheer at the harder stunts.

This was where I belonged, performing, speaking with my body in a way I couldn't do with words.

We struck our final pose, and it was as though the veil had lifted. Suddenly, I heard and saw with full clarity the crowd rising to their feet, cheering for us, cheering for me. My smile grew so wide my cheeks hurt. I breathed deeply, trying to catch my breath as we left the field.

Right outside the gates, my mom caught me in a hug. "Great job, sweet pea!"

I grinned. "Thanks, Mom."

"The only part you got wrong was the six-count there at the end."

My smile fell. "Thanks, Mom."

She patted my cheek. "Nationals are coming up. We have to be perfect."

I nodded, all business. She meant well, but *we* weren't the ones who had spent hours in grueling practices, who had tried diet after diet that just wasn't working. No, that was me.

She handed me my coat and said, "I'll see you at home?"

I nodded and went to find my friends. Cori, Des, Faith, and Nadira cheered for me as I reached them.

"That is so going on my YouTube channel!" Des said.

I blanched, thinking of her hundred thousand followers seeing me dance. "Seriously?"

"Oh yeah," she said. "Already posted."

"Can't wait to see the comments," I muttered. "At least we weren't wearing pink, so they can't make any pig jokes."

Nadira rolled her eyes. "At least they won't call you a Dalmatian."

I winced at the term. She had vitiligo, which made her ebony skin lose pigment in places. Personally, I thought it was beautiful, but apparently some people didn't agree.

Cori pulled her boyfriend's letterman jacket tighter around herself and said, "Don't worry about them. You're fabulous, remember?"

I smiled. "Right."

The conversation changed to the game we were watching. It was neck and neck, and if Emerson won, we'd be on our way to the State Championship game. As the final seconds ticked down, Emerson's quarterback threw a long pass to Ryker, which he caught right in the end zone.

"YES!" Cori screamed beside me, jumping to her feet.

Laughing, I stood to cheer as well. For five girls who hardly cared about football before this year, we sure were invested in this game.

As soon as the teams did the customary postgame handshake, we followed Cori to the field. She beelined to her boyfriend, Ryker, jumping into his arms. He caught her easily, grinning between kisses.

I tried not to stare at how absolutely cute they were.

"Hey, Adriel, right?"

I turned to see who'd spoken to find a guy from my chem class standing next to me. "Yeah, Carter?" I pretended not to know his name, but there was no way I couldn't. He weightlifted competitively and had made a name for himself as one of California's best and youngest bodybuilders. I wasn't surprised he didn't quite know me. Emerson was a small school, but people pretty much ran in their own circles.

He nodded and grinned at me, showing off stark white teeth that contrasted his beautiful dark skin. "Good job tonight," he said. "That dance was incredible."

My cheeks blushed, and I wished the stadium lights weren't so bright because there was no way he didn't see. I tried to keep my voice even as I said, "Thank you."

"Of course. You'll have to show me how sometime." He gave me another make-your-knees-weak smile and walked away, congratulating the guys on the football team.

Des nudged my side. "Was that the bodybuilder talking to you?"

I nodded, in disbelief myself.

"What did he say?" she asked.

"That I did a good job," I said dumbly.

Des giggled and shimmied her shoulders. "I bet he loved seeing you shake it."

I rolled my eyes, blushing more now than I was before. "Stop it!"

"Stop what?" Ryker asked, his arm slung around Cori's shoulder. His class ring glinted where it hung on a chain around her neck. Gah, could they get any cuter?

I shook my head. "Nothing. By the way, I heard there was more to congratulate you on than *the winning pass!*"

Ryker batted his hand in the air.

"Don't be modest, babe," Cori said.

"Yeah," I agreed. It was incredible that they both got offers from both schools. "Getting into U of Hawaii *and* Brentwood U is amazing! You two are totally a power couple."

Cori grinned up at him. "I really am proud of you. Now we just have to hope you decide the same place as me."

He held her tighter, resting his cheek on the top of her head. "I've done enough stupid stuff to last a lifetime. I told you I wasn't letting you go, and I meant it."

My heart melted for them. Maybe someday, after nationals, I would have a love like that. But after watching Cori have her heart torn in two and stitched back together again, I knew I couldn't afford a distraction like that.

Love was fine, but I liked the taste of gold even better.

Want to see the conversation Ray and Ryker had together off-screen? You can get it for free today!

Use this QR code to access the free bonus story!

Continue reading Adriel's story in Curvy Girls Can't Dance!

EPILOGUE

Use this code to discover Adriel's story!

ALSO BY KELSIE STELTING

The Curvy Girl Club

Curvy Girls Can't Date Quarterbacks

Curvy Girls Can't Date Billionaires

Curvy Girls Can't Date Cowboys

Curvy Girls Can't Date Bad Boys

Curvy Girls Can't Date Best Friends

Curvy Girls Can't Date Bullies

Curvy Girls Can't Dance

Curvy Girls Can't Date Soldiers

Curvy Girls Can't Date Princes

The Texas High Series

Chasing Skye: Book One

Becoming Skye: Book Two

Loving Skye: Book Three

Anika Writes Her Soldier

Abi and the Boy Next Door: Book One

Abi and the Boy Who Lied: Book Two

Abi and the Boy She Loves: Book Three

The Pen Pal Romance Series

Dear Adam

Fabio Vs. the Friend Zone

Sincerely Cinderella

The Sweet Water High Series: A Multi-Author Collaboration

Road Trip with the Enemy: A Sweet Standalone Romance

YA Contemporary Romance Anthology

The Art of Taking Chances

Nonfiction

Raising the West

AUTHOR'S NOTE

Bullying is such a taboo subject, especially for curvy girls who are often made to feel less-than because of their weight. From the very beginning of the Curvy Girl Club, we've seen mean girls say hurtful things that cut to the core of the worries the main characters already had about themselves.

Isn't that true to life? Bullies are so skilled at finding your insecurities and picking them apart, pouring salt into the wound. Cori was the perfect person to match a bully. This girl has incredible self-worth, and I can only wish I valued myself as a teen the way she does! Instead of falling into the trap of being ashamed of her size, she made it an asset, a nonissue.

What if we each stopped trying to reason why

we deserve to take up space? What if we didn't say "yeah, I might be big, but I have a great personality"? What if we just said "I have a great personality" and owned it?

What if we stood up to everyone who ever bullied us because of our size?

As an adult, I've learned that most people who feel the need to hurt others are operating on flawed logic. They either feel terrible on the inside, have been taught to interact with others in a certain way, or are searching for their own significance. Many times, trauma is involved.

Knowing these things helps me take bullying a little less personally and has helped me unsubscribe from the beliefs I accepted about myself as a teenager. What beliefs about yourself have you accepted from someone else's rhetoric? What if you chose to believe something else? Something that would serve you better?

I'm still figuring it out, but here's how I started out: I told myself I am fearfully and wonderfully made. That my humanity deserves humane treatment. That my preciousness isn't determined by what I do but who I *am*.

What can you tell yourself today to replace the beliefs your bullies gave you?

ACKNOWLEDGMENTS

The older I get, the more appreciative I become of those people close to me who are there no matter what. I wrote this book during a hard time when I had to question who was really on my team. My husband, my boys, our families, Sally Henson, and The HALO Project in Oklahoma City, thank you for being *my* people. I love having you in my corner.

Speaking of people in my corner, I feel like I can count on Tricia Harden with some of my most precious work. I was worried about this story, and she reminded me just how wonderful of a teammate and cheerleader she is on this writing journey. I appreciate you!

To you, dear reader, I am so thankful for your

love of The Curvy Girl Club. You inspire me to keep writing strong girls with hearts of gold, and I hope you see the best parts of you in each of these characters. Thank you for picking up this story. You make being an author so fun.

GLOSSARY

Latin Phrases

Ad Meliora: School motto meaning "toward better things."
Audentes fortuna iuvat: Motto of *Dulce Periculum* meaning "Fortune favors the bold."
Dulce Periculum: means "danger is sweet" - local secret club that performs stunts
Multum in Parvo: means "much in little"

Locations

Town Name: Emerson
Location: Halfway between Los Angeles and San Francisco

Surrounding towns: Brentwood, Seaton, Heywood

Emerson Academy: Private school Rory and Beckett attend

Brentwood Academy: Rival private school

Walden Island: Tourism island off the coast, only accessible by helicopter or ferry

MAIN HANGOUTS

Emerson Elementary Library: Where Rory tutors Anna, open to students K-7

Emerson Field: Massive park in the center of Emerson

Emerson Memorial: Local hospital

Emerson Shoppes: Shopping mall

Emerson Trails: Hiking trails in Emerson, near Emerson Field

Halfway Café: Expensive dining option in Emerson, frequented by celebrities

La La Pictures: Movie theater in Emerson

Ripe: Major health food store serving the tri-city area

Roasted: Popular coffee shop in Emerson

JJ Cleaning: Cleaning service owned by Jordan's mom

Seaton Bakery: Delicious dining and drink option in Seaton where Beckett works
Seaton Beach: Beach near Seaton – rougher than the beach near Brentwood
Seaton Pier: Fishing pier near Seaton
Spike's: Local 18-and-under club
Waldo's Diner: local diner, especially popular after sporting events

APPS

Rush+: Game app designed by Kai Rush and his father
Sermo: chat app used by private school students

IMPORTANT ENTITIES

Bhatta Productions: Production company owned by Zara's father
Brentwood Badgers: Professional football team
Heywood Market: Big ranch/distributor where everyone can purchase their meat locally
Invisible Mountains: Local major nonprofit - Callie's dad is the CEO
Dugan Industries: Owns and manages Brent-

wood Marina, along with other entities. Owned by Ryker Dugan's father, Trent Dugan.

ABOUT THE AUTHOR

Kelsie Stelting is a body positive romance author who writes love stories with strong characters, deep feelings, and happy endings.

She currently lives in Colorado. You can often find her writing, spending time with family, and soaking up too much sun wherever she can find it.

Visit www.kelsiestelting.com to get a free story and sign up for her readers' group!

facebook.com/kelsiesteltingcreative
twitter.com/kelsiestelting
instagram.com/kelsiestelting

Printed in Great Britain
by Amazon